A Texas Ranger
by
William MacLeod Raine

GP
GRINDL PRESS

This edition contains the complete and unabridged manuscript of *A Texas Ranger*, by William MacLeod Raine. A few minor changes have been made, limited to spelling and word replacement, appropriate to modern conventions. Original edition copyrighted in 1910.

All content not in the public domain in the United States, is original to this edition. Content in the public domain in the United States includes the novel manuscript and the the photograph (digitally altered) on the cover and title page

Copyright © 2013 by C. Wade Naney

All rights reserved. No part of the original content or design of this book may be reproduced in any form or by any means, electronic or mechanical. Printed in the United States of America.

ISBN:1490910247

GP

GRINDL PRESS
grindlpress.com

This book is one of numerous titles in the
OLD WEST CLASSICS SERIES
from Grindl Press.

Other Series from Grindl Press
available at
grindlpress.com

Contemporary Editions

Vocabulary From the Classics

Ethnic Studies

Regional Classics

Secondary Education Editions

PART I — THE MAN FROM THE PANHANDLE
(IN WHICH STEVE PLAYS SECOND FIDDLE)

CHAPTER I — A DESERT MEETING

AS SHE LAY CROUCHED in the bear-grass there came to the girl clearly the crunch of wheels over disintegrated granite. The trap had dipped into a draw, but she knew that presently it would reappear on the winding road. The knowledge smote her like a blast of winter, sent chills racing down her spine, and shook her as with an ague. Only the desperation of her plight spurred her flagging courage.

Round the bend came a pair of bays hitched to a single-seated open rig. They were driven by a young man, and as he reached the summit he drew up opposite her and looked down into the valley.

It lay in a golden glow at their feet, a basin of pure light and silence stretching mile on mile to the distant edge of jagged mountain-line which formed its lip. Sunlight strong as wine flooded a clean world, an amber Eden slumbering in an unbroken, hazy dream primeval.

"Don't move!"

At the summons the driver swung his head sharply to a picture he will never forget. A young woman was standing on the bank at the edge of the road covering him with a revolver, having apparently just stepped from behind the trunk of the cottonwood beside her. The color had fled her cheeks even to the edge of the dull red-copper waves of hair, but he could detect in her slim young suppleness no doubt or uncertainty. On the contrary, despite her girlish freshness, she looked very much like business. She was like some young wild creature of the forest cornered and brought to bay, but the very terror in her soul rendered her more dangerous. Of the heart beating like a trip-hammer the gray unwinking eyes that looked into hers read nothing. She had schooled her taut nerves to obedience, and they answered her resolute will steadily despite fluttering pulses.

"Don't move!" she said again.

"What do you want?" he asked harshly.

"I want your team," she panted.

"What for?"

"Never mind. I want it."

The rigor of his gaze slowly softened to a smile compound both of humor and grimness. He was a man to appreciate a piquant situation, none the less because it was at his expense. The spark that gleamed in his bold eye held some spice of the devil.

"All right. This is your hold-up, ma'am. I'll not move," he said, almost genially.

She was uneasily aware that his surrender had been too tame. Strength lay in that close-gripped salient jaw, in every line of the reckless sardonic face, in the set of the lean muscular shoulders. She had nerved herself to meet resistance, and instead he was yielding with complacent good nature.

"Get out!" she commanded.

He stepped from the rig and offered her the reins. As she reached for them his right hand shot out and caught the wrist that held the weapon, his left encircled her waist and drew her to him. She gave a little cry of fear and strained from him, fighting with all her lissom strength to free herself.

For all the impression she made the girdle round her waist might have been of steel. Without moving, he held her as she struggled, his brown muscular fingers slowly tightening round her wrist. Her stifled cry was of pain this time, and before it had died the revolver fell to the ground from her paralyzed grip.

But her exclamation had been involuntary and born of the soft tender flesh. The wild eyes that flamed into his asked for no quarter and received none. He drew her slowly down toward him, inch by inch, till she lay crushed and panting against him, but still unconquered. Though he held the stiff resistant figure motionless she still flashed battle at him.

He looked into the storm and fury of her face, hiding he knew not what of terror, and laughed in insolent delight. Then, very deliberately, he kissed her lips.

"You—coward!" came instantly her choking defiance.

"Another for that," he laughed, kissing her again.

Her little fist beat against his face and he captured it, but as he looked at her something that had come into the girl's face moved his not very accessible heart. The salt of the adventure was gone, his victory worse than a barren one. For stark fear stared at him, naked and unconcealed, and back of that he glimpsed a subtle something that he dimly recognized for the outraged maidenly modesty he had so ruthlessly trampled upon. His hands fell to his side reluctantly.

She stumbled back against the tree trunk, watching him with fascinated eyes that searched him anxiously. They found their answer, and with a long ragged breath the girl turned and burst into hysterical tears.

The man was amazed. A moment since the fury of a tigress had possessed her. Now she was all weak womanish despair. She leaned against the cottonwood and buried her face in her arm, the while uneven sobs shook her slender body. He frowned resentfully at this change of front, and because his calloused conscience was disturbed he began to justify himself. Why didn't she play it out instead of coming the baby act on him? She had undertaken to hold him up and he had made her pay forfeit. He didn't see that she had any kick coming. If she was this kind of a boarding-school kid she ought not to have monkeyed with the buzz-saw. She was lucky he didn't take her to El Paso with him and have her jailed.

"I reckon we'll listen to explanations now," he said grimly after a minute of silence interrupted only by her sobs.

The little fist that had struck at his face now bruised itself in unconscious blows at the bark of the tree. He waited till the staccato breaths had subsided, then took her by the shoulders and swung her round.

"You have the floor, ma'am. What does this gun-play business mean?"

Through the tears her angry eyes flashed starlike.

"I sha'n't tell you," she flamed. "You had no right to—How dared you insult me as you have?"

"Did I insult you?" he asked, with suave gentleness. "Then if you feel insulted I expect you lay claim to being a lady. But I reckon that don't fit in with holding up strangers at the end of a gun. If I've insulted you I'll ce'tainly apologize, but you'll have to show me I have. We're in Texas, which is next door but one to Missouri, ma'am."

"I don't want your apologies. I detest and hate you," she cried,

"That's your privilege, ma'am, and it's mine to know whyfor I'm held up with a gun when I'm traveling peaceably along the road," he answered evenly.

"I'll not tell you."

He spoke softly as if to himself. "That's too bad. I kinder hate to take her to jail, but I reckon I must."

She shrank back, aghast and white.

"No, no! You don't understand. I didn't mean to—I only wanted—Why, I meant to pay you for the team."

"I'll understand when you tell me," he said placidly.

"I've told you. I needed the team. I was going to let you have one of our horses and seventy-five dollars. It's all I have with me."

"One of your horses, you say? With seventy-five dollars to boot? And you was intending to arrange the trade from behind that gun. I expect you needed a team right bad."

His steady eyes rested on her, searched her, appraised her, while he meditated aloud in a low easy drawl.

"Yes, you ce'tainly must need the team. Now I wonder why? Well, I'd hate to refuse a lady anything she wants as bad as you do that." He swiftly swooped down and caught up her revolver from the ground, tossed it into the air so as to shift his hold from butt to barrel, and handed it to her with a bow. "Allow me to return the pop-gun you dropped, ma'am."

She snatched it from him and leveled it at him so that it almost touched his forehead. He looked at her and laughed in delighted mockery.

"All serene, ma'am. You've got me dead to rights again."

His very nonchalance disarmed her. What could she do while his low laughter mocked her?

"When you've gone through me complete I think I'll take a little *pasear* over the hill and have a look at your hawss. Mebbe we might still do business."

As he had anticipated, his suggestion filled her with alarm. She flew to bar the way.

"You can't go. It isn't necessary."

"Sho! Of course it's necessary. Think I'm going to buy a hawss I've never seen?" he asked, with deep innocence.

"I'll bring it here."

"In Texas, ma'am, we wait on the ladies. Still, it's your say-so when you're behind that big gun."

He said it laughing, and she threw the weapon angrily into the seat of the rig.

"Thank you, ma'am. I'll amble down and see what's behind the hill."

By the flinch in her eyes he tested his center shot and knew it true. Her breast was rising and falling tumultuously. A shiver ran through her.

"No—no. I'm not hiding—anything," she gasped.

"Then if you're not you can't object to my going there."

She caught her hands together in despair. There was about him something masterful that told her she could not prevent him from investigating; and it was impossible to guess how he would act after he knew. The men she had known had been bound by convention to respect a woman's wishes, but even her ignorance of his type made guess that this steel-eyed, close-knit young Westerner—or was he a Southerner?—would be impervious to appeals founded upon the rules of the society to which she had been accustomed. A glance at his stone-wall face, at the lazy confidence of his manner, made her dismally aware that the data gathered by her experience of the masculine gender were insufficient to cover this specimen.

"You can't go."

But her imperative refusal was an appeal. For though she hated him from the depths of her proud, untamed heart for the humiliation he had put upon her, yet for the sake of that ferocious hunted animal she had left lying under a cottonwood she must bend her spirit to win him.

"I'm going to sit in this game and see it out," he said, not unkindly.

"Please!"

Her sweet slenderness barred the way about as electively as a mother quail does the road to her young. He smiled, put his big hands on her elbows, and gently lifted her to one side. Then he strode forward lightly, with the long, easy, tireless stride of a beast of prey, striking direct for his quarry.

A bullet whizzed by his ear, and like a flash of light his weapon was unscabbarded and ready for action. He felt a flame of fire scorch his cheek and knew a second shot had grazed him.

"Hands up! Quick!" ordered the traveler.

Lying on the ground before him was a man with close-cropped hair and a villainous scarred face. A revolver in his hand showed the source of the bullets.

Eye to eye the men measured strength, fighting out to the last ditch the moral battle which was to determine the physical one. Sullenly, at the last, the one on the ground shifted his gaze and dropped his gun with a vile curse.

"Run to earth," he snarled, his lip lifting from the tobacco-stained upper teeth in an ugly fashion.

The girl ran toward the Westerner and caught at his arm. "Don't shoot," she implored.

Without moving his eyes from the man on the ground he swept her back.

"This outfit is too prevalent with its hardware," he growled. "Chew out an explanation, my friend, or you're liable to get spoiled."

It was the girl that spoke, in a low voice and very evidently under a tense excitement.

"He is my brother and he has—hurt himself. He can't ride any farther and we have seventy miles still to travel. We didn't know what to do, and so—"

"You started out to be a road-agent and he took a pot-shot at the first person he saw. I'm surely obliged to you both for taking so much interest in me, or rather in my team. Robbery and murder are quite a family pastime, ain't they?"

The girl went white as snow, seemed to shrink before his sneer as from a deadly weapon; and like a flash of light some divination of the truth pierced the Westerner's brain. They were fugitives from justice, making for the Mexican line. That the man was wounded a single glance had told him. It was plain to be seen that the wear and tear of keeping the saddle had been too much for him.

"I acted on an impulse," the girl explained in the same low tone. "I saw you coming and I didn't know—hadn't money enough to buy the team—besides—"

He took the words out of her mouth when she broke down.

"Besides, I might have happened to be a sheriff. I might be, but then I'm not."

The traveler stepped forward and kicked the wounded man's revolver beyond his reach, then swiftly ran a hand over him to make sure he carried no other gun.

The fellow on the ground eyed him furtively. "What are you going to do with me?" he growled.

The other addressed himself to the girl, ignoring him utterly.

"What has this man done?"

"He has—broken out from—from prison."

"Where?"

"At Yuma."

"Damn you, you're snitching," interrupted the criminal in a scream that was both wheedling and threatening.

The young man put his foot on the burly neck and calmly ground it into the dust. Otherwise he paid no attention to him, but held the burning eyes of the girl that stared at him from a bloodless face.

"What was he in for?"

"For holding up a train."

She had answered in spite of herself, by reason of something compelling in him that drew the truth from her.

"How long has he been in the penitentiary?"

"Seven years." Then, miserably, she added: "He was weak and fell into bad company. They led him into it."

"When did he escape?"

"Two days ago. Last night he knocked at my window—at the window of the room where I lodge in Fort Lincoln. I had not heard of his escape, but I took him in. There were horses in the barn. One of them was mine. I saddled, and after I had dressed his wound we started. He couldn't get any farther than this."

"Do you live in Fort Lincoln?"

"I came there to teach school. My home was in Wisconsin before."

"You came out here to be near him?"

"Yes. That is, near as I could get a school. I was to have got in the Tucson schools next year. That's much nearer."

"You visited him at the penitentiary?"

"No. I was going to during the Thanksgiving vacation. Until last night I had not seen him since he left home. I was a child of seven then."

The Texan looked down at the ruffian under his feet.

"Do you know the road to Mexico by the Arivaca cut-off?"

"Yes."

"Then climb into my rig and hit the trail hard—burn it up till you've crossed the line."

The fellow began to whine thanks, but the man above would have none of them, "I'm giving you this chance for your sister's sake. You won't make anything of it. You're born for meanness and deviltry. I know your kind from El Paso to Dawson. But she's game and she's white clear through, even if she is your sister and a plumb little fool. Can you walk to the road?" he ended abruptly.

"I think so. It's in my ankle. Some hell-hound gave it me while we were getting over the wall," the fellow growled.

"Don't blame him. His intentions were good. He meant to blow out your brains."

The convict cursed vilely, but in the midst of his impotent rage the other stopped and dragged him to his feet.

"That's enough. You padlock that ugly mouth and light a shuck."

The girl came forward and the man leaned heavily on her as he limped to the road. The Texan followed with the buckskin she had been riding and tied it to the back of the road-wagon.

"Give me my purse," the girl said to the convict after they were seated.

She emptied it and handed the roll of bills it contained to the owner of the team. He looked at it and at her, then shook his head.

"You'll need it likely. I reckon I can trust you. Schoolmarms are mostly reliable."

"I had rather pay now," she answered tartly.

"What's the rush?"

"I prefer to settle with you now."

"All right, but I'm in no sweat for my money. My team and the wagon are worth two hundred and fifty dollars. Put this plug at forty and it would be high." He jerked his head toward the brush where the other saddle-horse was. "That leaves me a balance of about two hundred and ten. Is that fair?"

She bit her lip in vexation. "I expect so, but I haven't that much with me. Can't I pay this seventy on account?"

"No, ma'am, you can't. All or none." There was a gleam of humor in his hard eyes. "I reckon you better let me come and collect after you get back to Fort Lincoln."

She took out a note-book and pencil. "If you will give me your name and address please."

He smiled hardily at her. "I've clean forgotten them."

There was a warning flash in her disdainful eye.

"Just as you like. My name is Margaret Kinney. I will leave the money for you at the First National Bank."

She gathered up the rains deftly.

"One moment." He laid a hand on the lines. "I reckon you think I owe you an apology for what happened when we first met."

A flood of spreading color dyed her cheeks. "I don't think anything about it."

"Oh, yes, you do," he contradicted. "And you're going to think a heap more about it. You're going to lay awake nights going over it."

Out of eyes like live coals she gave him one look. "Will you take your hands from these reins please?"

"Presently. Just now I'm talking and you're listening."

"I don't care to hear any apologies, sir," she said stiffly.

"I'm not offering any," he laughed, yet stung by her words.

"You're merely insulting me again, I presume?"

"Some young women need punishing. I expect you're one."

She handed him the horsewhip, a sudden pulse of passion beating fiercely in her throat. "Very well. Make an end of it and let me see the last of you," she challenged.

He cracked the lash expertly so that the horses quivered and would have started if his strong hand had not tightened on the lines.

The Westerner laughed again. "You're game anyhow."

"When you are quite through with me," she suggested, very quietly.

But he noticed the fury of her deep-pupiled eyes, the turbulent rise and fall of her bosom.

"I'll not punish you that way this time." And he gave back the whip.

"If you won't use it I will."

The lash flashed up and down, twined itself savagely round his wrist, and left behind a bracelet of crimson. Startled, the horses leaped forward. The reins slipped free from his numbed fingers. Miss Kinney had made her good-by and was descending swiftly into the valley.

The man watched the rig sweep along that branch of the road which led to the south. Then he looked at his wrist and laughed.

"The plucky little devil! She's a thoroughbred for fair. You bet I'll make her pay for this. But ain't she got sand in her craw? She's surely hating me proper." He laughed again in remembrance of the whole episode, finding in it something that stirred his blood immensely.

After the trap had swept round a curve out of sight he disappeared in the mesquite and bear-grass, presently returning with the roan that had been ridden by the escaped convict.

"Whoever would suppose she was the sister of that scurvy scalawag with jailbird branded all over his hulking hide? He ain't fit to wipe her little feet on. She's as fine as silk. Think of her going through what she is to save that coyote, and him as crooked as a dog's hind leg. There ain't any limit to what a good woman will do for a man when she thinks he's got a claim on her, more especially if he's a ruffian."

With this bit of philosophic observation he rolled a cigarette and lit it.

"Him fall into bad company and be led away?" he added in disgust. "There ain't any worse than him. But he'll work her to the limit before she finds it out."

Leisurely he swung to the saddle and rode down into the valley of the San Xavier, which rolled away from his feet in numberless tawny waves of unfeatured foot-hills and mesas and washes. Almost as far as the eye could see there stretched a sea of hilltops bathed in sun. Only on the west were they bounded, by the irregular saw-toothed edge of the Frenchman Hills, silhouetted against an incomparable blue. For a stretch of many miles the side of the range was painted scarlet by millions of poppies splashed broadcast.

"Nature's gone to flower-gardening for fair on the mountains," murmured the rider. "What with one thing and another I've got a notion I'm going to take a liking to this country."

The man was plainly very tired with rapid travel, and about the middle of the afternoon the young man unsaddled and picketed the animal near a water-hole. He lay down in the shadow of a cottonwood, flat on his back, face upturned to the deep cobalt sky. Presently the drowse of the afternoon crept over him. The slumberous valley grew hazy to his nodding eyes. The reluctant lids ceased to open and he was fast asleep.

CHAPTER II — LIEUTENANT FRASER INTERFERES

THE SUN HAD DECLINED almost to a saddle in the Cuesta del Burro when the sleeper reopened his eyes. Even before he had shaken himself free of sleep he was uneasily aware of something wrong. Hazily the sound of voices drifted to him across an immense space. Blurred figures crossed before his unfocused gaze.

The first thing he saw clearly was the roan, still grazing in the circle of its picket-rope. Beside the bronco were two men looking the animal over critically.

"Been going some," he heard one remark, pointing at the same time to the sweat-stains that streaked the shoulders and flanks.

"If he had me on his back he'd still be burning the wind, me being in his boots," returned the second, with a grating laugh, jerking his head toward the sleeper. "Whatever led the durned fool to stop this side of the line beats me."

"If he was hiking for Chihuahua he's been hitting a mighty crooked trail. I don't savvy it, him knowing the country as well as they say he does," the first speaker made answer.

The traveler's circling eye now discovered two more men, each of them covering him with a rifle. A voice from the rear assured him there was also a fifth member to the party.

"Look out! He's awake," it warned.

The young man's hand inadvertently moved toward his revolver-butt. This drew a sharp imperative order from one of the men in front.

"Throw up your hands, and damn quick!"

"You seem to have the call, gentlemen," he smiled. "Would you mind telling me what it's all about?"

"You know what it's all about as well as we do. Collect his gun, Tom."

"This hold-up business seems to be a habit in this section. Second time to-day I've been the victim of it," said the victim easily.

"It will be the last," retorted one of the men grimly.

"If you're after the mazuma you've struck a poor bank."

"You've got your nerve," cried one of the men in a rage; and another demanded: "Where did you get that hawss?"

"Why, I got it—" The young man stopped in the middle of his sentence. His jaw clamped and his eyes grew hard. "I expect you better explain what right you got to ask that question."

The man laughed without cordiality. "Seeing as I have owned it three years I allow I have some right."

"What's the use of talking? He's the man we want, broke in another impatiently.

"Who is the man you want?" asked their prisoner.

"You're the man we want, Jim Kinney."

"Wrong guess. My name is Larry Neill. I'm from the Panhandle and I've never been in this part of the country till two days ago."

"You may have a dozen names. We don't care what you call yourself. Of course you would deny being the man we're after. But that don't go with us."

"All right. Take me back to Fort Lincoln, or take me to the prison officials. They will tell you whether I am the man."

The leader of the party pounced on his slip. "Who mentioned prison? Who told you we wanted an escaped prisoner?"

"He's give himself away," triumphed the one edged Tom. "I guess that clinches it. He's riding Maloney's hawss. He's wounded; so's the man we want. He answers the description—gray eyes, tall, slim, muscular. Same gun—automatic Colt. Tell you there's nothin' to it, Duffield."

"If you're not Kinney, how come you with this hawss? He stole it from a barn in Fort Lincoln last night. That's known," said the leader, Duffield.

The imperilled man thought of the girl bearing toward the border with her brother and the remembrance padlocked his tongue.

"Take me to the proper authorities and I'll answer questions. But, I'll not talk here. What's the use? You don't believe a word I say."

"You spoke the truth that time," said one.

"If you ever want to do any explaining now's the hour," added another.

"I'll do mine later, gentlemen."

They looked at each other and one of them spoke.

"It will be too late to explain then."

"Too late?"

Some inkling of the man's hideous meaning seared him and ran like an ice-blast through him.

"You've done all the meanness you'll ever do in this world. Poor Dave Long is the last man you'll ever kill. We're going to do justice right now."

"Dave Long! I never heard of him," the prisoner repeated mechanically. "Good God, do you think I'm a murderer?"

One of the men thrust himself forward. "We know it. Y'u and that hellish partner of yours shot him while he was locking the gate. But y'u made a mistake when y'u come to Fort Lincoln. He lived there before he went to be a guard at the Arizona penitentiary. I'm his brother. These gentlemen are his neighbors. Y'u're not going back to prison. Y'u're going to stay right here under this cottonwood."

If the extraordinary menace of the man appalled Neill he gave no sign of it. His gray eye passed from one to another of them quietly without giving any sign of the impotent tempest raging within him.

"You're going to lynch me then?"

"Y'u've called the turn."

"Without giving me a chance to prove my innocence?"

"Without giving y'u a chance to escape or sneak back to the penitentiary."

The thing was horribly unthinkable. The warm mellow afternoon sunshine wrapped them about. The horses grazed with quiet unconcern. One of these hard-faced frontiersmen was chewing tobacco with machine-like regularity. Another was rolling a cigarette. There was nothing of dramatic effect. Not a man had raised his voice. But Neill knew there was no appeal. He had come to the end of the passage through a horrible mistake. He raged in bitter resentment against his fate, against these men who stood so quietly about him ready to execute it, most of all against the girl who had let him sacrifice himself by concealing the vital fact that her brother had murdered a guard to effect his escape. Fool that he had been, he had stumbled into a trap, and she had let him do it without a word of warning. Wild, chaotic thoughts crowded his brain furiously.

But the voice with which he addressed them was singularly even and colorless.

"I am a stranger to this country. I was born in Tennessee, brought up in the Panhandle. I'm an irrigation engineer by profession. This is my vacation. I'm headed now for the Mal Pais mines. Friends of mine are interested in a property there with me and I have been sent to look the ground over and make a report. I never heard of Kinney till to-day. You've got the wrong man, gentlemen."

"We'll risk it," laughed one brutally. "Bring that riata, Tom."

Neill did not struggle or cry out frantically. He stood motionless while they adjusted the rope round his bronzed throat. They had judged him for a villain; they should at least know him a man. So he stood there straight and lithe, wide-shouldered and lean-flanked, a man in a thousand. Not a twitch of the well-packed muscles, not a quiver of the eyelash nor a swelling of the throat betrayed any fear. His cool eyes were quiet and steady.

"If you want to leave any message for anybody I'll see it's delivered," promised Duffield.

"I'll not trouble you with any."

"Just as you like."

"He didn't give poor Dave any time for messages," cried Tom Long bitterly.

"That's right," assented another with a curse.

It was plain to the victim they were spurring their nerves to hardihood.

"Who's that?" cried one of the men, pointing to a rider galloping toward them.

The newcomer approached rapidly, covered by their weapons, and flung himself from his pony as he dragged it to a halt beside the group.

"Steve Fraser," cried Duffield in surprise, and added, "He's an officer in the rangers."

"Right, gentlemen. Come to claim my prisoner," said the ranger promptly.

"Y'u can't have him, Steve. We took him and he's got to hang."

The lieutenant of rangers shook his dark curly head.

"Won't do, Duffield. Won't do at all," he said decisively. "You'd ought to know law's on top in Texas these days."

Tom Long shouldered his way to the front. "Law! Where was the law when this ruffian Kinney shot down my poor brother Dave? I guess a rope and a cottonwood's good enough law for him. Anyhow, that's what he gits."

Fraser, hard-packed, lithe, and graceful, laid a friendly hand on the other's shoulder and smiled sunnily at him.

"I know how you feel, Tom. We all thought a heap of Dave and you're his brother. But Dave died for the law. Both you boys have always stood for order. He'd be troubled if he knew you were turned enemy to it on his account."

"I'm for justice, Steve. This skunk deserves death and I'm going to see he gits it."

"No, Tom."

"I say yes. Y'u ain't sitting in this game, Steve."

"I reckon I'll have to take a hand then."

The ranger's voice was soft and drawling, but his eyes were

indomitably steady. Throughout the Southwest his reputation for fearlessness was established even among a population singularly courageous. The audacity of his daredevil recklessness was become a proverb.

"We got a full table. Better ride away and forget it," said another.

"That ain't what I'm paid for, Jack," returned Fraser good-naturedly. "Better turn him over to me peaceable, boys. He'll get what's coming to him all right."

"He'll get it now, Steve, without any help of yours. We don't aim to allow any butting in."

"Don't you?"

There was a flash of steel as the ranger dived forward. Next instant he and the prisoner stood with their backs to the cottonwood, a revolver having somehow leaped from its scabbard to his hand. His hunting-knife had sheared at a stroke the riata round the engineer's neck.

"Take it easy, boys," urged Fraser, still in his gentle drawl, to the astonished vigilantes whom his sudden sally had robbed of their victim. "Think about it twice. We'll all be a long time dead. No use in hurrying the funerals."

Nevertheless he recognized battle as inevitable. Friends of his though they were, he knew these sturdy plainsmen would never submit to be foiled in their purpose by one man. In the momentary silence before the clash the quiet voice of the prisoner made itself heard.

"Just a moment, gentlemen. I don't want you spilling lead over me. I'm the wrong man, and I can prove it if you'll give me time. Here's the key to my room at the hotel in San Antonio. In my suit-case you'll find letters that prove—"

"We don't need them. I've got proof right here," cut in Fraser, remembering.

He slipped a hand into his coat pocket and drew out two photographs. "Boys, here are the pictures and descriptions of the two men that escaped from Yuma the other day. I hadn't had time to see this gentleman before he spoke, being some busy explaining the situation to you, but a blind jackass could see he don't favor either Kinney or Struve, You're sure barking up the wrong tree."

The self-appointed committee for the execution of justice and the man from the Panhandle looked the prison photographs over blankly. Between the hard, clean-cut face of their prisoner and those that looked at them from the photographs it was impossible to find any resemblance. Duffield handed the prints back with puzzled chagrin.

"I guess you're right, Steve. But I'd like this gentleman to explain how come he to be riding the horse one of these miscreants stole from Maloney's barn last night."

Steve looked at the prisoner. "It's your spiel, friend," he said.

"All right. I'll tell you some facts. Just as I was coming down from the Roskruge range this mo'ning I was held up for my team. One of these fellows—the one called Kinney—had started from Fort Lincoln on this roan here, but he was wounded and broke down. There was some gun-play, and he gave me this scratch on the cheek. The end of it was that he took my team and left me with his worn-out bronc. I plugged on all day with the hawss till about three mebbe, then seeing it was all in I unsaddled and picketed. I lay down and dropped asleep. Next I knew the necktie-party was in session."

"What time was it y'u met this fellow Kinney?" asked Long sharply.

"Must have been about nine or nine-thirty I judge."

"And it's five now. That's eight hours' start, and four more before we can cut his trail on Roskruge. By God, we've lost him!"

"Looks like," agreed another ruefully.

"Make straight for the Arivaca cut-off and you ought to stand a show," suggested Fraser.

"That's right. If we ride all night, might beat him to it." Each of the five contributed a word of agreement.

Five minutes later the Texan and the ranger watched a dust-cloud drifting to the south. In it was hidden the posse disappearing over the hilltop.

Steve grinned. "I hate to disappoint the boys. They're so plumb anxious. But I reckon I'll strike the telephone line and send word to Moreno for one of the rangers to cut out after Kinney. Going my way, seh?"

"If you're going mine."

"I reckon I am. And just to pass the time you might tell me the real story of that hold-up while we ride."

"The real story?"

"Well, I don't aim to doubt your word, but I reckon you forgot to tell some of it." He turned on the other his wry smile. "For instance, seh, you ain't asking me to believe that you handed over your rig to Kinney so peaceful and that he went away and clean forgot to unload from you that gun you pack."

The eyes of the two met and looked into each other's as clear and straight as Texas sunshine. Slowly Neill's relaxed into a smile.

"No, I won't ask you to believe that. I owe you something because you saved my life—"

"Forget it," commanded the lieutenant crisply.

"And I can't do less than tell you the whole story."

He told it, yet not the whole of it either; for there was one detail he omitted completely. It had to do with the cause for existence of the little black-and-blue bruise under his right eye and the purple ridge that seamed his wrist. Nor with all his acuteness could Stephen Fraser guess that the one swelling had been made by a gold ring on the clenched fist of an angry girl held tight in Larry Neill's arms, the other by the lash of a horsewhip wielded by the same young woman.

CHAPTER III — A DISCOVERY

THE ROAN, HAVING BEEN much refreshed by a few hours on grass, proved to be a good traveller. The two men took a road-gait and held it steadily till they reached a telephone-line which stretched across the desert and joined two outposts of civilization. Steve strapped on his climbing spurs and went up a post lightly with his test outfit. In a few minutes he had Moreno on the wire and was in touch with one of his rangers.

"Hello! This you, Ferguson? This is Fraser. No, Fraser— Lieutenant Fraser. Yes. How many of the boys can you get in touch with right away? Two? Good. I want you to cover the Arivaca cut-off. Kinney is headed that way in a rig. His sister is with him. She is not to be injured under any circumstances. Understand? Wire me at the Mal Pais mines to-morrow your news. By the way, Tom Long and some of the boys are headed down that way with notions of lynching Kinney. Dodge them if you can and rush your man up to the Mal Pais. Good-bye."

"Suppose they can't dodge them?" ventured Neill after Steve had rejoined him.

"I reckon they can. If not—well, my rangers are good boys; I expect they won't give up a prisoner."

"I'm right glad to find you are going to the Mal Pais mines with me, lieutenant. I wasn't expecting company on the way."

"I'll bet a dollar Mex against two plunks gold that you're wondering whyfor I'm going."

Larry laughed. "You're right. I was wondering."

"Well, then, it's this way. What with all these boys on Kinney's trail he's as good as rounded up. Fact is, Kinney's only a weak sister anyhow. He turned State's witness at the trial, and it was his testimony that convicted Struve. I know something about this because I happened to be the man that caught Struve. I had just joined the rangers. It was my first assignment. The other three got away. Two of them escaped and the third was not tried for lack of sufficient evidence. Now, then: Kinney rides the roads from Yuma to Marfa and is now or had ought to be somewhere in this valley between Posa Buena and Taylor's ranch. But where is Struve, the hardier ruffian of the two? He ain't been seen since they broke out. He sure never reached Ft. Lincoln. My notion is that he dropped off the train in the darkness about Casa Grande, then rolled his tail for the Mal Pais country. Your eyes are asking whys mighty loud, my friend; and my answer is that there's a man up there mebbe who has got to hide Struve if he shows up. That's only a guess, but it looks good to me. This man was the brains of the whole outfit, and folks say that he's got cached the whole haul the gang made from that S. P. hold-up. What's more, he scattered gold so liberal that his name wasn't even mentioned at the trial. He's a big man now, a millionaire copper king and into gold-mines up to the hocks. In the Southwest those things happen. It doesn't always do to look too closely at a man's past.

"We'll say Struve drops in on him and threatens to squeak. Mebbe he has got evidence; mebbe he hasn't. Anyhow, our big duck wants to forget the time he was wearing a mask and bending a six-gun for a living. Also and moreover, he's right anxious to have other folks get a chance to forget. From what I can hear he's clean mashed on some girl at Amarillo, or maybe it's Fort Lincoln. See what a twist Strove's got on him if he can slip into the Mal Pais country on the q. t."

"And you're going up there to look out for him?"

"I'm going in to take a casual look around. There's no telling what a man might happen onto accidentally if he travels with his ear to the ground."

The other nodded. He could now understand easily why Fraser was going into the Mal Pais country, but he could not make out why the ranger, naturally a man who lived under his own hat and kept his own counsel, had told him so much as he had. The officer shortly relieved his mind on this point.

"I may need help while I'm there. May I call on you if I do, seh?"

Neill felt his heart warm toward this hard-faced, genial frontiersman, who knew how to judge so well the timbre of a casual acquaintance.

"You sure may, lieutenant."

"Good. I'll count on you then."

So, in these few words, the compact of friendship and alliance was sealed between them. Each of them was strangely taken with the other, but it is not the way of the Anglo-Saxon fighting man to voice his sentiment. Though each of them admired the stark courage and the flawless fortitude he knew to dwell in the other, impassivity sat on their faces like an ice-mask. For this is the hall-mark of the Southwest, that a man must love and hate with the same unchanging face of iron, save only when a woman is in consideration.

They were to camp that night by Cottonwood Spring, and darkness caught them still some miles from their camp. They were on no road, but were travelling across country through washes and over countless hills. The ranger led the way, true as an arrow, even after velvet night had enveloped them.

"It must be right over this mesa among the cottonwoods you see rising from that arroyo," he announced at last.

He had scarcely spoken before they struck a trail that led them direct to the spring. But as they were descending this in a circle Fraser's horse shied.

"Hyer you, Pinto! What's the matter with—"

The ranger cut his sentence in two and slid from the saddle. When his companion reached him and drew rein the ranger was bending over a dark mass stretched across the trail. He looked up quietly.

"Man's body," he said briefly.

"Dead?"

"Yes."

Neill dismounted and came forward. The moon-crescent was up by now and had lit the country with a chill radiance. The figure was dressed in the coarse striped suit of a convict.

"I don't savvy this play," Fraser confessed softly to himself.

"Do you know him?"

"Suppose you look at him and see if you know him."

Neill looked into the white face and shook his head.

"No, I don't know him, but I suppose it is Struve."

From his pocket the ranger produced a photograph and handed it to him.

"Hyer, I'll strike a match and you'll see better."

The match flared up in the slight breeze and presently went out, but not before Neill had seen that it was the face of the man who lay before them.

"Did you see the name under the picture, seh?"

"No."

Another match flared and the man from the Panhandle read a name, but it was not the one he had expected to see. The words printed there were "James Kinney."

"I don't understand. This ain't Kinney. He is a heavy-set man with a villainous face. There's some mistake."

"There ce'tainly is, but not at this end of the line. This is Kinney all right. I've seen him at Yuma. He was heading for the Mal Pais country and he died on the way. See hyer. Look at these soaked bandages. He's been wounded—shot mebbe—and the wound broke out on him again so that he bled to death."

"It's all a daze to me. Who is the other man if he isn't Kinney?"

"We're coming to that. I'm beginning to see daylight," said Steve, gently. "Let's run over this thing the way it might be. You've got to keep in mind that this man was weak, one of those spineless fellows that stronger folks lead around by the nose. Well, they make their getaway at Yuma after Struve has killed a guard. That killing of Dave Long shakes Kinney up a lot, he being no desperado but only a poor lost-dog kind of a guy. Struve notices it and remembers that this fellow weakened before. He makes up his mind to take no chances. From that moment he watches for a chance to make an end of his pardner. At Casa Grande they drop off the train they're riding and cut across country toward the Mal Pais. Mebbe they quarrel or mebbe Struve gets his chance and takes it. But after he has shot his man he sees he has made a mistake. Perhaps they were seen travelling in that direction. Anyhow, he is afraid the body will be found since he can't bury it right. He changes his plan and takes a big chance; cuts back to the track, boards a freight, and reaches Fort Lincoln."

"My God!" cried the other, startled for once out of his calm.

The officer nodded. "You're on the trail right enough. I wish we were both wrong, but we ain't."

"But surely she would have known he wasn't her brother, surely—"

The ranger shook his head. "She hadn't seen the black sheep since she was a kid of about seven. How would she know what he looked like? And Struve was primed with all the facts he had heard Kinney blat out time and again. She wasn't suspecting any imposition and he worked her to a fare-you-well."

Larry Neill set his teeth on a wave of icy despair.

"And she's in that devil's power. She would be as safe in a den of rattlers. To think that I had my foot on his neck this mo'ning and didn't break it."

"She's safe so long as she is necessary to him. She's in deadly peril as soon as he finds her one witness too many. If he walks into my boys' trap at the Arivaca cut-off, all right. If not, God help her! I've shut the door to Mexico and safety in his face. He'll strike back for the Mal Pais country. It's his one chance, and he'll want to travel light and fast."

"If he starts back Tom Long's party may get him."

"That's one more chance for her, but it's a slim one. He'll cut straight across country; they're following the trail. No, seh, our best bet is my rangers. They'd ought to land him, too."

"Oh, ought to," derided the other impatiently. "Point is, if they don't. How are we going to save her? You know this country. I don't."

"Don't tear your shirt, amigo," smiled the ranger. "We'll arrive faster if we don't go off half-cocked. Let's picket the broncs, amble down to the spring, and smoke a cigarette. We've got to ride twenty miles for fresh hawsses and these have got to have a little rest."

They unsaddled and picketed, then strolled to the spring.

"I've been thinking that maybe we have made a mistake. Isn't it possible the man with Miss Kinney is not Struve?" asked Neill.

"That's easy proved. You saw him this mo'ning." The lieutenant went down into his pocket once more for a photograph. "Does this favor the man with Miss Kinney?"

Under the blaze of another match, shielded by the ranger's hands, Larry looked into the scowling, villainous face he had seen earlier in the day. There could be no mistaking those leering, cruel eyes nor the ratlike, shifty look of the face, not to mention the long scar across it. His heart sank.

"It's the man."

"Don't you blame yourself for not putting his lights out. How could you tell who he was?"

"I knew he was a ruffian, hide and hair."

"But you thought he was her brother and that's a whole lot different. What do you say to grubbing here? We've got to go to the Halle ranch for hawsses and it's a long jog."

They lit a fire and over their coffee discussed plans. In the midst of these the Southerner picked up idly a piece of wrapping-paper. Upon it was pencilled a wavering scrawl:

Bleeding has broke out again. Can't stop it. Struve shot me and left me for dead ten miles back. I didn't kill the guard or know he meant to. J. KINNEY.

Neill handed the paper to the ranger, who read it through, folded it, and gave it back to the other.

"Keep that paper. We may need it." His grave eyes went up the trail to where the dark figure lay motionless in the cold moonlight. "Well, he's come to the end of the trail—the only end he could have reached. He wasn't strong enough to survive as a bad man. Poor devil!"

They buried him in a clump of cottonwoods and left a little pile of rocks to mark the spot.

CHAPTER IV — LOST!

AFTER HER PRECIPITATE LEAVE-TAKING of the man whose team she had bought or borrowed, Margaret Kinney nursed the fires of her indignation in silence, banking them for future use against the time when she should meet him again in the event that should ever happen. She brought her whip-lash snapping above the backs of the horses, and there was that in the supple motion of the small strong wrist which suggested that nothing would have pleased her more than having this audacious Texan there in place of the innocent animals. For whatever of inherited savagery lay latent in her blood had been flogged to the surface by the circumstances into which she had been thrust. Never in all her placid life had she known the tug of passion any closer than from across the footlights of a theatre.

She had had, to be sure, one stinging shame, but it had been buried in far-away Arizona, quite beyond the ken of the convention-bound people of the little Wisconsin town where she dwelt. But within the past twelve hours Fate had taken hold of her with both hands and thrust her into Life. She sensed for the first time its roughness, its nakedness, its tragedy. She had known the sensations of a hunted wild beast, the flush of shame for her kinship to this coarse ruffian by her side, and the shock of outraged maiden modesty at kisses ravished from her by force. The teacher hardly knew herself for the same young woman who but yesterday was engrossed in multiplication tables and third readers.

A sinister laugh from the man beside her brought the girl back to the present.

She looked at him and then looked quickly away again. There was something absolutely repulsive in the creature—in the big ears that stood out from the close-cropped head, in the fishy eyes that saw everything without ever looking directly at anything, in the crooked mouth with its irregular rows of stained teeth from which several were missing. She had often wondered about her brother, but never at the worst had she imagined anything so bad as this. The memory would be enough to give one the shudders for years.

"Guess I ain't next to all that happened there in the mesquite," he sneered, with a lift of the ugly lip.

She did not look at him. She did not speak. There seethed in her a loathing and a disgust beyond expression.

"Guess you forgot that a fellow can sometimes hear even when he can't see. Since I'm chaperooning you I'll make out to be there next time you meet a good-looking lady-killer. Funny, the difference it makes, being your brother. You ain't seen me since you was a kid, but you plumb forgot to kiss me."

There was a note in his voice she had not heard before, some hint of leering ribaldry in the thick laugh that for the first time stirred unease in her heart. She did not know that the desperate, wild-animal fear in him, so overpowering that everything else had been pushed to the background, had obscured certain phases of him that made her presence here such a danger as she could not yet conceive. That fear was now lifting, and the peril loomed imminent.

He put his arm along the back of the seat and grinned at her from his loose-lipped mouth.

"But o' course it ain't too late to begin now, my dearie."

Her fearless level eyes met squarely his shifty ones and read there something she could dread without understanding, something that was an undefined sacrilege of her sweet purity. For woman-like her instinct leaped beyond reason.

"Take down your arm," she ordered.

"Oh, I don't know, sis. I reckon your brother—"

"You're no brother of mine," she broke in. "At most it is an accident of birth I disown. I'll have no relationship with you of any sort."

"Is that why you're driving with me to Mexico?" he jeered.

"I made a mistake in trying to save you. If it were to do over again I should not lift a hand."

"You wouldn't, eh?"

There was something almost wolfish in the facial malignity that distorted him.

"Not a finger."

"Perhaps you'd give me up now if you had a chance?"

"I would if I did what was right."

"And you'd sure want to do what was right," he snarled.

"Take down your arm," she ordered again, a dangerous glitter in her eyes.

He thrust his evil face close to hers and showed his teeth in a blind rage that forgot everything else.

"Listen here, you little locoed baby. I got something to tell you that'll make your hair curl. You're right, I ain't your brother. I'm Nick Struve—Wolf Struve if you like that better. I lied you into believing me your brother, who ain't ever been anything but a skim-milk quitter. He's dead back there in the cactus somewhere, and I killed him!"

Terror flooded her eyes. Her very breathing hung suspended. She gazed at him in a frozen fascination of horror.

"Killed him because he gave me away seven years ago and was gittin' ready to round on me again. Folks don't live long that play Wolf Struve for a lamb. A wolf! That's what I am, a born wolf, and don't you forget it."

The fact itself did not need his words for emphasis. He fairly reeked the beast of prey. She had to nerve herself against faintness. She must not swoon. She dared not.

"Think you can threaten to give me up, do you? 'Fore I'm through with you you'll wish you had never been born. You'll crawl on your knees and beg me to kill you."

Such a devil of wickedness she had never seen in human eyes before. The ruthlessness left no room for appeal. Unless the courage to tame him lay in her she was lost utterly.

He continued his exultant bragging, blatantly, ferociously.

"I didn't tell you about my escape; how a guard tried to stop me and I put the son of a gun out of business. There's a price on my head. D'ye think I'm the man to give you a chance to squeal on me? D'ye think I'll let a pink-and-white chit send me back to be strangled?" he screamed.

The stark courage in her rose to the crisis. Not an hour before she had seen the Texan cow him. He was of the kind would take the whip whiningly could she but wield it. Her scornful eyes fastened on him contemptuously, chiseled into the cur heart of him.

"What will you do?" she demanded, fronting the issue that must sooner or later rise.

The raucous jangle of his laugh failed to disturb the steadiness of her gaze. To reassure himself of his mastery he began to bluster, to threaten, turning loose such a storm of vile abuse as she had never heard. He was plainly working his nerve up to the necessary pitch.

In her first terror she had dropped the reins. Her hands had slipped unconsciously under the lap-robe. Now one of them touched something chilly on the seat beside her. She almost gasped her relief. It was the selfsame revolver with which she had tried to hold up the Texan.

In the midst of Struve's flood of invective the girl's hand leaped quickly from the lap-robe. A cold muzzle pressed against his cheek brought the convict's outburst to an abrupt close.

"If you move I'll fire," she said quietly.

For a long moment their gazes gripped, the deadly clear eyes of the young woman and the furtive ones of the miscreant. Underneath the robe she felt a stealthy movement, and cried out quickly: "Hands up!"

With a curse he threw his arms into the air.

"Jump out! Don't lower your hands!"

"My ankle," he whined.

"Jump!"

His leap cleared the wheel and threw him to the ground. She caught up the whip and slashed wildly at the horses. They sprang forward in a panic, flying wildly across the open plain. Margaret heard a revolver bark twice. After that she was so busy trying to regain control of the team that she could think of nothing else. The horses were young and full of spirit, so that she had all she could do to keep the trap from being upset. It wound in and out among the hills, taking perilous places safely to her surprise, and was at last brought to a stop only by the narrowing of a draw into which the animals had bolted.

They were quiet now beyond any chance of farther runaway, even had it been possible. Margaret dropped the lines on the dashboard and began to sob, at first in slow deep breaths and then in quicker uneven ones. Plucky as she was, the girl had had about all her nerves could stand for one day. The strain of her preparation for flight, the long night drive, and the excitement of the last two hours were telling on her in a hysterical reaction.

She wept herself out, dried her eyes with dabs of her little kerchief, and came back to a calm consideration of her situation. She must get back to Fort Lincoln as soon as possible, and she must do it without encountering the convict. For in the course of the runaway the revolver had been jolted from the trap.

Not quite sure in which direction lay the road, she got out from the trap, topped the hill to her right, and looked around. She saw in all directions nothing but rolling hilltops, merging into each other even to the horizon's edge. In her wild flight among these hills she had lost count of direction. She had not yet learned how to know north from south by the sun, and if she had it would have helped but little since she knew only vaguely the general line of their travel.

She felt sure that from the top of the next rise she could locate the road, but once there she was as uncertain as before. Before giving up she breasted a third hill to the summit. Still no signs of the road. Reluctantly she retraced her steps, and at the foot of the hill was uncertain whether she should turn to right or left. Choosing the left, from the next height she could see nothing of the team. She was not yet alarmed. It was ridiculous to suppose that she was lost. How could she be when she was within three or four hundred yards of the rig? She would cut across the shoulder into the wash and climb the hillock beyond. For behind it the team must certainly be.

But at her journey's end her eyes were gladdened by no sight of the horses. Every draw was like its neighbor, every rolling rise a replica of the next. The truth came home to a sinking heart. She was lost in one of the great deserts of Texas. She would wander for days as others had, and she would die in the end of starvation and thirst. Nobody would know where to look for her, since she had told none where she was going. Only yesterday at her boarding-house she had heard a young man tell how a tenderfoot had been found dead after he had wandered round and round in intersecting circles. She sank down and gave herself up to despair.

But not for long. She was too full of grit to give up without a long fight. How many hours she wandered Margaret Kinney did not know. The sun was high in the heavens when she began. It had given place to flooding moonlight long before her worn feet and aching heart gave up the search for some human landmark. Once at least she must have slept, for she stared up from a spot where she had sunk down to look up into a starry sky that was new to her.

The moon had sailed across the vault and grown chill and faint with dawn before she gave up, completely exhausted, and when her eyes opened again it was upon a young day fresh and sweet. She knew by this time hunger and an acute thirst. As the day increased, this last she knew must be a torment of swollen tongue and lime-kiln throat. Yesterday she had cried for help till her voice had failed. A dumb despair had now driven away her terror.

And then into the awful silence leaped a sound like a messenger of hope. It was a shot, so close that she could see the smoke rise from an arroyo near. She ran forward till she could look down into it and caught sight of a man with a dead bird in his hand. He had his back toward her and was stooping over a fire. Slithering down over the short dry grass, she was upon him almost before she could stop.

"I've been lost all night and all yesterday," she sobbed.

He snatched at the revolver lying beside him and whirled like a flash as if to meet an attack. The girl's pumping heart seemed to stand still. The man snarling at her was the convict Struve.

CHAPTER V — LARRY NEILL TO THE RESCUE

THE SNARL GAVE WAY slowly to a grim more malign than his open hostility.

"So you've been lost! And now you're found—come safe back to your loving brother. Ain't that luck for you? Hunted all over Texas till you found him, eh? And it's a powerful big State, too."

She caught sight of something that made her forget all else.

"Have you got water in that canteen?" she asked, her parched eyes staring at it.

"Yes, dearie."

"Give it me."

He squatted tailor-fashion on the ground, put the canteen between his knees, and shoved his teeth in a crooked grin.

"Thirsty?"

"I'm dying for a drink."

"You look like a right lively corpse."

"Give it to me."

"Will you take it now or wait till you get it?"

"My throat's baked. I want water," she said hoarsely.

"Most folks want a lot they never get."

She walked toward him with her hand outstretched.

"I tell you I've got to have it."

He laughed evilly. "Water's at a premium right now. Likely there ain't enough here to get us both out of this infernal hole alive. Yes, it's sure at a premium."

He let his eye drift insolently over her and take stock of his prey, in the same feline way of a cat with a mouse, gloating over her distress and the details of her young good looks. His tainted gaze got the faint pure touch of color in her face, the reddish tinge of her wavy brown hair, the desirable sweetness of her rounded maidenhood. If her step dragged, if dusky hollows shadowed her lids, if the native courage had been washed from the hopeless eyes, there was no spring of manliness hid deep within him that rose to refresh her exhaustion. No pity or compunction stirred at her sweet helplessness.

"Do you want my money?" she asked wearily.

"I'll take that to begin with."

She tossed him her purse. "There should be seventy dollars there.

May I have a drink now?"

"Not yet, my dear. First you got to come up to me and put your arms round—"

He broke off with a curse, for she was flying toward the little circle of cottonwoods some forty yards away. She had caught a glimpse of the water-hole and was speeding for it.

"Come back here," he called, and in a rage let fly a bullet after her.

She paid no heed, did not stop till she reached the spring and threw herself down full length to drink, to lave her burnt face, to drink again of the alkali brackish water that trickled down her throat like nectar incomparably delicious.

She was just rising to her feet when Struve hobbled up.

"Don't you think you can play with me, missie. When I give the word you stop in your tracks, and when I say 'Jump!' step lively."

She did not answer. Her head was lifted in a listening attitude, as if to catch some sound that came faintly to her from a distance.

"You're mine, my beauty, to do with as I please, and don't you forget it."

She did not hear him. Her ears were attuned to voices floating to her across the desert. Of course she was beginning to wander in her mind. She knew that. There could be no other human beings in this sea of loneliness. They were alone; just they two, the degenerate ruffian and his victim. Still, it was strange. She certainly had imagined the murmur of people talking. It must be the beginning of delirium.

"Do you hear me?" screamed Struve, striking her on the cheek with his fist. "I'm your master and you're my squaw."

She did not cringe as he had expected, nor did she show fight. Indeed the knowledge of the blow seemed scarcely to have penetrated her mental penumbra. She still had that strange waiting aspect, but her eyes were beginning to light with new-born hope. Something in her manner shook the man's confidence; a dawning fear swept away his bluster. He, too, was now listening intently.

Again the low murmur, beyond a possibility of doubt. Both of them caught it. The girl opened her throat in a loud cry for help. An answering shout came back clear and strong. Struve wheeled and started up the arroyo, bending in and out among the cactus till he disappeared over the brow.

Two horsemen burst into sight, galloping down the steep trail at breakneck speed, flinging down a small avalanche of shale with them. One of them caught sight of the girl, drew up so short that his horse slid to its haunches, and leaped from the saddle in a cloud of dust.

He ran toward her, and she to him, hands out to meet her rescuer.

"Why didn't you come sooner? I've waited so long," she cried pathetically, as his arms went about her.

"You poor lamb! Thank God we're in time!" was all he could say.

Then for the first time in her life she fainted.

The other rider lounged forward, a hat in his hand that he had just picked up close to the fire.

"We seem to have stampeded part of this camping party. I'll just take a run up this hill and see if I can't find the missing section and persuade it to stay a while. I don't reckon you need me hyer, do you?" he grinned, with a glance at Neill and his burden.

"All right. You'll find me here when you get back, Fraser," the other answered.

Larry carried the girl to the water-hole and set her down beside it. He sprinkled her face with water, and presently her lids trembled and fluttered open. She lay there with her head on his arm and looked at him quite without surprise.

"How did you find me?"

"Mainly luck. We followed your trail to where we found the rig. After that it was guessing where the needle was in the haystack It just happened we were cutting across country to water when we heard a shot."

"That must have been when he fired at me," she said.

"My God! Did he shoot at you?"

"Yes. Where is he now?" She shuddered.

"Cutting over the hills with Steve after him."

"Steve?"

"My friend, Lieutenant Fraser. He is an officer in the ranger force."

"Oh!" She relapsed into a momentary silence before she said: "He isn't my brother at all. He is a murderer." She gave a sudden little moan of pain as memory pierced her of what he had said. "He bragged to me that he had killed my brother. He meant to kill me, I think."

"Sho! It doesn't matter what the coyote meant. It's all over now. You're with friends."

A warm smile lit his steel-blue eyes, softened the lines of his lean, hard face. Never had shipwrecked mariner come to safer harbor than she. She knew that this slim, sun-bronzed Westerner was a man's man, that strength and nerve inhabited his sinewy frame. He would fight for her because she was a woman as long as he could stand and see.

A touch of color washed back into her cheeks, a glow of courage into her heart. "Yes, it's all over. The weary, weary hours—and the fear—and the pain—and the dreadful thirst—and worst of all, him!"

She began to cry softly, hiding her face in his coat-sleeve.

"I'm crying because—it's all over. I'm a little fool, just as—as you said I was."

"I didn't know you then," he smiled. "I'm right likely to make snap-shot judgments that are 'way off."

"You knew me well enough to—" She broke off in the middle, bathed in a flush of remembrance that brought her coppery head up from his arm instantly.

"Be careful. You're dizzy yet."

"I'm all right now, thank you," she answered, her embarrassed profile haughtily in the air. "But I'm ravenous for something to eat. It's been twenty-four hours since I've had a bite. That's why I'm weepy and faint. I should think you might make a snap-shot judgment that breakfast wouldn't hurt me."

He jumped up contritely. "That's right. What a goat I am!"

His long, clean stride carried him over the distance that separated him from his bronco. Out of the saddle-bags he drew some sandwiches wrapped in a newspaper.

"Here, Miss Margaret! You begin on these. I'll have coffee ready in two shakes of a cow's tail. And what do you say to bacon?"

He understood her to remark from the depths of a sandwich that she said "Amen!" to it, and that she would take everything he had and as soon as he could get it ready. She was as good as her word. He found no cause to complain of her appetite. Bacon and sandwiches and coffee were all consumed in quantities reasonable for a famished girl who had been tramping actively for a day and a night, and, since she was a child of impulse, she turned more friendly eyes on him who had appeased her appetite.

"I suppose you are a cowboy like everybody else in this country?" she ventured amiably after her hunger had become less sharp.

"No, I belong to the government reclamation service."

"Oh!" She had a vague idea she had heard of it before. "Who is it you reclaim? Indians, I suppose."

"We reclaim young ladies when we find them wandering about the desert," he smiled.

"Is that what the government pays you for?"

"Not entirely. Part of the time I examine irrigation projects and report on their feasibility. I have been known to build dams and bore tunnels."

"And what of the young ladies you reclaim? Do you bore them?" she asked saucily.

"I understand they have hitherto always found me very entertaining," he claimed boldly, his smiling eyes on her.

"Indeed!"

"But young ladies are peculiar. Sometimes we think we're entertaining them when we ain't."

"I'm sure you are right."

"And other times they're interested when they pretend they're not."

"It must be comforting to your vanity to think that," she said coldly. For his words had recalled similar ones spoken by him twenty-four hours earlier, which in turn had recalled his unpardonable sin.

The lieutenant of rangers appeared over the hill and descended into the draw. Miss Kinney went to meet him.

"He got away?" she asked.

"Yes, ma'am. I lost him in some of these hollows, or rather I never found him. I'm going to take my hawss and swing round in a circle."

"What are you going to do with me?" she smiled.

"I been thinking that the best thing would be for you to go to the Mal Pais mines with Mr. Neill."

"Who is Mr. Neill?"

"The gentleman over there by the fire."

"Must I go with him? I should feel safer in your company, lieutenant."

"You'll be safe enough in his, Miss Kinney."

"You know me then?" she asked.

"I've seen you at Fort Lincoln. You were pointed out to me once as a new teacher."

"But I don't want to go to the Mal Pais mines. I want to go to Fort Lincoln. As to this gentleman, I have no claims on him and shall not trouble him to burden himself with me."

Steve laughed. "I don't reckon he would think, it a terrible burden, ma'am. And about the Mal Pais—this is how it is. Fort Lincoln is all of sixty miles from here as the crow flies. The mines are about seventeen. My notion was you could get there and take the stage tomorrow to your town."

"What shall I do for a horse?"

"I expect Mr. Neill will let you ride his. He can walk beside the hawss."

"That won't do at all. Why should I put him to that inconvenience? I'll walk myself."

The ranger flashed his friendly smile at her. He had an instinct that served him with women. "Any way that suits you and him suits me. I'm right sorry that I've got to leave you and take out after that hound Struve, but you may take my word for it that this gentleman will look after you all right and bring you safe to the Mal Pais."

"He is a stranger to me. I've only met him once and on that occasion not pleasantly. I don't like to put myself under an obligation to him. But of course if I must I must."

"That's the right sensible way to look at it. In this little old world we got to do a heap we don't want to do. For instance, I'd rather see you to the Mal Pais than hike over the hills after this fellow," he concluded gallantly.

Neill, who had been packing the coffee-pot and the frying-pan, now sauntered forward with his horse.

"Well, what's the program?" he wanted to know.

"It's you and Miss Kinney for the Mal Pais, me for the trail. I ain't very likely to find Mr. Struve, but you can't always sometimes tell. Anyhow, I'm going to take a shot at it," the ranger answered.

"And at him?" his friend suggested.

"Oh, I reckon not. He may be a sure-enough wolf, but I expect this ain't his day to howl."

Steve whistled to his pony, swung to the saddle when it trotted up, and waved his hat in farewell.

His "Adios!" drifted back to them from the crown of the hill just before he disappeared over its edge.

CHAPTER VI — SOMEBODY'S ACTING MIGHTY FOOLISH.

LARRY NEILL WATCHED HIM vanish and then turned smiling to Miss Kinney.

"All aboard for the Mal Pais," he sang out cheerfully.

Too cheerfully perhaps. His assurance that all was well between them chilled her manner. He might forgive himself easily if he was that sort of man; she would at least show him she was no party, to it. He had treated her outrageously, had manhandled her with deliberate intent to insult. She would show him no one alive could treat her so and calmly assume to her that it was all right.

Her cool eyes examined the horse, and him.

"I don't quite see how you expect to arrange it, Mr. Neill. That is your name, isn't it?" she added indifferently.

"That's my name—Larry Neill. Easiest thing in the world to arrange. We ride pillion if it suits you; if not, I'll walk."

"Neither plan suits me," she announced curtly, her gaze on the far-away hills.

He glanced at her in quick surprise, then made the mistake of letting himself smile at her frosty aloofness instead of being crestfallen by it. She happened to look round and catch that smile before he could extinguish it. Her petulance hardened instantly to a resolution.

"I don't quite know what we're going to do about it—unless you walk," he proposed, amused at the absurdity of his suggestion.

"That's just what I'm going to do," she retorted promptly.

"What!" He wheeled on her with an astonished smile on his face.

This served merely to irritate her.

"I said I was going to walk."

"Walk seventeen miles?"

"Seventy if I choose."

"Nonsense! Of course you won't."

Her eyebrows lifted in ironic demurrer. "I think you must let me be the judge of that," she said gently.

"Walk!" he reiterated. "Why, you're walked out. You couldn't go a mile. What do you take me for? Think I'm going to let you come that on me."

"I don't quite see how you can help it, Mr. Neill," she answered.

"Help it! Why, it ain't reasonable. Of course you'll ride."

"Of course I won't."

She set off briskly, almost jauntily, despite her tired feet and aching limbs.

"Well, if that don't beat—" He broke off to laugh at the situation. After she had gone twenty steps he called after her in a voice that did not suppress its chuckle: "You ain't going the right direction, Miss Kinney."

She whirled round on him in anger. How dared he laugh at her?

"Which is the right way?" she choked.

"North by west is about it."

She was almost reduced to stamping her foot.

Without condescending to ask more definite instructions she struck off at haphazard, and by chance guessed right. There was nothing for it but to pursue. Wherefore the man pursued. The horse at his heels hampered his stride, but he caught up with her soon.

"Somebody's acting mighty foolish," he said.

She said nothing very eloquently.

"If I need punishing, ma'am, don't punish yourself, but me. You ain't able to walk and that's a fact."

She gave her silent attention strictly to the business of making progress through the cactus and the sand.

"Say I'm all you think I am. You can trample on me proper after we get to the Mal Pais. Don't have to know me at all if you don't want to. Won't you ride, ma'am? Please!"

His distress filled her with a fierce delight. She stumbled defiantly forward.

He pondered a while before he asked quietly:

"Ain't you going to ride, Miss Kinney?"

"No, I'm not. Better go on. Pray don't let me detain you."

"All right. See that peak with the spur to it? Well, you keep that directly in line and make straight for it. I'll say good-by now, ma'am. I got to hurry to be in time for dinner. I'll send some one out from the camp to meet you that ain't such a villain as I am."

He swung to the saddle, put spurs to his pony, and cantered away. She could scarce believe it, even when he rode straight over the hill without a backward glance. He would never leave her. Surely he would not do that. She could never reach the camp, and he knew it. To be left alone in the desert again; the horror of it broke her down, but not immediately. She went proudly forward with her head in the air at first. He might look round. Perhaps he was peeping at her from behind some cholla. She would not gratify him by showing any interest in his whereabouts. But presently she began to lag, to scan draws and mesas anxiously for him, even to call aloud in an ineffective little voice which the empty hills echoed faintly. But from him there came no answer.

She sat down and wept in self-pity. Of course she had told him to go, but he knew well enough she did not mean it. A magnanimous man would have taken a better revenge on an exhausted girl than to leave her alone in such a spot, and after she had endured such a terrible experience as she had. She had read about the chivalry of Western men. Yet these two had ridden away on their horses and left her to live or die as chance willed it.

"Now, don't you feel so bad, Miss Margaret. I wasn't aiming really to leave you, of course," a voice interrupted her sobs to say.

She looked through the laced fingers that covered her face, mightily relieved, but not yet willing to confess it. The engineer had made a circuit and stolen up quietly behind.

"Oh! I thought you had gone," she said as carelessly as she could with a voice not clear of tears.

"Were you crying because you were afraid I hadn't?" he asked.

"I ran a cactus into my foot. And I didn't say anything about crying."

"Then if your foot is hurt you will want to ride. That seventeen miles might be too long a stroll before you get through with it."

"I don't know what I'll do yet," she answered shortly.

"I know what you'll do."

"Yes?"

"You'll quit your foolishness and get on this hawss."

She flushed angrily. "I won't!"

He stooped down, gathered her up in his arms, and lifted her to the saddle.

"That's what you're going to do whether you like it or not," he informed her.

"How are you going to make me stay here, now you have put me here?"

"I'm going to get on behind and hold you if it's necessary."

He was sensible enough of the folly of it all, but he did not see what else he could do. She had chosen to punish him through herself in a way that was impossible. It was a childish thing to do, born of some touch of hysteria her experience had induced, and he could only treat her as a child till she was safely back in civilization.

Their wills met in their eyes, and the man's, masculine and dominant, won the battle. The long fringe of hers fell to the soft cheeks.

"It won't be at all necessary," she promised.

"Are you sure?"

"Quite sure."

"That's the way to talk."

"If you care to know," she boiled over, "I think you the most hateful man I ever met."

"That's all right," he grinned ruefully. "You're the most contrary woman I ever bumped into, so I reckon honors are easy."

He strode along beside the horse, mile after mile, in a silence which neither of them cared to break. The sap of youth flowed free in him, was in his elastic tread, in the set of his broad shoulders, in the carriage of his small, well-shaped head. He was as lean-loined and lithe as a panther, and his stride ate up the miles as easily.

They nooned at a spring in the dry wash of Bronco Creek. After he had unsaddled and picketed he condescended to explain to her.

"We'll stay here three hours or mebbe four through the heat of the day."

"Is it far now?" she asked wearily.

"Not more than seven miles I should judge. Are you about all in?"

"Oh, no! I'm all right, thank you," she said, with forced sprightliness.

His shrewd, hard gaze went over her and knew better.

"You lie down under those live-oaks and I'll get some grub ready."

"I'll cook lunch while you lie down. You must be tired walking so far through the sun," said Miss Kinney.

"Have I got to pick you up again and carry you there?"

"No, you haven't. You keep your hands off me," she flashed.

But nevertheless she betook herself to the shade of the live-oaks and lay down. When he went to call her for lunch he found her fast asleep with her head pillowed on her arm. She looked so haggard that he had not the heart to rouse her.

"Let her sleep. It will be the making of her. She's fair done. But ain't she plucky? And that spirited! Ready to fight so long as she can drag a foot. And her so sorter slim and delicate. Funny how she hangs onto her grudge against me. Sho! I hadn't ought to have kissed her, but I'll never tell her so."

He went back to his coffee and bacon, dined, and lay down for a siesta beneath a cottonwood some distance removed from the live-oaks where Miss Kinney reposed. For two or three hours he slept soundly, having been in the saddle all night. It was mid-afternoon when he awoke, and the sun was sliding down the blue vault toward the sawtoothed range to the west. He found the girl still lost to the world in deep slumber.

The man from the Panhandle looked across the desert that palpitated with heat, and saw through the marvelous atmosphere the smoke of the ore-mills curling upward. He was no tenderfoot, to suppose that ten minutes' brisk walking would take him to them. He guessed the distance at about two and a half hour's travel.

"This is ce'tainly a hot evening. I expect we better wait till sundown before moving," he said aloud.

Having made up his mind, it was characteristic of him that he was asleep again in five minutes. This time she wakened before him, to look into a wonderful sea of gold that filled the crotches of the hills between the purple teeth. No sun was to be seen—it had sunk behind the peaks—but the trail of its declension was marked by that great pool of glory into which she gazed.

Margaret crossed the wash to the cottonwood under which her escort was lying. He was fast asleep on his back, his gray shirt open at the bronzed, sinewy neck. The supple, graceful lines of him were relaxed, but even her inexperience appreciated the splendid shoulders and the long rippling muscles. The maidenly instinct in her would allow but one glance at him, and she was turning away when his eyes opened.

Her face, judging from its tint, might have absorbed some of the sun-glow into which she had been gazing.

"I came to see if you were awake," she explained.

"Yes, ma'am, I am," he smiled.

"I was thinking that we ought to be going. It will be dark before we reach Mal Pais."

He leaped to his feet and faced her.

"C'rect."

"Are you hungry?"

"Yes."

He relit the fire and put on the coffee-pot before he saddled the horse. She ate and drank hurriedly, soon announcing herself ready for the start.

She mounted from his hand; then without asking any questions he swung to a place behind her.

"We'll both ride," he said.

The stars were out before they reached the outskirts of the mining-camp. At the first house of the rambling suburbs Neill slipped to the ground and walked beside her toward the old adobe plaza of the Mexican town.

People passed them on the run, paying no attention to them, and others dribbled singly or in small groups from the houses and saloons. All of them were converging excitedly to the plaza.

"Must be something doing here," said her guide. "Now I wonder what!"

Round the next turn he found his answer. There must have been present two or three hundred men, mostly miners, and their gazes all focussed on two figures which stood against a door at the top of five or six steps. One of the forms was crouched on its knees, abject, cringing terror stamped on the white villainous face upturned to the electric light above. But the other was on its feet, a revolver in each hand, a smile of reckless daring on the boyish countenance that just now stood for law and order in Mal Pais.

The man beside the girl read the situation at a glance. The handcuffed figure groveling on the steps belonged to the murderer Struve, and over him stood lightly the young ranger Steve Fraser. He was standing off a mob that had gathered to lynch his prisoner, and one glance at him was enough to explain how he had won his reputation as the most dashing and fearless member of a singularly efficient force. For plain to be read as the danger that confronted him was the fact that peril was as the breath of life to his nostrils.

CHAPTER VII — ENTER MR. DUNKE

"HE'S MY PRISONER AND you can't have him," the girl heard the ranger say.

The answer came in a roar of rage. "By God, we'll show you!"

"If you want him, take him. But don't come unless you are ready to pay the price!" warned the officer.

He was bareheaded and his dark-brown curly hair crisped round his forehead engagingly. Round his right hand was tied a blood-stained handkerchief. A boy he looked, but his record was a man's, and so the mob that swayed uncertainly below him knew. His gray eyes were steady as steel despite the fire that glowed in them. He stood at ease, with nerve unshaken, the curious lifted look of a great moment about the poise of his graceful figure.

"It is Lieutenant Fraser," cried Margaret, but as she looked down she missed her escort.

An instant, and she saw him. He was circling the outskirts of the crowd at a run. For just a heart-beat she wondered what he was about, but her brain told her before her eye. He swung in toward the steps, shoulders down, and bored a way through the stragglers straight to the heart of the turmoil. Taking the steps in two jumps, he stood beside the ranger.

"Hello, Tennessee," grinned that young man. "Come to be a pall-bearer?"

"Hello, Texas! Can't say, I'm sure. Just dropped in to see what's doing."

Steve's admiring gaze approved him a man from the ground up. But the ranger only laughed and said: "The band's going to play a right lively tune, looks like."

The man from the Panhandle had his revolvers out already. "Yes, there will be a hot time in the old town to-night, I shouldn't wonder."

But for the moment the attackers were inclined to parley. Their leader stepped out and held up a hand for a suspension of hostilities. He was a large man, heavily built, and powerful as a bear. There was about him an air of authority, as of one used to being obeyed. He was dressed roughly enough in corduroy and miner's half-leg boots, but these were of the most expensive material and cut. His cold gray eye and thin lips denied the manner of superficial heartiness he habitually carried. If one scratched the veneer of good nature it was to find a hard selfishness that went to his core.

"It's Mr. Dunke!" the young school-teacher cried aloud in surprise.

"I've got something to say to you, Mr. Lieutenant Ranger," he announced, with importance.

"Uncork it," was Fraser's advice.

"We don't want to have any trouble with you, but we're here for business. This man is a cold-blooded murderer and we mean to do justice on him."

Steve laughed insolently. "If all them that hollers for justice the loudest got it done to them, Mr. Dunke, there'd be a right smart shrinkage in the census returns."

Dunke's eye gleamed with anger. "We're not here to listen to any smart guys, sir. Will you give up Struve to us or will you not?"

"That's easy. I will not."

The mob leader turned to the Tennessean. "Young man, I don't know who you are, but if you mean to butt into a quarrel that ain't yours all I've got to say is that you're hunting an early grave."

"We'll know about that later, seh."

"You stand pat, do you?"

"Well, seh, I draw to a pair that opens the pot anyhow," answered Larry, with a slight motion of his weapons.

Dunke fell back into the mob, a shot rang out into the night, and the crowd swayed forward. But at that instant the door behind Fraser swung open. A frightened voice sounded in his ear.

"Quick, Steve!"

The ranger slewed his head, gave an exclamation of surprise, and hurriedly threw his prisoner into the open passage.

"Back, Larry! Lively, my boy!" he ordered.

Neill leaped back in a spatter of bullets that rained round him. Next moment the door was swung shut again.

"You all right, Nell?" asked Fraser quickly of the young woman who had opened the door, and upon her affirmative reply he added: "Everybody alive and kicking? Nobody get a pill?"

"I'm all right for one," returned Larry. "But we had better get out of this passage. I notice our friends the enemy are sending their cards through the door after us right anxious."

As he spoke a bullet tore a jagged splinter from a panel and buried itself in the ceiling. A second and a third followed.

"That's c'rect. We'd better be 'Not at home' when they call. Eh, Nell?"

Steve put an arm affectionately round the waist of the young woman who had come in such timely fashion to their aid and ran through the passage with her to the room beyond, Neill following with the prisoner.

"You're wounded, Steve," the young woman cried.

He shrugged. "Scratch in the hand. Got it when I arrested him. Had to shoot his trigger finger off."

"But I must see to it."

"Not now; wait till we're out of the woods." He turned to his friend: "Nell, let me introduce to you Mr. Neill, from the Panhandle. Mr. Neill, this is my sister. I don't know how come she to drop down behind us like an angel from heaven, but that's a story will wait. The thing we got to do right now is to light a shuck out of here."

His friend nodded, listening to the sound of blows battering the outer door. "They'll have it down in another minute. We've got to burn the wind seven ways for Sunday."

"What I'd like to know is whether there are two entrances to this rat-trap. Do you happen to know, Nell?" asked Fraser of his sister.

"Three," she answered promptly. "There's a back door into the court and a trap-door to the roof. That's the way I came."

"And it's the way we'll go. I might a-known you'd know all about it give you a quarter of a chance," her brother said admiringly. "We'll duck through the roof and let Mr. Dunke hold the sack. Lead the way, sis."

She guided them along another passageway and up some stairs to the second story. The trap-door that opened to the flat roof was above the bed about six feet. Neill caught the edges of the narrow opening, drew himself up, and wriggled through. Fraser lifted his sister by the waist high enough for Larry to catch her hands and draw her up.

"Hurry, Steve," she urged. "They've broken in. Hurry, dear."

The ranger unlocked his prisoner's handcuffs and tossed them up to the Tennessean.

"Get a move on you, Mr. Struve, unless you want to figure in a necktie party," he advised.

But the convict's flabby muscles were unequal to the task of getting him through the opening. Besides which, his wounded hand, tied up with a blood-soaked rag, impeded him. He had to be pulled from above and boosted from behind. Fraser, fit to handle his weight in wildcats, as an admirer had once put it, found no trouble in following. Steps were already heard on the stairs below when Larry slipped the cover to its place and put upon it a large flat stone which he found on the roof for that purpose. The fugitives crawled along the roof on their hands and knees so as to escape the observation of the howling mob outside the house. Presently they came into the shadows, and Nell rose, ran forward to a little ladder which led to a higher roof, and swiftly ascended. Neill, who was at her heels, could not fail to note the light supple grace with which she moved. He thought he had never seen a more charming woman in appearance. She still somehow retained the slim figure and taking ways of a girl, in conjunction with the soft rounded curves of a present-day Madonna.

Two more roofs were crossed before they came to another open trap-door. A lamp in the room below showed it to be a bedroom with two cots in it. Two children, one of them a baby, were asleep in these. A sweet-faced woman past middle age looked anxiously up with hands clasped together as in prayer.

"Is it you, Nellie?" she asked.

"Yes, mother, and Steve, and his friend. We're all right."

Fraser dropped through, and his sister let herself down into his arms. Struve followed, and was immediately handcuffed. Larry put back the trap and fastened it from within before he dropped down.

"We shall have to leave at once, mother, without waiting to dress the children," explained Fraser. "Wrap them in blankets and take some clothes along. I'll drop you at the hotel and slip my prisoner into the jail the back way if I can; that is, if another plan I have doesn't work."

The oldest child awoke and caught sight of Fraser. He reached out his hands in excitement and began to call: "Uncle Steve! Uncle Steve back again."

Fraser picked up the youngster. "Yes, Uncle Steve is back. But we're going to play a game that Indians are after us. Webb must be good and keep very, very still. He mustn't say a word till uncle tells him he may."

The little fellow clapped his hands. "Goody, goody! Shall we begin now?"

"Right this minute, son. Better take your money with you, mother. Is father here?"

"No, he is at the ranch. He went down in the stage to-day."

"All right, friends. We'll take the back way. Tennessee, will you look out for Mr. Struve? Sis will want to carry the baby."

They passed quietly down-stairs and out the back door. The starry night enveloped them coldly, and the moon looked down through rifted clouds. Nature was peaceful as her own silent hills, but the raucous jangle of cursing voices from a distance made discord of the harmony. They slipped along through the shadows, meeting none except occasional figures hurrying to the plaza. At the hotel door the two men separated from the rest of the party, and took with them their prisoner.

"I'm going to put him for safe-keeping down the shaft of a mine my father and I own," explained Steve. "He wouldn't be safe in the jail, because Dunke, for private reasons, has made up his mind to put out his lights."

"Private reasons?" echoed the engineer.

"Mighty good ones, too. Ain't that right?" demanded the ranger of Struve.

The convict cursed, though his teeth still chattered with fright from the narrow escape he had had, but through his prison jargon ran a hint of some power he had over the man Dunke. It was plain he thought the latter had incited the lynching in order to shut the convict's mouth forever.

"Where is this shaft?" asked Neill.

"Up a gulch about half a mile from here."

Fraser's eyes fixed themselves on a young man who passed on the run. He suddenly put his fingers to his lips and gave a low whistle. The running man stopped instantly, his head alert to catch the direction from which the sound had come. Steve whistled again and the stranger turned toward them.

"It's Brown, one of my rangers," explained the lieutenant.

Brown, it appeared, had just reached town and stabled his horse when word came to him that there was trouble on the plaza. He had been making for it when his officer's whistle stopped him.

"It's all over except getting this man to safety. I'm going to put him down an abandoned shaft of the Jackrabbit. He'll be safe there, and nobody will think to look for him in any such place," said Fraser.

The man from the Panhandle drew his friend to one side. "Do you need me any longer? I left Miss Kinney right on the edge of that mob, and I expect I better look around and see where she is now."

"All right. No, we don't need you. Take care you don't let any of these miners recognize you. They might make you trouble while they're still hot. Well, so-long. See you to-morrow at the hotel."

The Tennessean looked to his guns to make sure they hung loose in the scabbards, then stepped briskly back toward the plaza.

CHAPTER VIII — WOULD YOU WORRY ABOUT ME?

MARGARET KINNEY'S HEART CEASED beating in that breathless instant after the two dauntless friends had flung defiance to two hundred. There was a sudden tightening of her throat, a fixing of dilated eyes on what would have been a thrilling spectacle had it not meant so much more to her. For as she leaned forward in the saddle with parted lips she knew a passionate surge of fear for one of the apparently doomed men that went through her like swift poison, that left her dizzy with the shock of it.

The thought of action came to her too late. As Dunke stepped back to give the signal for attack she cried out his name, but her voice was drowned in the yell of rage that filled the street. She tried to spur her horse into the crowd, to force a way to the men standing with such splendid fearlessness above this thirsty pack of wolves. But the denseness of the throng held her fixed even while revolvers flashed.

And then the miracle happened. She saw the door open and limned in a penumbra of darkness the white comely face of a woman. She saw the beleaguered men sway back and the door close in the faces of the horde. She saw bullets go crashing into the door, heard screams of baffled fury, and presently the crash of axes into the panels of the barrier that held them back. It seemed to fade away before her gaze, and instead of it she saw a doorway full of furious crowding miners.

Then presently her heart stood still again. From her higher place in the saddle, well back in the outskirts of the throng, in the dim light she made out a figure crouching on the roof; then another, and another, and a fourth. She suffered an agony of fear in the few heartbeats before they began to slip away. Her eyes swept the faces near her. One and all they were turned upon the struggling mass of humanity at the entrance to the passage. When she dared look again to the roof the fugitives were gone. She thought she perceived them swarming up a ladder to the higher roof, but in the surrounding grayness she could not be sure of this.

The stamping of feet inside the house continued. Once there was the sound of an exploding revolver. After a long time a heavy figure struggled into view through the roof-trap. It was Dunke himself. He caught sight of the ladder, gave a shout of triumph, and was off in pursuit of his flying prey. As others appeared on the roof they, too, took up the chase, a long line of indistinct running figures.

There were other women on the street now, most of them Mexicans, so that Margaret attracted little attention. She moved up opposite the house that had become the scene of action, expecting every moment to hear the shots that would determine the fate of the victims.

But no shots came. Lights flashed from room to room, and presently one light began to fill a room so brilliantly that she knew a lamp must have been overturned and set the house on fire. Dunke burst from the front door, scarce a dozen paces from her. There was a kind of lurid fury in his eyes. He was as ravenously fierce as a wolf balked of its kill. She chose that moment to call him.

"Mr. Dunke!"

Her voice struck him into a sort of listening alertness, and again she pronounced his name.

"You, Miss Kinney—here?" he asked in amazement.

"Yes—Miss Kinney."

"But—What are you doing here? I thought you were at Fort Lincoln."

"I was, but I'm here now."

"Why? This is no place for you to-night. Hell's broke loose."

"So it seems," she answered, with shining eyes.

"There's trouble afoot, Miss Margaret. No girl should be out, let alone an unprotected one."

"I did not come here unprotected. There was a man with me. The one, Mr. Dunke, that you are now looking for to murder!"

She gave it to him straight from the shoulder, her eyes holding his steadily.

"Struve?" he gasped, taken completely aback.

"No, not Struve. The man who stood beside Lieutenant Fraser, the one you threatened to kill because he backed the law."

"I guess you don't know all the facts, Miss Kinney." He came close and met her gaze while he spoke in a low voice. "There ain't many know what I know. Mebbe there ain't any beside you now. But I know you're Jim Kinney's sister."

"You are welcome to the knowledge. It is no secret. Lieutenant Fraser knows it. So does his friend. I'm not trying to hide it. What of it?"

Her quiet scorn drew the blood to his face.

"That's all right. If you do want to keep it quiet I'm with you. But there's something more. Your brother escaped from Yuma with this fellow Struve. Word came over the wire an hour or two ago that Struve had been captured and that it was certain he had killed his pal, your brother. That's why I mean to see him hanged before mo'ning."

"He did kill my brother. He told me so himself." Her voice carried a sob for an instant, but she went on resolutely. "What has that to do with it? Isn't there any law in Texas? Hasn't he been captured? And isn't he being taken back to his punishment?"

"He told you so himself!" the man echoed. "When did he tell you? When did you see him?"

"I was alone with him for twelve hours in the desert."

"Alone with you?" His puzzled face showed how he was trying to take this in, "I don't understand. How could he be alone with you?"

"I thought he was my brother and I was helping him to escape from Fort Lincoln."

"Helping him to escape! Helping Wolf Struve to escape! Well, I'm darned if that don't beat my time. How come you to think him your brother?" the man asked suspiciously.

"It doesn't matter how or why. I thought so. That's enough."

"And you were alone with him—why, you must have been alone with him all night," cried Dunke, coming to a fresh discovery.

"I was," she admitted very quietly.

A new suspicion edged itself into his mind. "What did you talk about? Did he say anything about—Did he—He always was a terrible liar. Nobody ever believed Wolf Struve."

Without understanding the reason for it, she could see that he was uneasy, that he was trying to discount the value of anything the convict might have told her. Yet what could Struve the convict, No. 9,432, have to do with the millionaire mine-owner, Thomas J. Dunke? What could there be in common between them? Why should the latter fear what the other had to tell? The thing was preposterous on the face of it, but the girl knew by some woman's instinct that she was on the edge of a secret Dunke held hidden deep in his heart from all the world. Only this much she guessed; that Struve was a sharer of his secret, and therefore he was set on lynching the man before he had time to tell it.

"They got away, didn't they?" she asked.

"They got away—for the present," he answered grimly. "But we're still hunting them."

"Can't you let the law take its course, Mr. Danke? Is it necessary to do this terrible thing?"

"Don't you worry any about it, Miss Kinney. This ain't a woman's job. I'll attend to it."

"But my friends," she reminded him.

"We ain't intending to hurt them any. Come, I'll see you home. You staying at the hotel?"

"I don't know. I haven't made any arrangements yet."

"Well, we'll go make them now."

But she did not move. "I'm not going in till I know how this comes out."

He was a man used to having his own brutal way, one strong by nature, with strength increased by the money upon which he rode rough-shod to success.

He laughed as he caught hold of the rein. "That's ridiculous!"

"But my business, I think," the girl answered sharply, jerking the bridle from his fingers.

Dunke stared at her. It was his night of surprises. He failed to recognize the conventional teacher he knew in this bright-eyed, full-throated young woman who fronted him so sure of herself. She seemed to him to swim brilliantly in a tide of flushed beauty, in spite of the dust and the stains of travel. She was in a shapeless khaki riding-suit and a plain, gray, broad-brimmed Stetson. But the one could not hide the flexible curves that made so frankly for grace, nor the other the coppery tendrils that escaped in fascinating disorder from under its brim.

"You hadn't ought to be out here. It ain't right."

"I don't remember asking you to act as a standard of right and wrong for me."

He laughed awkwardly. "We ain't quarreling, are we, Miss Margaret?"

"Certainly I am not. I don't quarrel with anybody but my friends."

"Well, I didn't aim to offend you anyway. You know me better than that." He let his voice fall into a caressing modulation and put a propitiatory hand on her skirt, but under the uncompromising hardness of her gaze the hand fell away to his side. "I'm your friend—leastways I want to be."

"My friends don't lynch men."

"But after what he did to your brother."

"The law will take care of that. If you want to please me call off your men before it is too late."

It was his cue to please her, for so far as it was in him the man loved her. He had set his strong will to trample on his past, to rise to a place where no man could shake his security with proof of his former misdeeds. He meant to marry her and to place her out of reach of those evil days of his. Only Struve was left of the old gang, and he knew the Wolf well enough to be sure that the fellow would delight in blackmailing him. The convict's mouth must be closed. But just now he must promise t she wanted, and he did.

The promise was still on his lips when a third person strode into their conversation.

"Sorry I had to leave you so hastily, Miss Kinney. I'm ready to take you to the hotel now if it suits you."

Both of them turned quickly, to see the man from the Panhandle sauntering forth from the darkness. There was a slight smile on his face, which did not abate when he nodded to Dunke amiably.

"You?" exclaimed the mine-owner angrily.

"Why, yes—me. Hope we didn't inconvenience you, seh, by postponing the coyote's journey to Kingdom Come. My friend had to take a hand because he is a ranger, and I sat in to oblige him. No hard feelings, I hope."

"Did you—Are you all safe?" Margaret asked.

"Yes, ma'am. Got away slick and clean."

"Where?" barked Dunke.

"Where what, my friend?"

"Where did you take him?"

Larry laughed in slow deep enjoyment. "I hate to disappoint you, but if I told that would be telling. No, I reckon I won't table my cards yet a while. If you're playing in this game of Hi-Spy go to it and hunt."

"Perhaps you don't know that I am T. J. Dunke."

"You don't say! And I'm General Grant. This lady hyer is Florence Nightingale or Martha Washington, I disremember which."

Miss Kinney laughed. "Whichever she is she's very very tired," she said. "I think I'll accept your offer to see me to the hotel, Mr. Neill."

She nodded a careless good night to the mine-owner, and touched the horse with her heel. At the porch of the rather primitive hotel she descended stiffly from the saddle.

Before she left the Southerner—or the Westerner, for sometimes she classified him as one, sometimes as the other—she asked him one hesitant question.

"Were you thinking of going out again tonight?"

"I did think of taking a turn out to see if I could find Fraser. Anything I can do for you?"

"Yes. Please don't go. I don't want to have to worry about you. I have had enough trouble for the present."

"Would you worry about me?" he asked quietly, his eyes steadily on her.

"I lie awake about the most unaccountable things sometimes."

He smiled in his slow Southern fashion. "Very well. I'll stay indoors. I reckon Steve ain't lost, anyhow. You're too tired to have to lie awake about me to-night. There's going to be lots of other nights for you to think of me."

She glanced at him with a quick curiosity. "Well, of all the conceit I ever heard!"

"I'm the limit, ain't I?" he grinned as he took himself off.

CHAPTER IX — DOWN THE JACKRABBIT SHAFT.

NEXT MORNING LARRY GOT up so late that he had to Order a special breakfast for himself, the dining-room being closed. He found one guest there, however, just beginning her oatmeal, and he invited himself to eat at her table.

"Good mawnin', Miss Kinney. You don't look like you had been lying awake worrying about me," he began by way of opening the conversation.

Nor did she. Youth recuperates quickly, and after a night's sound sleep she was glowing with health and sweet vitality. He could see a flush beat into the fresh softness of her flesh, but she lifted her dark lashes promptly to meet him, and came to the sex duel gaily.

"I suppose you think I had to take a sleeping-powder to keep me from it?" she flashed back.

"Oh, well, a person can dream," he suggested.

"How did you know? But you are right. I did dream of you."

To the waiter he gave his order before answering her. "Some oatmeal and bacon and eggs. Yes, coffee. And some hot cakes, Charlie. Did you honest dream about me?" This last not to the Chinese waiter who had padded soft-footed to the kitchen.

"Yes."

She smiled shyly at him with sweet innocence, and he drew his chair a trifle closer.

"Tell me."

"I don't like to."

"But you must. Go on."

"Well," very reluctantly. "I dreamed I was visiting the penitentiary and you were there in stripes. You were in for stealing a sheep, I think. Yes, that was it, for stealing a sheep."

"Couldn't you make it something more classy if you're bound to have me in?" he begged, enjoying immensely the rise she was taking out of him.

"I have to tell it the way it was," she insisted, her eyes bubbling with fun. "And it seems you were the prison cook. First thing I knew you were standing in front of a wall and two hundred of the prisoners were shooting at you. They were using your biscuits as bullets."

"That was a terrible revenge to take on me for baking them."

"It seems you had your sheep with you—the one you stole, and you and it were being pelted all over."

"Did you see a lady hold-up among those shooting at me?" he inquired anxiously.

She shook her head. "And just when the biscuits were flying thickest the wall opened and Mr. Fraser appeared. He caught you and the sheep by the back of your necks, and flung you in. Then the wall closed, and I awoke."

"That's about as near the facts as dreams usually get."

He was very much pleased, for it would have been a great disappointment to him if she had admitted dreaming about him for any reason except to make fun of him. The thing about her that touched his imagination most was something wild and untamed, some quality of silken strength in her slim supple youth that scoffed at all men and knew none as master. He meant to wrest from her if he could an interest that would set him apart in her mind from all others, but he wanted the price of victory to cost him something. Thus the value of it would be enhanced.

"But tell me about your escape—all about it and what became of Lieutenant Fraser. And first of all, who the lady was that opened the door for you," she demanded.

"She was his sister."

"Oh! His sister." Her voice was colorless. She observed him without appearing to do so. "Very pretty, I thought her. Didn't you?"

"Right nice looking. Had a sort of an expression made a man want to look at her again."

"Yes."

Innocently unaware that he was being pumped, he contributed

more information. "And that game."

"She was splendid. I can see her now opening the door in the face of the bullets."

"Never a scream out of her either. Just as cool."

"That is the quality men admire most, isn't it—courage?"

"I don't reckon that would come first. Course it wouldn't make a hit with a man to have a woman puling around all the time."

"My kind, you mean."

Though she was smiling at him with her lips, it came to him that his words were being warped to a wrong meaning.

"No, I don't," he retorted bluntly.

"As I remember it, I was bawling every chance I got yesterday and the day before," she recalled, with fine contempt of herself.

"Oh, well! You had reason a-plenty. And sometimes a woman cries just like a man cusses. It don't mean anything. I once knew a woman wet her handkerchief to a sop crying because her husband forgot one mo'ning to kiss her good-by. She quit irrigating to run into a burning house after a neighbor's kids."

"I accept your apology for my behavior if you'll promise I won't do it again," she laughed. "But tell me more about Miss Fraser. Does she live here?"

For a moment he was puzzled. "Miss Fraser! Oh! She gave up that name several years ago. Mrs. Collins they call her. And say, you ought to see her kiddies. You'd fall in love with them sure."

The girl covered her mistake promptly with a little laugh. It would never do for him to know she had been yielding to incipient jealousy. "Why can't I know them? I want to meet her too."

The door opened and a curly head was thrust in. "Dining-room closes for breakfast at nine. My clock says it's ten-thirty now. Pretty near work to keep eating that long, ain't it? And this Sunday, too! I'll have you put in the calaboose for breaking the Sabbath."

"We're only bending it," grinned Neill. "Good mo'ning, Lieutenant. How is Mrs. Collins, and the pickaninnies?"

"First rate. Waiting in the parlor to be introduced to Miss Kinney."

"We're through," announced Margaret, rising.

"You too, Tennessee? The proprietor will be grateful."

The young women took to each other at once. Margaret was very fond of children, and the little boy won her heart immediately. Both he and his baby sister were well-trained, healthy, and lovable little folks, and they adopted "Aunt Peggy" enthusiastically.

Presently the ranger proposed to Neill an adjournment.

"I got to take some breakfast down the Jackrabbit shaft to my prisoner. Wanter take a stroll that way?" he asked.

"If the ladies will excuse us."

"Glad to get rid of you," Miss Kinney assured him promptly, but with a bright smile that neutralized the effect of her sauciness. "Mrs. Collins and I want to have a talk."

The way to the Jackrabbit lay up a gulch behind the town. Up one incline was a shaft-house with a great gray dump at the foot of it. This they left behind them, climbing the hill till they came to the summit.

The ranger pointed to another shaft-house and dump on the next hillside.

"That's the Mal Pais, from which the district is named. Dunke owns it and most of the others round here. His workings and ours come together in several places, but we have boarded up the tunnels at those points and locked the doors we put in. Wonder where Brown is? I told him to meet me here to let us down."

At this moment they caught sight of him coming up a timbered draw. He lowered them into the shaft, which was about six hundred feet deep. From the foot of the shaft went a tunnel into the heart of the mountain. Steve led the way, flashing an electric searchlight as he went.

"We aren't working this part of the mine any more," he explained. "It connects with the newer workings by a tunnel. We'll go back that way to the shaft."

"You've got quite a safe prison," commented the other.

"It's commodious, anyhow; and I reckon it's safe. If a man was to get loose he couldn't reach the surface without taking somebody into partner-ship with him. There ain't but three ways to daylight; one by the shaft we came down, another by way of our shaft-house, and the third by Dunke's, assuming he could break through into the Mal Pais. He'd better not break loose and go to wandering around. There are seventeen miles of workings down here in the Jackrabbit, let alone the Mal Pais. He might easily get lost and starve to death. Here he is at the end of this tunnel."

Steve flashed the light twice before he could believe his eyes. There was no sign of Struve except the handcuffs depending from an iron chain connected by a heavy staple with the granite wall. Apparently he had somehow managed to slip from the gyves by working at them constantly.

The officer turned to his friend and laughed. "I reckon I'm holding the sack this time. See. There's blood on these cuffs. He rasped his hands some before he got them out."

"Well, you've still got him safe down here somewhere."

"Yes, I have or Dunke has. The trouble is both the mines are shut down just now. He's got about forty miles of tunnel to play hide-and-go-seek in. He's in luck if he doesn't starve to death."

"What are you going to do about it?"

"I'll have to get some of my men out on search-parties—just tell them there's a man lost down here without telling them who. I reckon we better say nothing about it to the ladies. You know how tender-hearted they are. Nellie wouldn't sleep a wink to-night for worrying."

"All right. We'd better get to it at once then."

Fraser nodded. "We'll go up and rustle a few of the boys that know the mine well. I expect before we find him Mr. Wolf Struve will be a lamb and right anxious for the shepherd to arrive."

All day the search proceeded without results, and all of the next day. The evening of this second day found Struve still not accounted for.

CHAPTER X — IN A TUNNEL OF THE MAL PAIS

ALTHOUGH MISS KINNEY HAD assured Neill that she was glad to be rid of him it occurred to her more than once in the course of the day that he was taking her a little too literally. On Sunday she did not see a glimpse of him after he left. At lunch he did not appear, nor was he in evidence at dinner. Next morning she learned that he had been to breakfast and had gone before she got down. She withheld judgment till lunch, being almost certain that he would be on hand to that meal. His absence roused her resentment and her independence. If he didn't care to see her she certainly did not want to see him. She was not going to sit around and wait for him to take her down into the mine he had promised she should see. Let him forget his appointment if he liked. He would wait a long time before she made any more engagements with him.

About this time Dunke began to flatter himself that he had made an impression. Miss Kinney was all smiles. She was graciously pleased to take a horseback ride over the camp with him, nor did he know that her roving eye was constantly on the lookout for a certain spare, clean-built figure she could recognize at a considerable distance by the easy, elastic tread. Monday evening the mine-owner called upon her and Mrs. Collins, whose brother also was among the missing, and she was delighted to accept his invitation to go through the Mal Pais workings with him.

"That is, if Mrs. Collins will go, too," she added as an afterthought.

That young woman hesitated. Though this man had led his miners against her brother, she was ready to believe the attack not caused by personal enmity. The best of feeling did not exist between the owners of the Jackrabbit and those of the Mal Pais. Dunke was suspected of boldly crossing into the territory of his neighbor where his veins did not lead. But there had been no open rupture. For the very reason that an undertow of feeling existed Nellie consented to join the party. She did not want by a refusal to put into words a hostility that he had always carefully veiled. She was in the position of not wanting to go at all, yet wanting still less to decline to do so.

"I shall be glad to go," she said.

"Fine. We'll start about nine, or nine-thirty say. I'll drive up in a surrey."

"And we'll have lunch for the party put up at the hotel here. I'll get some fruit to take along," said Margaret.

"We'll make a regular picnic of it," added Dunke heartily. "You'll enjoy eating out of a dinner-pail for once just like one of my miners, Miss Kinney."

After he had gone Margaret mentioned to Mrs. Collins her feeling concerning him. "I don't really like him. Or rather I don't give him my full confidence. He seems pleasant enough, too." She laughed a little as she added: "You know he does me the honor to admire me."

"Yes, I know that. I was wondering how you felt about it."

"How ought one to feel about one of the great mining kings of the West?"

"Has that anything to do with it, my dear? I mean his being a mining king?" asked Mrs. Collins gently.

Margaret went up to her and kissed her. "You're a romantic little thing. That's because you probably married a heaven-sent man. We can't all be fortunate."

"We none of us need to marry where we don't love."

"Goodness me! I'm not thinking of marrying Mr. Dunke's millions. The only thing is that I don't have a Croesus to exhibit every day at my chariot wheels. It's horrid of course, but I have a natural feminine reluctance to surrendering him all at once. I don't object in the least to trampling on him, but somehow I don't feel ready for his declaration of independence."

"Oh, if that's all!" her friend smiled.

"That's quite all."

"Perhaps you prefer Texans who come from the Panhandle."

Mrs. Collins happened to be looking straight at her out of her big brown eyes. Wherefore she could not help observing the pink glow that deepened in the soft cheeks.

"He hasn't preferred me much lately."

Nellie knitted her brow in perplexity. "I don't understand. Steve's been away, too, nearly all the time. Something is going on that we don't know about."

"Not that I care. Mr. Neill is welcome to stay away."

Her new friend shot a swift slant look at her. "I don't suppose you trample on him much."

Margaret flushed. "No, I don't. It's the other way. I never saw anybody so rude. He does not seem to have any saving sense of the proper thing."

"He's a man, dearie, and a good one. He may be untrammeled by convention, but he is clean and brave. He has eyes that look through cowardice and treachery, fine strong eyes that are honest and unafraid."

"Dear me, you must have studied them a good deal to see all that in them," said Miss Peggy lightly, yet pleased withal.

"My dear," reproached her friend, so seriously that Peggy repented.

"I didn't really mean it," she laughed. "I've heard already on good authority that you see no man's eyes except the handsome ones in the face of Mr. Tim Collins."

"I do think Tim has fine eyes," blushed the accused.

"No doubt of it. Since you have been admiring my young man I must praise yours," teased Miss Kinney.

"Am I to wish you joy? I didn't know he was your young man," flashed back the other.

"I understand that you have been trying to put him off on me."

"You'll find he does not need any 'putting off' on anybody."

"At least, he has a good friend in you. I think I'll tell him, so that when he does condescend to become interested in a young woman he may refer her to you for a recommendation."

The young wife borrowed for the occasion some of Miss Peggy's audacity. "I'm recommending him to that young woman now, my dear," she made answer.

Dunke's party left for the mine on schedule time, Water-proof coats and high lace-boots had been borrowed for the ladies as a protection against the moisture they were sure to meet in the tunnels one thousand feet below the ground. The mine-owner had had the hoisting-engine started for the occasion, and the cage took them down as swiftly and as smoothly as a metropolitan elevator. Nevertheless Margaret clung tightly to her friend, for if was her first experience of the kind. She had never before dropped nearly a quarter of a mile straight down into the heart of the earth and she felt a smothered sensation, a sense of danger induced by her unaccustomed surroundings. It is the unknown that awes, and when she first stepped from the cage and peered down the long, low tunnel through which a tramway ran she caught her breath rather quickly. She had an active imagination, and she conjured cave-ins, explosions, and all the other mine horrors she had read about.

Their host had spared no expense to make the occasion a gala one. Electric lights were twinkling at intervals down the tunnel, and an electric ore-car with a man in charge was waiting to run them into the workings nearly a mile distant. Dunke dealt out candles and assisted his guests into the car, which presently carried them deep into the mine. Margaret observed that the timbered sides of the tunnel leaned inward slightly and that the roof was heavily cross-timbered.

"It looks safe," she thought aloud.

"It's safe enough," returned Dunke carelessly. "The place for cave-

A TEXAS RANGER

ins is at the head of the workings, before we get drifts timbered."

"Are we going into any of those places?"

"I wouldn't take you into any place that wasn't safe, Miss Margaret."

"Is it always so dreadfully warm down here?" she asked.

"You must remember we're somewhere around a thousand feet in the heart of the earth. Yes, it's always warm."

"I don't see how the men stand it and work."

"Oh, they get used to it."

They left the car and followed a drift which took them into a region of perpetual darkness, into which the electric lights did not penetrate. Margaret noticed that her host carried his candle with ease, holding it at an angle that gave the best light and most resistance to the air, while she on her part had much ado to keep hers from going out. Frequently she had to stop and let the tiny flame renew its hold on the base of supplies. So, without his knowing it, she fell behind gradually, and his explanations of stopes, drifts, air-drills, and pay-streaks fell only upon the already enlightened ears of Mrs. Collins.

The girl had been picking her way through some puddles of water that had settled on the floor, and when she looked up the lights of those ahead had disappeared. She called to them faintly and hurried on, appalled at the thought of possibly losing them in these dreadful underground catacombs where Stygian night forever reigned. But her very hurry delayed her, for in her haste the gust of her motion swept out the flame. She felt her way forward along the wall, in a darkness such as she had never conceived before. Nor could she know that by chance she was following the wrong wall. Had she chosen the other her hand must have come to a break in it which showed that a passage at that point deflected from the drift toward the left. Unconsciously she passed this, already frightened but resolutely repressing her fear.

"I'll not let them know what an idiot I am. I'll not! I'll not!" she told herself.

Therefore she did not call yet, thinking she must come on them at any moment, unaware that every step was taking her farther from the gallery into which they had turned. When at last she cried out it was too late. The walls hemmed in her cry and flung it back tauntingly to her—the damp walls against which she crouched in terror of the subterranean vault in which she was buried. She was alone with the powers of darkness, with the imprisoned spirits of the underworld that fought inarticulately against the audacity of the puny humans who dared venture here. So her vivid imagination conceived it, terrorizing her against both will and reason.

How long she wandered, a prey to terror, calling helplessly in the blackness, she did not know. It seemed to her that she must always wander so, a perpetual prisoner condemned to this living grave. So that it was with a distinct shock of glad surprise she heard a voice answer faintly her calls. Calling and listening alternately, she groped her way in the direction of the sounds, and so at last came plump against the figure of the approaching rescuer.

"Who is it?" a hoarse voice demanded.

But before she could answer a match flared and was held close to her face. The same light that revealed her to him told the girl who this man was that had met her alone a million miles from human aid. The haggard, drawn countenance with the lifted upper lip and the sunken eyes that glared into hers belonged to the convict Nick Struve.

The match went out before either of them spoke.

"You—you here!" she exclaimed, and was oddly conscious that her relief at meeting even him had wiped out for the present her fear of the man.

"For God's sake, have you got anything to eat?" he breathed thickly.

It had been part of the play that each member of their little party should carry a dinner-pail just like an ordinary miner. Wherefore she had hers still in her hand.

"Yes, and I have a candle here. Have you another match?"

He lit the candle with a shaking hand.

"Gimme that bucket," he ordered gruffly, and began to devour ravenously the food he found in it, tearing at sandwiches and gulping them down like a hungry dog.

"What day is this?" he stopped to ask after he had stayed the first pangs.

She told him Tuesday.

"I ain't eaten since Saturday," he told her. "I figured it was a week. There ain't any days in this place—nothin' but night. Can't tell one from another."

"It's terrible," she agreed.

His appetite was wolfish. She could see that he was spent, so weak with hunger that he had reeled against the wall as she handed him the dinner-pail. Pallor was on the sunken face, and exhaustion in the trembling hands and unsteady gait.

"I'm about all in, what with hunger and all I been through. I thought I was out of my head when I heard you holler." He snatched up the candle from the place where he had set it and searched her face by its flame. "How come you down here? You didn't come alone. What you doin' here?" he demanded suspiciously.

"I came down with Mr. Dunke and a friend to look over his mine. I had never been in one before."

"Dunke!" A spasm of rage swept the man's face. "You're a friend of his, are you? Where is he? If you came with him how come you to be roaming around alone?"

"I got lost. Then my light went out."

"So you're a friend of Dunke, that damned double-crosser! He's a millionaire, you think, a big man in this Western country. That's what he claims, eh?" Struve shook a fist into the air in a mad burst of passion. "Just watch me blow him higher'n a kite. I know what he is, and I got proof. The Judas! I keep my mug shut and do time while he gets off scot-free and makes his pile. But you listen to me, ma'am. Your friend ain't nothin' but an outlaw. If he got his like I got mine he'd be at Yuma to-day. Your brother could a-told you. Dunke was at the head of the gang that held up that train. We got nabbed, me and Jim. Burch got shot in the Catalinas by one of the rangers, and Smith died of fever in Sonora. But Dunke, curse him, he sneaks out and buys the officers off with our plunder. That's what he done—let his partners get railroaded through while he sails out slick and easy. But he made one mistake, Mr. Dunke did. He wrote me a letter and told me to keep mum and he would fix it for me to get out in a few months. I believed him, kept my mouth padlocked, and served seven years without him lifting a hand for me. Then, when I make my getaway he tries first off to shut my mouth by putting me out of business. That's what your friend done, ma'am."

"Is this true?" asked the girl whitely.

"So help me God, every word of it."

"He let my brother go to prison without trying to help him?"

"Worse than that. He sent him to prison. Jim was all right when he first met up with Dunke. It was Dunke that got him into his wild ways and led him into trouble. It was Dunke took him into the hold-up business. Hadn't been for him Jim never would have gone wrong."

She made no answer. Her mind was busy piecing out the facts of her brother's misspent life. As a little girl she remembered her big brother before he went away, good-natured, friendly, always ready to play with her. She was sure he had not been bad, only fatally weak. Even this man who had slain him was ready to testify to that.

She came back from her absorption to find Struve outlining what he meant to do.

"We'll go back this passage along the way you came. I want to find Mr. Dunke. I allow I've got something to tell him he will be right interested in hearing."

He picked up the candle and led the way along the tunnel. Margaret followed him in silence.

CHAPTER XI — THE SOUTHERNER TAKES A RISK

THE CONVICT SHAMBLED FORWARD through the tunnel till he came to a drift which ran into it at a right angle.

"Which way now?" he demanded.

"I don't know."

"Don't know," he screamed. "Didn't you just come along here? Do you want me to get lost again in this hell-hole?"

The stricken fear leaped into his face. He had forgotten her danger, forgotten everything but the craven terror that engulfed him. Looking at him, she was struck for the first time with the thought that he might be on the verge of madness.

His cry still rang through the tunnel when Margaret saw a gleam of distant light. She pointed it out to Struve, who wheeled and fastened his eyes upon it. Slowly the faint yellow candle-rays wavered toward them. A man was approaching through the gloom, a large man whom she presently recognized as Dunke. A quick gasp from the one beside her showed that he too knew the man. He took a dozen running steps forward, so that in his haste the candle flickered out.

"That you, Miss Margaret?" the mine-owner called.

Neither she nor Struve answered. The latter had stopped and was waiting tensely his enemy's approach. When he was within a few yards of the other Dunke raised his candle and peered into the blackness ahead of him.

"What's the matter? Isn't it you, Miss Peggy?"

"No, it ain't. It's your old pal, Nick Struve. Ain't you glad to see him, Joe?"

Dunke looked him over without a word. His thin lips set and his gaze grew wall-eyed. The candle passed from right to left hand.

Struve laughed evilly. "No, I'm not going to pay you that way—not yet; nor you ain't going to rid yourself of me either. Want to know why, Mr. Millionaire Dunke, what used to be my old pal? Want to know why it ain't going to do you any good to drop that right hand any closer to your hip pocket?"

Still Dunke said nothing, but the candle-glow that lit his face showed an ugly expression.

"Don't you whip that gun out, Joe Dunke. Don't you! 'Cause why? If you do you're a goner."

"What do you mean?"

"I mean that I kept the letter you wrote me seven years ago, and have put it where it will do you no good if anything happens to me. That's why you won't draw that gun, Joe Dunke. If you do it will send you to Yuma. Millionaire you may be, but that won't keep you from wearing stripes."

Struve's voice rang exultantly. From the look in the face of his old comrade in crime who had prospered at his expense, as he chose to think, he saw that for the time being he had got the whip-hand.

There was a long silence before Dunke asked hoarsely:

"What do you want?"

"I want you to hide me. I want you to get me out of this country. I want you to divvy up with me. Didn't we grub-stake you with the haul from the Overland? Don't we go share and share alike, the two of us that's left? Ain't that fair and square? You wouldn't want to do less than right by an old pal, cap, you that are so respectable and proper now. You ain't forgot the man that lay in the ditch with you the night we held up the flyer, the man that rode beside you when you shot—"

"For God's sake don't rake up forgotten scrapes. We were all young together then. I'll do what's right by you, but you got to keep your mouth shut and let me manage this."

"The way you managed it before when you let me rot at Yuma seven years," jeered Struve.

"I couldn't help it. They were on my trail and I had to lie low. I tell you I'll pull you through if you do as I say."

"And I tell you I don't believe a word you say. You double-crossed me before and you will again if you get a chance. I'll not let you out of my sight."

"Don't be a fool, Nick. How can I help you if I can't move around to make the arrangements for running you across the line?"

"And what guarantee have I got you ain't making arrangements to have me scragged? Think I'm forgetting Saturday night?"

The girl in the blackness without the candle-shine moved slightly.

"What's that?" asked Dunke, startled.

"What's what?"

"That noise. Some one moved."

Dunke's revolver came swiftly from his pocket.

"I reckon it must a-been the girl."

"What girl? Miss Kinney?"

Dunke's hard eyes fastened on the other like steel augers.

Margaret came forward and took wraithlike shape.

"I want you to take me to Mrs. Collins, Mr. Dunke," she said.

The steel probes shifted from Struve to her.

"What did you hear, Miss Kinney? This man is a storehouse of lies. I let him run on to see how far he would go."

Struve's harsh laugh filled the tunnel.

"Take me to Mrs. Collins," she reiterated wearily.

"Not till I know what you heard," answered Dunke doggedly.

"I heard everything," she avowed boldly. "The whole wretched, miserable truth."

She would have pushed past him, but he caught her arm.

"Let me go!"

"I tell you it's all a mistake. I can explain it. Give me time."

"I won't listen, I want never to see either of you again. What have I ever done that I should be mixed up with such men?" she cried, with bitter despair.

"Don't go off half-cocked. 'Course I'll take you to Mrs. Collins if you like. But you got to listen to what I say."

Another candle glimmered dimly in the tunnel and came toward them. It presently stopped, and a voice rolled along the vault.

"Hello, there!"

Margaret would have known that voice anywhere among a thousand. Now it came to her sweet as water after a drought. She slipped past Dunke and ran stumbling through the darkness to its source.

"Mr. Neill! Mr. Neill!"

The pitiful note in her voice, which he recognized instantly, stirred him to the core. Astonished that she should be in the mine and in trouble, he dashed forward, and his candle went out in the rush. Groping in the darkness her hands encountered his. His arms closed round her, and in her need of protection that brushed aside conventions and non-essentials, the need that had spoken in her cry of relief, in her hurried flight to him, she lay panting and trembling in his arms. He held her tight, as one who would keep his own against the world.

"How did you get here—what has happened?" he demanded.

Hurriedly she explained.

"Oh, take me away, take me away!" she concluded, nestling to him with no thought now of seeking to disguise her helpless dependence upon him, of hiding from herself the realization that he was the man into whose keeping destiny had ordained that she was to give her heart.

"All right, honey. You're sure all safe now," he said tenderly, and in the blackness his lips sought and met hers in a kiss that sealed the understanding their souls had reached.

At the sound of Neill's voice Dunke had extinguished the candle and vanished in the darkness with Struve, the latter holding him by the arm in a despairing grip. Neill shouted again and again, as he relighted his candle, but there came no answer to his calls.

"We had better make for the shaft," he said.

They set out on the long walk to the opening that led up to the light and the pure air. For a while they walked on in silence. At last he took her hand and guided her fingers across the seam on his wrist.

"It don't seem only four days since you did that, honey," he murmured.

"Did I do that?" Her voice was full of self-reproach, and before he could stop her she lifted his hand and kissed the welt.

"Don't, sweet. I deserved what I got and more. I'm ready with that apology you didn't want then, Peggy."

"But I don't want it now, either. I won't have it. Didn't I tell you I wouldn't? Besides," she added, with a little leap of laughter in her voice, "why should you ask pardon for kissing the girl you were meant to—to——"

He finished it for her.

"To marry, Peggy. I didn't know it then, but I knew it before you said good-by with your whip."

"And I didn't know it till next morning," she said.

"Did you know it then, when you were so mean to me?"

"That was why I was so mean to you. I had to punish myself and you because I—liked you so well."

She buried her face shyly in his coat to cover this confession.

It seemed easy for both of them to laugh over nothing in the exuberance of their common happiness. His joy pealed now delightedly.

"I can't believe it—that four days ago you wasn't on the earth for me. Seems like you always belonged; seems like I always enjoyed your sassy ways."

"That's just the way I feel about you. It's really scandalous that in less than a week—just a little more than half a week—we should be engaged. We are engaged, aren't we?"

"Very much."

"Well, then—it sounds improper, but it isn't the least bit. It's right. Isn't it?"

"It ce'tainly is."

"But you know I've always thought that people who got engaged so soon are the same kind of people that correspond through matrimonial papers. I didn't suppose it would ever happen to me."

"Some right strange things happen while a person is alive, Peggy."

"And I don't really know anything at all about you except that you say your name is Larry Neill. Maybe you are married already."

She paused, startled at the impossible thought.

"It must have happened before I can remember, then," he laughed.

"Or engaged. Very likely you have been engaged a dozen times. Southern people do, they say."

"Then I'm an exception."

"And me—you don't know anything about me."

"A fellow has to take some risk or quit living," he told her gaily.

"When you think of my temper doesn't it make you afraid?"

"The samples I've had were surely right exhilarating," he conceded. "I'm expecting enough difference of opinion to keep life interesting."

"Well, then, if you won't be warned you'll just have to take me and risk it."

And she slipped her arm into his and held up her lips for the kiss awaiting her.

CHAPTER XII — EXIT DUNKE

DUNKE PLOWED BACK THROUGH the tunnel in a blind whirl of passion. Rage, chagrin, offended vanity, acute disappointment, all blended with a dull heartache to which he was a stranger. He was a dangerous man in a dangerous mood, and so Wolf Struve was likely to discover. But the convict was not an observant man. His loose upper lip lifted in the ugly sneer to which it was accustomed.

"Got onto you, didn't she?"

Dunke stuck his candle in a niche of the ragged granite wall, strode across to his former partner in crime, and took the man by the throat.

"I'll learn you to keep that vile tongue of yours still," he said between set teeth, and shook the hapless man till he was black in the face.

Struve hung, sputtering and coughing, against the wall where he had been thrown. It was long before he could do more than gasp.

"What—what did you do—that for?" His furtive ratlike face looked venomous in its impotent anger. "I'll pay you for this—and don't you—forget it, Joe Dunke!"

"You'd shoot me in the back the way you did Jim Kinney if you got a chance. I know that; but you see you won't get a chance."

"I ain't looking for no such chance. I—"

"That's enough. I don't have to stand for your talk even if I do have to take care of you. Light your candle and move along this tunnel lively."

Something in Dunke's eye quelled the rebellion the other contemplated. He shuffled along, whining as he went that he would never have looked for his old pal to treat him so. They climbed ladders to the next level, passed through an empty stope, and stopped at the end of a drift.

"I'll arrange to get you out of here to-night and have you run across the line. I'm going to give you three hundred dollars. That's the last cent you'll ever get out of me. If you ever come back to this country I'll see that you're hanged as you deserve."

With that Dunke turned on his heel and was gone. But his contempt for the ruffian he had cowed was too fearless. He would have thought so if he could have known of the shadow that dogged his heels through the tunnel, if he could have seen the bare fangs that had gained Struve his name of "Wolf," if he could have caught the flash of the knife that trembled in the eager hand. He did not know that, as he shot up in the cage to the sunlight, the other was filling the tunnel with imprecations and wild threats, that he was hugging himself with the promise of a revenge that should be sure and final.

Dunke went about the task of making the necessary

arrangements personally. He had his surrey packed with food, and about eleven o'clock drove up to the mine and was lowered to the ninth level. An hour later he stepped out of the cage with a prisoner whom he kept covered with a revolver.

"It's that fellow Struve," he explained to the astonished engineer in the shaft-house. "I found him down below. It seems that Fraser took him down the Jackrabbit and he broke loose and worked through to our ground."

"Do you want any help in taking him downtown, sir? Shall I phone for the marshal?"

His boss laughed scornfully.

"When I can't handle one man after I've got him covered I'll let you know, Johnson."

The two men went out into the starlit night and got into the surrey. The play with the revolver had hitherto been for the benefit of Johnson, but it now became very real. Dunke jammed the rim close to the other's temple.

"I want that letter I wrote you. Quick, by Heaven! No fairy-tales, but the letter!"

"I swear, Joe—"

"The letter, you villain! I know you never let it go out of your possession. Give it up! Quick!"

Struve's hand stole to his breast, came out slowly to the edge of his coat, then leaped with a flash of something bright toward the other's throat. Simultaneously the revolver rang out. A curse, the sound of a falling body, and the frightened horses leaped forward. The wheels slipped over the edge of the narrow mountain road, and surrey, horses, and driver plunged a hundred feet down to the sharp, broken rocks below.

Johnson, hearing the shot, ran out and stumbled over a body lying in the road. By the bright moonlight he could see that it was that of his employer. The surrey was nowhere in sight, but he could easily make out where it had slipped over the precipice. He ran back into the shaft-house and began telephoning wildly to town.

CHAPTER XIII — STEVE OFFERS CONGRATULATIONS

WHEN FRASER REACHED THE dining-room for breakfast his immediate family had finished and departed. He had been up till four o'clock and his mother had let him sleep as long as he would. Now, at nine, he was up again and fresh as a daisy after a morning bath.

He found at the next table two other late breakfasters.

"Mo'ning, Miss Kinney. How are you, Tennessee?" he said amiably.

Both Larry and the young woman admitted good health, the latter so blushingly that Steve's keen eyes suggested to him that he might not be the only one with news to tell this morning.

"What's that I hear about Struve and Dunke?" asked Neill at once.

"Oh, you've heard it. Well, it's true. I judge Dunke was arranging to get him out of the country. Anyhow, Johnson says he took the fellow out to his surrey from the shaft-house of the Mal Pais under his gun. A moment later the engineer heard a shot and ran out. Dunke lay in the road dead, with a knife through his heart. We found the surrey down in the canyon. It had gone over the edge of the road. Both the hawsses were dead, and Struve had disappeared. How the thing happened I reckon never will be known unless the convict tells it. My guess would be that Dunke attacked him and the convict was just a little bit more than ready for him."

"Have you any idea where Struve is?"

"The obvious guess would be that he is heading for Mexico. But I've got another notion. He knows that's where we will be looking for him. His record shows that he used to trail with a bunch of outlaws up in Wyoming. That was most twenty years ago. His old pals have disappeared long since. But he knows that country up there. He'll figure that down here he's sure to be caught and hanged sooner or later. Up there he'll have a chance to hide under another name."

Neill nodded. "That's a big country up there and the mountains are full of pockets. If he can reach there he will be safe."

"Maybe," the ranger amended quietly.

"Would you follow him?"

The officer's opaque gaze met the eyes of his friend. "We don't aim to let a prisoner make his getaway once we get our hands on him. Wyoming ain't so blamed far to travel after him—if I learn he is there."

For a moment all of them were silent. Each of them was thinking of the fellow and the horrible trail of blood he had left behind him in one short week. Margaret looked at her lover and shuddered. She had not the least doubt that this man sitting opposite them would bring the criminal back to his punishment, but the sinister grotesque shadow of the convict seemed to fall between her and her happiness.

Larry caught her hand under the table and gave it a little pressure of reassurance. He spoke in a low voice. "This hasn't a thing to do with us, Peggy—not a thing. They were already both out of your life."

"Yes, I know, but—"

"There aren't any buts." He smiled warmly, and his smile took the other man into their confidence. "You've been having a nightmare. That's past. See the sunshine on those hills. It's bright mo'ning, girl. A new day for you and for me."

Steve grinned. "This is awful sudden, Tennessee. You must a-been sawing wood right industrious on the hawssback ride and down in the tunnel. I expect there wasn't any sunshine down there, was there?"

"You go to grass, Steve."

"No, Tennessee is ce'tainly no two-bit man. Lemme see. One—two—three—four days. That's surely going some," the ranger soliloquized.

"Mr. Fraser," the young woman reproved with a blush.

"Don't mind him, Peggy. He's merely jealous," came back Larry.

"Course I'm jealous. Whyfor not? What license have these Panhandle guys to come in and tote off our girls? But don't mind me. I'll pay strict attention to my ham and eggs and not see a thing that's going on."

"Lieutenant!" Miss Margaret was both embarrassed and shocked.

"Want me to shut my eyes, Tennessee?"

"Next time we get engaged you'll not be let in on the ground floor," Neill predicted.

"Four days! My, my! If that ain't rapid transit for fair!"

"You're a man of one idea, Steve. Cayn't you see that the fact's the main thing, not the time it took to make it one?"

"And counting out Sunday and Monday, it only leaves two days."

"Don't let that interfere with your breakfast. You haven't been elected timekeeper for this outfit, you know!"

Fraser recovered from his daze and duly offered congratulations to the one and hopes for unalloyed joy to the other party to the engagement.

"But four days!" he added in his pleasant drawl. "That's sure some precipitous. Just to look at him, ma'am"—this innocently to Peggy—"a man wouldn't think he had it in him to locate, stake out, and do the necessary assessment work on such a rich claim as the Margaret Kinney all in four days. Mostly a fellow don't strike such high-grade ore without a lot of—"

"That will do for you, lieutenant," interrupted Miss Kinney, with merry, sparkling eyes. "You needn't think we're going to let you trail this off into a compliment now. I'm going to leave you and see what Mrs. Collins says. She won't sit there and parrot 'Four days' for the rest of her life."

With which Mistress Peggy sailed from the room in mock hauteur.

When Larry came back from closing the door after her, his friend fell upon him with vigorous hands to the amazement of Wun Hop, the waiter.

"You blamed lucky son of a gun," he cried exuberantly between punches. "You've ce'tainly struck pure gold, Tennessee. Looks like Old Man Good Luck has come home to roost with you, son."

The other, smiling, shook hands with him. "I'm of that opinion myself, Steve," he said.

PART II — THE GIRL OF LOST VALLEY

CHAPTER I — IN THE FIRE ZONE

"SAY, YOU TEDDY HAWSS, I'm plumb fed up with sagebrush and scenery. I kinder yearn for co'n bread and ham. I sure would give six bits for a drink of real wet water. Yore sentiments are similar, I reckon, Teddy."

The Texan patted the neck of his cow pony, which reached round playfully and pretended to nip his leg. They understood each other, and were now making the best of a very unpleasant situation. Since morning they had been lost on the desert. The heat of midday had found them plowing over sandy wastes. The declining sun had left them among the foothills, wandering from one to another, in the vain hope that each summit might show the silvery gleam of a windmill, or even that outpost of civilization, the barb-wire fence. And now the stars looked down indifferently, myriads of them, upon the travelers still plodding wearily through a land magically transformed by moonlight to a silvery loveliness that blotted out all the garish details of day.

The Texan drew rein. "We all been discovering that Wyoming is a powerful big state. Going to feed me a cigarette, Teddy. Too bad a hawss cayn't smoke his troubles away," he drawled, and proceeded to roll a cigarette, lighting it with one sweeping motion of his arm, that passed down the leg of his chaps and ended in the upward curve at his lips.

The flame had not yet died, when faintly through the illimitable velvet night there drifted to him a sound.

"Did you hear that, pardner?" the man demanded softly, listening intently for a repetition of it.

It came presently, from away over to the left, and, after it, what might have been taken for the popping of a distant bunch of firecrackers.

"Celebrating the Fourth some premature, looks like. What? Think not, Teddy! Some one getting shot up? Sho! You are romancin', old hawss."

Nevertheless he swung the pony round and started rapidly in the direction of the shots. From time to time there came a renewal of them, though the intervals grew longer and the explosions were now individual ones. He took the precaution to draw his revolver from the holster and to examine it carefully.

"Nothing like being sure. It's a heap better than being sorry afterward," he explained to the cow pony.

For the first time in twelve hours, he struck a road. Following this as it wound up to the summit of a hill, he discovered that the area of disturbance was in the valley below. For, as he began his descent, there was a flash from a clump of cotton-woods almost at his feet.

"Did yo' git him?" a voice demanded anxiously.

"Don't know, dad," the answer came, young, warm, and tremulous.

"Hello! There's a kid there," the Texan decided. Aloud, he asked quietly: "What's the row, gentlemen?"

One of the figures whirled—it was the boyish one, crouched behind a dead horse—and fired at him.

"Hold on, sonny! I'm a stranger. Don't make any more mistakes like that."

"Who are you?"

"Steve Fraser they call me. I just arrived from Texas. Wait a jiff, and I'll come down and explain."

He stayed for no permission, but swung from the saddle, trailed the reins, and started down the slope. He could hear a low-voiced colloquy between the two dark figures, and one of them called roughly:

"Hands up, friend! We'll take no chances on yo'."

The Texan's hands went up promptly, just as a bullet flattened itself against a rock behind him. It had been fired from the bank of the dry wash, some hundred and fifty yards away.

"That's no fair! Both sides oughtn't to plug at me," he protested, grinning.

The darkness which blurred detail melted as Fraser approached, and the moonlight showed him a tall, lank, unshaven old mountaineer, standing behind a horse, his shotgun thrown across the saddle.

"That's near enough, Mr. Fraser from Texas," said the old man, in a slow voice that carried the Southern intonation. "This old gun is loaded with buckshot, and she scatters like hell. Speak yore little piece. How came yo' here, right now?"

"I got lost in the Wind River bad lands this mo'ning, and I been playing hide and go seek with myself ever since."

"Where yo' haided for?"

"Gimlet Butte."

"Huh! That's right funny, too."

"Why?"

"Because all yo' got to do to reach the butte is to follow this road and yore nose for about three miles."

A bullet flung up a spurt of sand beside the horse.

The young fellow behind the dead horse broke in, with impatient alarm: "He's all right, dad. Can't you tell by his way of talking that he's from the South? Make him lie down."

Something sweet and vibrant in the voice lingered afterward in the Texan's mind almost like a caress, but at the time he was too busy to think of this. He dropped behind a cottonwood, and drew his revolver.

"How many of them are there?" he asked of the lad, in a whisper.

"About six, I think. I'm sorry I shot at you."

"What's the row?"

"They followed us out of Gimlet Butte. They've been drinking. Isn't that some one climbing up the side of the ridge?"

"I believe it is. Let me have your rifle, kid."

"What for?" The youngster took careful aim, and fired.

A scream from the sagebrush—just one, and then no more.

"Bully for you', Arlie," the old man said.

None of them spoke for some minutes, then Fraser heard a sob—a stifled one, but unmistakable none the less.

"Don't be afraid, kid. We'll stand 'em off," the Texan encouraged.

"I ain't afraid, but I—I——Oh, God, I've killed a man."

The Texan stared at him, where he lay in the heavy shadows, shaken with his remorse. "Holy smoke! Wasn't he aiming to kill you? He likely isn't dead, anyhow. You got real troubles to worry about, without making up any."

He could see the youngster shaking with the horror of it, and could hear the staccato sobs forcing themselves through the closed teeth. Something about it, some touch of pathos he could not account for, moved his not very accessible heart. After all, he was a slim little kid to be engaged in such a desperate encounter Fraser remembered his own boyhood and the first time he had ever seen bloodshed, and, recalling it, he slipped across in the darkness and laid an arm across the slight shoulder.

"Don't you worry, kid. It's all right. You didn't mean—"

He broke off in swift, unspeakable amazement. His eye traveled up the slender figure from the telltale skirt. This was no boy at all, but a girl. As he took in the mass of blue-black hair and the soft but cleancut modeling from ear to chin, his hand fell from her shoulder. What an idiot he had been not to know from the first that such a voice could have come only from a woman! He had been deceived by the darkness and by the slouch hat she wore. He wanted to laugh in sardonic scorn of his perception.

But on the heel of that came a realization of her danger. He must get her out of there at once, for he knew that the enemy must be circling round, to take them on the flank too. It was not a question of whether they could hold off the attackers. They might do that, and yet she might be killed while they were doing it. A man used to coping with emergencies, his brain now swiftly worked out a way of escape.

"Yore father and I will take care of these coyotes. You slip along those shadows up the hill to where my Teddy hawss is, and burn the wind out of here," he told her.

"I'll not leave dad," she said quickly.

The old mountaineer behind the horse laughed apologetically. "I been trying to git her to go, but she won't stir. With the pinto daid, o' course we couldn't both make it."

"That's plumb foolishness," the Texan commented irritably.

"Mebbe," admitted the girl; "but I reckon I'll stay long as dad does."

"No use being pigheaded about it."

Her dark eyes flashed. "Is this your say-so, Mr. Whatever-your-name-is?" she asked sharply, less because she resented what he said than because she was strung to a wire edge.

His troubled gaze took in again her slim girlishness. The frequency of danger had made him proof against fear for himself, but just now he was very much afraid for her. Hard man as he was, he had the Southerner's instinctive chivalry toward woman.

"You better go, Arlie," her father counseled weakly.

"Well, I won't," she retorted emphatically.

The old man looked whimsically at the Texan. "Yo' see yo'self how it is, stranger."

Fraser saw, and the girl's stanchness stirred his admiration even while it irritated him. He made his decision immediately.

"All right. Both of you go."

"But we have only one horse," the girl objected. "They would catch us."

"Take my Teddy."

"And leave you here?" The dark eyes were full on him again, this time in a wide-open surprise.

"Oh, I'll get out once you're gone. No trouble about that."

"How?"

"We couldn't light out, and leave yo' here," the father interrupted.

"Of course we couldn't," the girl added quickly. "It isn't your quarrel, anyhow."

"What good can you do staying here?" argued Fraser. "They want you, not me. With you gone, I'll slip away or come to terms with them. They haven't a thing against me."

"That's right," agreed the older man, rubbing his stubbly beard with his hand. "That's sho'ly right."

"But they might get you before they understood," Arlie urged.

"Oh, I'll keep under cover, and when it's time, I'll sing out and let them know. Better leave me that rifle, though." He went right on, taking it for granted that she had consented to go: "Slip through those shadows up that draw. You'll have no trouble with Teddy. Whistle when you're ready, and your father will make a break up the hill on his hawss. So-long. See you later some time, mebbe."

She went reluctantly, not convinced, but overborne by the quality of cheerful compulsion that lay in him. He was not a large man, though the pack and symmetry of his muscles promised unusual strength. But the close-gripped jaw, the cool serenity of the gray eyes that looked without excitement upon whatever they saw, the perfect poise of his carriage—all contributed to a personality plainly that of a leader of men.

It was scarce a minute later that the whistle came from the hilltop. The mountaineer instantly swung to the saddle and set his pony to a canter up the draw. Fraser could see him join his daughter in the dim light, for the moon had momentarily gone behind a cloud, but almost at once the darkness swallowed them.

Some one in the sagebrush called to a companion, and the Texan knew that the attackers had heard the sound of the galloping horses. Without waiting an instant, he fired twice in rapid succession.

"That'll hold them for a minute or two," he told himself. "They won't understand it, and they'll get together and have a powwow."

He crouched behind the dead horse, his gaze sweeping the wash, the sagebrush, and the distant group of cottonwoods from which he had seen a shot fired. Though he lay absolutely still, without the least visible excitement, he was alert and tense to the finger tips. Not the slightest sound, not the smallest motion of the moonlit underbrush, escaped his unwavering scrutiny.

The problem before him was to hold the attackers long enough for Arlie and her father to make their escape, without killing any of them or getting killed himself. He knew that, once out of the immediate vicinity, the fugitives would leave the road and take to some of the canyons that ran from the foothills into the mountains. If he could secure them a start of fifteen minutes that ought to be enough.

A voice from the wash presently hailed him:

"See here! We're going to take you back with us, old man. That's a cinch. We want you for that Squaw Creek raid, and we're going to have you. You done enough damage. Better surrender peaceable, and we'll promise to take you back to jail. What say?"

"Gimme five minutes to think it over," demanded the Texan.

"All right, five minutes. But you want to remember that it's all off with you if you don't give up. Billy Faulkner's dead, and we'll sure come a-shooting."

Fraser waited till his five minutes was nearly up, then plunged across the road into the sagebrush growing thick there. A shot or two rang out, without stopping him. Suddenly a man rose out of the sage in front of him, a revolver in his hand.

For a fraction of a second, the two men faced each other before either spoke.

"Who are you?"

Fraser's answer was to dive for the man's knees, just as a football tackle does. They went down together, but it was the Texan got up first. A second man was running toward him.

"Hands up, there!" the newcomer ordered.

Fraser's hand went up, but with his forty-five in it. The man pitched forward into the sage. The Southerner twisted forward again, slid down into the dry creek, and ran along its winding bed for a hundred yards. Then he left it, cutting back toward the spot where he had lain behind the dead horse. Hiding in the sage, he heard the pursuit pouring down the creek, waited till it was past, and quickly recrossed the road. Here, among the cow-backed hills, he knew he was as safe as a needle in a haystack.

"I had to get that anxious guy, but it might have been a whole lot worse. I only plugged his laig for him," he reflected comfortably. "Wonder why they wanted to collect the old man's scalp, anyhow? The little girl sure was game. Just like a woman, though, the way she broke down because she hit that fellow."

Within five minutes he was lost again among the thousand hills that rose like waves of the sea, one after another. It was not till nearly morning that he again struck a road.

He was halted abruptly by a crisp command from behind a boulder:

"Up with your hands—quick!"

"Who are you, my friend?" the Texan asked mildly.

"Deputy sheriff," was the prompt response. "Now, reach for the sky, and prompt, too."

"Just as you say. You've ce'tainly got the crawl on me."

The deputy disarmed his captive, and drove him into town before him. When morning dawned, Fraser found himself behind the bars. He was arrested for the murder of Faulkner.

CHAPTER II — A COMPACT

AFTER THE JAILER HAD brought his breakfast, Fraser was honored by a visit from the sheriff, a big, rawboned Westerner, with the creases of fifty outdoor years stamped on his brown, leathery face.

He greeted his prisoner pleasantly enough, and sat down on the bed.

"Treating you right, are they?" he asked, glancing around. "Breakfast up to the mark?"

"I've got no kick coming, thank you," said Fraser.

"Good!"

The sheriff relapsed into sombre silence. There was a troubled look in the keen eyes that the Texan did not understand. Fraser waited for the officer to develop the object of his visit, and it was set down to his credit. A weaker man would have rushed at once into excuses and explanations. But in the prisoner's quiet, steely eyes, in the close-shut mouth and salient jaw, in the set of his well-knit figure, Sheriff Brandt found small room for weakness. Whoever he was, this man was one who could hold his own in the strenuous game of life.

"My friend," said the sheriff abruptly, "you and I are up against it. There is going to be trouble in town to-night."

The level, gray eyes looked questioningly at the sheriff.

"You butted into grief a-plenty when you lined up with the cattlemen in this sheep war. Who do you ride for?"

"I'm not riding for anybody," responded Fraser. "I just arrived from Texas. Didn't even know there was a feud on."

Brandt laughed incredulously. "That will sound good to a jury, if your case ever comes to that stage. How do you expect to explain Billy Faulkner's death?"

"Is there any proof I killed him?"

"Some. You were recognized by two men last night while you were trying to escape. You carried a rifle that uses the same weight bullet as the one we dug out of Billy. When you attacked Tom Peake you dropped that rifle, and in your getaway hadn't time to pick it up again. That is evidence enough for a Wyoming jury, in the present state of public opinion."

"What do you mean by 'in the present state of public opinion'?"

"I mean that this whole country is pretty nearly solid against the Cedar Mountain cattlemen, since they killed Campeau and Jennings in that raid on their camp. You know what I mean as well as I do."

Fraser did not argue the point. He remembered now having seen an account of the Squaw Creek raid on a sheep camp, ending in a battle that had resulted in the death of two men and the wounding of three others. He had been sitting in a hotel at San Antonio, Texas, when he had read the story over his after-dinner cigar. The item had not seemed even remotely connected with himself. Now he was in prison at Gimlet Butte, charged with murder, and unless he was very much mistaken the sheriff was hinting at a lynching. The Squaw Creek raid had come very near to him, for he knew the fight he had interrupted last night had grown out of it.

"What do you mean by trouble to-night?" he asked, in an even, conversational tone.

The sheriff looked directly at him. "You're a man, I reckon. That calls for the truth. Men are riding up and down this country to-day, stirring up sentiment against your outfit. To-night the people will gather in town, and the jail will be attacked."

"And you?"

"I'll uphold the law as long as I can."

Fraser nodded. He knew Brandt spoke the simple truth. What he had sworn to do he would do to the best of his ability. But the Texan knew, too, that the ramshackle jail would be torn to pieces and the sheriff overpowered.

From his coat pocket he drew a letter, and presented it to the other. "I didn't expect to give this to you under these circumstances, Mr. Brandt, but I'd like you to know that I'm on the level when I say I don't know any of the Squaw Creek cattlemen and have never ridden for any outfit in this State."

Brandt tore open the letter, and glanced hurriedly through it. "Why, it's from old Sam Slauson! We used to ride herd together when we were boys." And he real aloud:

"Introducing Steve Fraser, lieutenant in the Texas Rangers."

He glanced up quickly. "You're not the Fraser that ran down Chacon and his gang of murderers?"

"Yes, I was on that job."

Brandt shook hands heartily. "They say it was a dandy piece of work. I read that story in a magazine. You delivered the goods proper."

The ranger was embarrassed. "Oh, it wasn't much of a job. The man that wrote it put in the fancy touches, to make his story sell, I expect."

"Yes, he did! I know all about that!" the sheriff derided. "I've got to get you out of this hole somehow. Do you mind if I send for Hilliard, the prosecuting attorney? He's a bright young fellow, loaded to the guards with ideas. What I want is to get at a legal way of fixing this thing up, you understand. I'll call him up on the phone, and have him run over."

Hilliard was shortly on the spot—a short, fat little fellow with eyeglasses. He did not at first show any enthusiasm in the prisoner's behalf.

"I don't doubt for a moment that you are the man this letter says you are, Mr. Fraser," he said suavely. "But facts are stubborn things. You were seen carrying the gun that killed Faulkner. We can't get away from that just because you happen to have a letter of introduction to Mr. Brandt."

"I don't want to get away from it," retorted. Fraser. "I have explained how I got into the fight. A man doesn't stand back and see two people, and one of them a girl, slaughtered by seven or eight."

The lawyer's fat forefinger sawed the air. "That's how you put it. Mind, I don't for a moment say it isn't the right way. But what the public wants is proof. Can you give evidence to show that Faulkner and his friends attacked Dillon and his daughter? Have you even got them on hand here to support your statement? Have you got a grain of evidence, apart from your bare word?"

"That letter shows—"

"It shows nothing. You might have written it yourself last night. Anyhow, a letter of introduction isn't quite an excuse for murder."

"It wasn't murder."

"That's what you say. I'll be glad to have you prove it."

"They followed Dillon—if that is his name—out of town."

"They put it that they were on their way home, when they were attacked."

"By an old man and his daughter," the Texan added significantly.

"There again we have only your statement for it. Half a dozen men had been in town during the day from the Cedar Mountain district. These men were witnesses in the suit that rose over a sheep raid. They may all have been on the spot, to ambush Faulkner's crowd."

Brandt broke in: "Are you personally convinced that this gentleman is Lieutenant Fraser of the Rangers?"

"Personally, I am of opinion that he is, but—"

"Hold your horses, Dave. Believing that, do you think that we ought to leave him here to be lynched to-night by Peake's outfit?"

"That isn't my responsibility, but speaking merely as a private citizen, I should say, No."

"What would you do with him then?"

"Why not take him up to your house?"

"Wouldn't be safe a minute, or in any other house in town."

"Then get out of town with him."

"It can't be done. I'm watched."

Hilliard shrugged.

The ranger's keen eyes went from one to another. He saw that what the lawyer needed was some personal interest to convert him into a partisan. From his pocket he drew another letter and some papers.

"If you doubt that I am Lieutenant Fraser you can wire my captain at Dallas. This is a letter of congratulation to me from the Governor of Texas for my work in the Chacon case. Here's my railroad ticket, and my lodge receipt. You gentlemen are the officers in charge. I hold you personally responsible for my safety—for the safety of a man whose name, by chance, is now known all over this country."

This was a new phase of the situation, and it went home to the lawyer's mind at once. He had been brought into the case willy nilly, and he would be blamed for anything that happened to this young Texan, whose deeds had recently been exploited broadcast in the papers. He stood for an instant in frowning thought, and as he did so a clause in the letter from the Governor of Texas caught and held his eye.

which I regard as the ablest, most daring, and, at the same time, the most difficult and most successful piece of secret service that has come to my knowledge....

Suddenly, Hilliard saw the way out—a way that appealed to him none the less because it would also serve his own ambitions.

"Neither you nor I have any right to help this gentleman to escape, sheriff. The law is plain. He is charged with murder. We haven't any right to let our private sympathies run away with us. But there is one thing we can do."

"What is that?" the sheriff asked.

"Let him earn his freedom."

"Earn it! How?"

"By serving the State in this very matter of the Squaw Creek raid. As prosecuting attorney, it is in my discretion to accept the service of an accomplice to a crime in fixing the guilt upon the principals. Before the law, Lieutenant Fraser stands accused of complicity. We believe him not guilty, but that does not affect the situation. Let him go up into the Cedar Mountain country and find out the guilty parties in the Squaw Creek raid."

"And admit my guilt by compromising with you?" the Texan scoffed.

"Not at all. You need not go publicly. In point of fact, you couldn't get out of town alive if it were known. No, we'll arrange to let you break jail on condition that you go up into the Lost Canyon district, and run down the murderers of Campeau and Jennings, That gives us an excuse for letting you go. You see the point—don't you?"

The Texan grinned. "That isn't quite the point, is it?" he drawled. "If I should be successful, you will achieve a reputation, without any cost to yourself. That's worth mentioning."

Hilliard showed a momentary embarrassment.

"That's incidental. Besides, it will help your reputation more than mine."

Brandt got busy at once with the details of the escape. "We'll loosen up the mortar round the bars in the south room. They are so rickety anyhow I haven't kept any prisoners there for years. After you have squeezed through you will find a horse saddled in the draw, back here. You'll want a gun of course."

"Always providing Lieutenant Fraser consents to the arrangement," the lawyer added smoothly.

"Oh, I'll consent," laughed Fraser wryly. "I have no option. Of course, if I win I get the reward—whatever it is."

"Oh, of course."

"Then I'm at your service, gentlemen, to escape whenever you say the word."

"The best time would be right after lunch. That would give you five hours before Nichols was in here again," the sheriff suggested.

"Suppose you draw a map, showing the route I'm to follow to reach Cedar Mountain. I reckon I had better not trouble folks to ask them the way." And the Texan grinned.

"That's right. I'll fix you up, and tell you later just where you'll find the horse," Brandt answered.

"You're an officer yourself, lieutenant," said the lawyer. "You know just how much evidence it takes to convict. Well, that's just how much we want. If you have to communicate with us, address 'T. L. Meredith, Box 117.' Better send your letter in cipher. Here's a little code I worked out that we sometimes use. Well, so-long. Good hunting, lieutenant."

Fraser nodded farewell, but did not offer to shake hands.

Brandt lingered for an instant. "Don't make any mistake, Fraser, about this job you've bit off. It's a big one, and don't you forget it. People are sore on me because I have fallen down on it. I can't help it. I just can't get the evidence. If you tackle it, you'll be in danger from start to finish. There are some bad men in this country, and the worst of them are lying low in Lost Valley."

The ranger smiled amiably. "Where is this Lost Valley?"

"Somewhere up in the Cedar Mountain district. I've never been there. Few men have, for it is not easy to find; and even if it were strangers are not invited."

"Well, I'll have to invite myself."

"That's all right. But remember this. There are men up there who would drill holes in a dying man. I guess Lost Valley is the country God forgot."

"Sounds right interesting."

"You'll find it all that, and don't forget that if they find out what you are doing there, it will be God help Steve Fraser!"

The ranger's eyes gleamed. "I'll try to remember it."

CHAPTER III — INTO LOST VALLEY

IT WAS ONE-TWENTY WHEN Fraser slipped the iron bar from the masonry into which it had been fixed and began to lower himself from the window. The back of the jail faced on the bank of a creek; and into the aspens, which ran along it at this point in a little grove, the fugitive pushed his way. He descended to the creek edge and crossed the mountain stream on boulders which filled its bed. From here he followed the trail for a hundred yards that led up the little river. On the way he passed a boy fishing and nodded a greeting to him.

"What time is it, mister?" the youngster asked.

A glance at his watch showed the Texan that it was one-twenty-five.

"The fish have quit biting. Blame it all, I'm going home. Say, mister, Jimmie Spence says they're going to lynch that fellow who killed Billy Faulkner—going to hang him to-night, Jimmie says. Do you reckon they will?"

"No, I reckon not."

"Tha's what I told him, but Jimmie says he heard Tom Peake say so. Jimmie says this town will be full o' folks by night."

Without waiting to hear any more of Jimmie's prophecies, Fraser followed the trail till it reached a waterfall Brandt had mentioned, then struck sharply to the right. In a little bunch of scrub oaks he found a saddled horse tied to a sapling. His instructions were to cross the road, which ran parallel with the stream, and follow the gulch that led to the river. Half an hour's travel brought him to another road. Into this he turned, and followed it.

In a desperate hurry though he was, Steve dared not show it. He held his piebald broncho to the ambling trot a cowpony naturally drops into. From his coat pocket he flashed a mouthharp for use in emergency.

Presently he met three men riding into town. They nodded at him, in the friendly, casual way of the outdoors West. The gait of the pony was a leisurely walk, and its rider was industriously executing, "I Met My Love In the Alamo."

"Going the wrong way, aren't you?" one of the three suggested.

"Don't you worry, I'll be there when y'u hang that guy they caught last night," he told them with a grin.

From time to time he met others. All travel seemed to be headed townward. There was excitement in the air. In the clear atmosphere voices carried a long way, and all the conversation that came to him was on the subjects of the war for the range, the battle of the previous evening, and the lynching scheduled to take place in a few hours. He realized that he had escaped none too soon, for it was certain that as the crowd in town multiplied, they would set a watch on the jail to prevent Brandt from slipping out with his prisoner.

About four miles from town he cut the telephone wires, for he knew that as soon as his escape became known to the jailer, the sheriff would be notified, and he would telephone in every direction the escape of his prisoner, just the same as if there had been no arrangement between them. It was certain, too, that all the roads leading from Gimlet Butte would be followed and patrolled immediately. For which reason he left the road after cutting the wires, and took to the hill trail marked out for him in the map furnished by Brandt.

By night, he was far up in the foothills. Close to a running stream, he camped in a little, grassy park, where his pony could find forage.

Brandt had stuffed his saddlebags with food, and had tied behind a sack, with a feed or two of oats for his horse. Fraser had ridden the range too many years to risk lighting a fire, even though he had put thirty-five miles between him and Gimlet Butte. The night was chill, as it always is in that altitude, but he rolled up in his blanket, got what sleep he could, and was off again by daybreak.

Before noon he was high in the mountain passes, from which he could sometimes look down into the green parks where nested the little ranches of small cattlemen. He knew now that he was beyond the danger of the first hurried pursuit, and that it was more than likely that any of these mountaineers would hide him rather than give him up. Nevertheless, he had no immediate intention of putting them to the test.

The second night came down on him far up on Dutchman Creek, in the Cedar Mountain district. He made a bed, where his horse found a meal, in a haystack of a small ranch, the buildings of which were strung along the creek. He was weary, and he slept deep. When he awakened next morning, it was to hear the sound of men's voices. They drifted to him from the road in front of the house.

Carefully he looked down from the top of his stack upon three horsemen talking to the bare-headed ranchman whom they had called out from his breakfast.

"No, I ain't seen a thing of him. Shot Billy Faulkner, you say? What in time for?" the rancher was innocently asking.

"You know what for, Hank Speed," the leader of the posse made sullen answer. "Well, boys, we better be pushing on, I expect."

Fraser breathed freer when they rode out of sight. He had overslept, and had had a narrow shave; for his pony was grazing in the alfalfa field within a hundred yards of them at that moment. No sooner had the posse gone than Hank Speed stepped across the field without an instant's hesitation and looked the animal over, after which he returned to the house and came out again with a rifle in his hands.

The ranger slid down the farther side of the stack and slipped his revolver from its holster. He watched the ranchman make a tour of the out-buildings very carefully and cautiously, then make a circuit of the haystack at a safe distance. Soon the rancher caught sight of the man crouching against it.

"Oh, you're there, are you? Put up that gun. I ain't going to do you any harm."

"What's the matter with you putting yours up first?" asked the Texan amiably.

"I tell you I ain't going to hurt you. Soon as I stepped out of the house I seen your horse. All I had to do was to say so, and they would have had you slick."

"What did you get your gun for, then?"

"I ain't taking any chances till folks' intentions has been declared. You might have let drive at me before I got a show to talk to you."

"All right. I'll trust you." Fraser dropped his revolver, and the other came across to him.

"Up in this country we ain't in mourning for Billy Faulkner. Old man Dillon told me what you done for him. I reckon we can find cover for you till things quiet down. My name is Speed."

"Call me Fraser."

"Glad to meet you, Mr. Fraser. I reckon we better move you back into the timber a bit. Deputy sheriffs are some thick around here right now. If you have to lie hid up in this country for a spell, we'll make an arrangement to have you taken care of."

"I'll have to lie hid. There's no doubt about that. I made my jail break just in time to keep from being invited as chief guest to a necktie party."

"Well, we'll put you where the whole United States Army couldn't find you."

They had been walking across the field and now crawled between the strands of fence wire.

"I left my saddle on top of the stack," the ranger explained.

"I'll take care of it. You better take cover on top of this ridge till I get word to Dillon you're here. My wife will fix you up some breakfast, and I'll bring it out."

"I've ce'tainly struck the good Samaritan," the Texan smiled.

"Sho! There ain't a man in the hills wouldn't do that much for a friend."

"I'm glad I have so many friends I never saw."

"Friends? The hills are full of them. You took a hand when old man Dillon and his girl were sure up against it. Cedar Mountain stands together these days. What you did for them was done for us all," Speed explained simply.

Fraser waited on the ridge till his host brought breakfast of bacon, biscuits, hard-boiled eggs, and coffee. While he ate, Speed sat down on a boulder beside him and talked.

"I sent my boy with a note to Dillon. It's a good thirty miles from here, and the old man won't make it back till some time to-morrow. Course, you're welcome at the house, but I judge it wouldn't be best for you to be seen there. No knowing when some of Brandt's deputies might butt in with a warrant. You can slip down again after dark and burrow in the haystack. Eh? What think?"

"I'm in your hands, but I don't want to put you and your friends to so much trouble. Isn't there some mountain trail off the beaten road that I could take to Dillon's ranch, and so save him from the trip after me?"

Speed grinned. "Not in a thousand years, my friend. Dillon's ranch ain't to be found, except by them that know every pocket of these hills like their own back yard. I'll guarantee you couldn't find it in a month, unless you had a map locating it."

"Must be in that Lost Valley, which some folks say is a fairy tale," the ranger said carelessly, but with his eyes on the other.

The cattleman made no comment. It occurred to Fraser that his remark had stirred some suspicion of him. At least, it suggested caution.

"If you're through with your breakfast, I'll take back the dishes," Speed said dryly.

The day wore to sunset. After dark had fallen the Texan slipped through the alfalfa field again and bedded in the stack. Before the morning was more than gray he returned to the underbrush of the ridge. His breakfast finished, and Speed gone, he lay down on a great flat, sun-dappled rock, and looked into the unflecked blue sky. The season was spring, and the earth seemed fairly palpitating with young life. The low, tireless hum of insects went on all about him. The air was vocal with the notes of nesting birds. Away across the valley he could see a mountain slope, with snow gulches glowing pink in the dawn. Little checkerboard squares along the river showed irrigated patches. In the pleasant warmth he grew drowsy. His eyes closed, opened, closed again.

He was conscious of no sound that awakened him, yet he was aware of a presence that drew him from drowsiness to an alert attention. Instinctively, his hand crept to his scabbarded weapon.

"Don't shoot me," a voice implored with laughter—a warm, vivid voice, that struck pleasantly on his memory.

The Texan turned lazily, and leaned on his elbow. She came smiling out of the brush, light as a roe, and with much of its slim, supple grace. Before, he had seen her veiled by night; the day disclosed her a dark, spirited young creature. The mass of blue-black hair coiled at the nape of the brown neck, the flash of dark eyes beneath straight, dark eyebrows, together with a certain deliberation of movement that was not languor, made it impossible to doubt that she was a Southerner by inheritance, if not by birth.

"I don't reckon I will," he greeted, smiling. "Down in Texas it ain't counted right good manners to shoot up young ladies."

"And in Wyoming you think it is."

"I judge by appearances, ma'am."

"Then you judge wrong. Those men did not know I was with dad that night. They thought I was another man. You see, they had just lost their suit for damages against dad and some more for the loss of six hundred sheep in a raid last year. They couldn't prove who did it." She flamed into a sudden passion of resentment. "I don't defend them any. They are a lot of coyotes, or they wouldn't have attacked two men, riding alone."

He ventured a rapier thrust. "How about the Squaw Creek raid? Don't your friends sometimes forget to fight fair, too?"

He had stamped the fire out of her in an instant. She drooped visibly. "Yes—yes, they do," she faltered. "I don't defend them, either. Dad had nothing to do with that. He doesn't shoot in the back."

"I'm glad to hear it," he retorted cheerfully. "And I'm glad to hear that your friends the enemy didn't know it was a girl they were attacking. Fact is, I thought you were a boy myself when first I happened in and you fanned me with your welcome."

"I didn't know. I hadn't time to think. So I let fly. But I was so excited I likely missed you a mile."

He took off his felt hat and examined with interest a bullet hole through the rim. "If it was a mile, I'd hate to have you miss me a hundred yards," he commented, with a little ripple of laughter.

"I didn't! Did I? As near as that?" She caught her hands together in a sudden anguish for what might have been.

"Don't you care, ma'am. A miss is as good as a mile. It ain't the first time I've had my hat ventilated. I mentioned it, so you wouldn't get discouraged at your shooting. It's plenty good. Good enough to suit me. I wouldn't want it any better."

"What about the man I wounded." she asked apprehensively. "Is he—is it all right?"

"Haven't you heard?"

"Heard what?" He could see the terror in her eyes.

"How it all came out?"

He could not tell why he did it, any more than he could tell why he had attempted no denial to the sheriff of responsibility for the death of Faulkner, but as he looked at this girl he shifted the burden from her shoulders to his. "You got your man in the ankle. I had worse luck after you left. They buried mine."

"Oh!" From her lips a little cry of pain forced itself. "It wasn't your fault. It was for us you did it. Oh, why did they attack us?"

"I did what I had to do. There is no blame due either you or me for it," he said, with quiet conviction.

"I know. But it seems so dreadful. And then they put you in jail—and you broke out! Wasn't that it?"

"That was the way of it, Miss Arlie. How did you know?"

"Henry Speed's note to father said you had broken jail. Dad wasn't at home. You know, the round-up is on now and he has to be there. So I saddled, and came right away."

"That was right good of you."

"Wasn't it?" There was a softened, almost tender, jeer in her voice. "Since you only saved our lives!"

"I ain't claiming all that, Miss Arlie."

"Then I'll claim it for you. I suppose you gave yourself up to them and explained how it was after we left."

"Not exactly that. I managed to slip away, through the sage. It was mo'ning before I found the road again. Soon as I did, a deputy tagged me, and said, 'You're mine.' He spoke for me so prompt and seemed so sure about what he was saying, I didn't argue the matter with him." He laughed gayly.

"And then?"

"Then he herded me to town, and I was invited to be the county's guest. Not liking the accommodations, I took the first chance and flew the coop. They missed a knife in my pocket when they searched me, and I chipped the cement away from the window bars, let myself down by the bed linen, and borrowed a cow-pony I found saddled at the edge of town. So, you see, I'm a hawss thief too, ma'am."

She could not take it so lightly as he did, even though she did not know that he had barely escaped with his life. Something about his debonair, smiling hardihood touched her imagination, as did also the virile competence of the man. If the cool eyes in his weatherbeaten face could be hard as agates, they could also light up with sparkling imps of mischief. Certainly he was no boy, but the close-cut waves of crisp, reddish hair and the ready smile contributed to an impression of youth that came and went.

"Willie Speed is saddling you a horse. The one you came on has been turned loose to go back when it wants to. I'm going to take you home with me," she told him.

"Well, I'm willing to be kidnapped."

"I brought your horse Teddy. If you like, you may ride that, and I'll take the other."

"Yore a gentleman, ma'am. I sure would."

When Arlie saw with what pleasure the friends met, how Teddy nickered and rubbed his nose up and down his master's coat and how the Texan put him through his little repertoire of tricks and fed him a lump of sugar from his coat pocket, she was glad she had ridden Teddy instead of her own pony to the meeting.

They took the road without loss of time. Arlie Dillon knew exactly how to cross this difficult region. She knew the Cedar Mountain district as a grade teacher knows her arithmetic. In daylight or in darkness, with or without a trail, she could have traveled almost a bee line to the point she wanted. Her life had been spent largely in the saddle—at least that part of it which had been lived outdoors. Wherefore she was able to lead her guest by secret trails that wound in and out among the passes and through unsuspected gorges to hazardous descents possible only to goats and cow ponies. No stranger finding his way in would have stood a chance of getting out again unaided.

Among these peaks lay hidden pockets and caches by hundreds, rock fissures which made the country a very maze to the uninitiated. The ranger, himself one of the best trailers in Texas, doubted whether he could retrace his steps to the Speed place.

After several hours of travel, they emerged from a gulch to a little valley known as Beaver Dam Park. The girl pointed out to her companion a narrow brown ribbon that wound through the park.

"There's the road again. That's the last we shall see of it—or it will be when we have crossed it. Once we reach the Twin Buttes that are the gateway to French Cañon you are perfectly safe. You can see the buttes from here. No, farther to the right."

"I thought I'd ridden some tough trails in my time, but this country ce'tainly takes the cake," Fraser said admiringly, as his gaze swept the horizon. "It puts it over anything I ever met up with. Ain't that right, Teddy hawss?"

The girl flushed with pleasure at his praise. She was mountain bred, and she loved the country of the great peaks.

They descended the valley, crossed the road, and in an open grassy spot just beyond, came plump upon four men who had unsaddled to eat lunch.

The meeting came too abruptly for Arlie to avoid it. One glance told her that they were deputies from Gimlet Butte. Without the least hesitation she rode forward and gave them the casual greeting of cattleland. Fraser, riding beside her, nodded coolly, drew to a halt, and lit a cigarette.

"Found him yet, gentlemen?" he asked.

"No, nor we ain't likely to, if he's reached this far," one of the men answered.

"It would be some difficult to collect him here," the Texan admitted impartially.

"Among his friends," one of the deputies put in, with a snarl.

Fraser laughed easily. "Oh, well, we ain't his enemies, though he ain't very well known in the Cedar Mountain country. What might he be like, pardner?"

"Hasn't he lived up here long?" asked one of the men, busy with some bacon over a fire.

"They say not."

"He's a heavy-set fellow, with reddish hair; not so tall as you, I reckon, and some heavier. Was wearing chaps and gauntlets when he made his getaway. From the description, he looks something like you, I shouldn't wonder."

Fraser congratulated himself that he had had the foresight to discard as many as possible of these helps to identification before he was three miles from Gimlet Butte. Now he laughed pleasantly.

"Sure he's heavier than me, and not so tall."

"It would be a good joke, Bud, if they took you back to town for this man," cut in Arlie, troubled at the direction the conversation was taking, but not obviously so.

"I ain't objecting any, sis. About three days of the joys of town would sure agree with my run-down system," the Texan answered joyously.

"When you cowpunchers do get in, you surely make Rome howl," one of the deputies agreed, with a grin. "Been in to the Butte lately?"

The Texan met his grin. "It ain't been so long."

"Well, you ain't liable to get in again for a while," Arlie said emphatically. "Come on, Bud, we've got to be moving."

"Which way is Dead Cow Creek?" one of the men called after them.

Fraser pointed in the direction from which he had just come.

After they had ridden a hundred yards, the girl laughed aloud her relief at their escape. "If they go the way you pointed for Dead Cow Creek, they will have to go clear round the world to get to it. We're headed for the creek now."

"A fellow can't always guess right," pleaded the Texan. "If he could, what a fiend he would be at playing the wheel! Shall I go back and tell him I misremembered for a moment where the creek is?"

"No, sir. You had me scared badly enough when you drew their attention to yourself. Why did you do it?"

"It was the surest way to disarm any suspicion they might have had. One of them had just said the man they wanted was like me. Presently, one would have been guessing that it was me." He looked at her drolly, and added: "You played up to me fine, sis."

A touch of deeper color beat into her dusky cheeks. "We'll drop the relationship right now, if you please. I said only what you made me say," she told him, a little stiffly.

But presently she relaxed to the note of friendliness, even of comradeship, habitual to her. She was a singularly frank creature, having been brought up in a country where women were few and far, and where conventions were of the simplest. Otherwise, she would not have confessed to him with unconscious naïveté, as she now did, how greatly she had been troubled for him before she received the note from Speed.

"It worried me all the time, and it troubled dad, too. I could see that. We had hardly left you before I knew we had done wrong. Dad did it for me, of course; but he felt mighty bad about it. Somehow, I couldn't think of anything but you there, with all those men shooting at you. Suppose you had waited too long before surrendering! Suppose you had been killed for us!" She looked at him, and felt a shiver run over her in the warm sunlight. "Night before last I was worn out. I slept some, but I kept dreaming they were killing you. Oh, you don't know how glad I was to get word from Speed that you were alive." Her soft voice had the gift of expressing feeling, and it was resonant with it now.

"I'm glad you were glad," he said quietly.

Across Dead Cow Creek they rode, following the stream up French Cañon to what was known as the Narrows. Here the great rock walls, nearly two thousand feet high, came so close together as to leave barely room for a footpath beside the creek which boiled down over great boulders. Unexpectedly, there opened in the wall a rock fissure, and through this Arlie guided her horse.

The Texan wondered where she could be taking him, for the fissure terminated in a great rock slide some two hundred yards ahead of them. Before reaching this she turned sharply to the left, and began winding in and out among the big boulders which had fallen from the summit far above.

Presently Fraser observed with astonishment that they were following a path that crept up the very face of the bluff. Up—up—up they went until they reached a rift in the wall, and into this the trail went precipitously. Stones clattered down from the hoofs of the horses as they clambered up like mountain goats. Once the Texan had to throw himself to the ground to keep Teddy from falling backward.

Arlie, working her pony forward with voice and body and knees, so that from her seat in the saddle she seemed literally to lift him up, reached the summit and looked back.

"All right back there?" she asked quietly.

"All right," came the cheerful answer. "Teddy isn't used to climbing up a wall, but he'll make it or know why."

A minute later, man and horse were beside her.

"Good for Teddy," she said, fondling his nose.

"Look out! He doesn't like strangers to handle him."

"We're not strangers. We're tillicums. Aren't we, Teddy?"

Teddy said "Yes" after the manner of a horse, as plain as words could say it.

From their feet the trail dropped again to another gorge, beyond which the ranger could make out a stretch of valley through which ran the gleam of a silvery thread.

"We're going down now into Mantrap Gulch. The patch of green you see beyond is Lost Valley," she told him.

"Lost Valley," he repeated, in amazement. "Are we going to Lost Valley?"

"You've named our destination."

"But—you don't live in Lost Valley."

"Don't I?"

"Do you?"

"Yes," she answered, amused at his consternation, if it were that.

"I wish I had known," he said, as if to himself.

"You know now. Isn't that soon enough? Are you afraid of the place, because people make a mystery of it?" she demanded impatiently.

"No. It isn't that." He looked across at the valley again, and asked abruptly: "Is this the only way in?"

"No. There is another, but this is the quickest."

"Is the other as difficult as this?"

"In a way, yes. It is very much more round-about. It isn't known much by the public. Not many outsiders have business in the valley."

She volunteered no explanation in detail, and the man beside her said, with a grim laugh:

"There isn't any general admission to the public this way, is there?"

"No. Oh, folks can come if they want to."

He looked full in her face, and said significantly: "I thought the way to Lost Valley was a sort of a secret—one that those who know are not expected to tell."

"Oh, that's just talk. Not many come in but our friends. We've had to be careful lately. But you can't call a secret what a thousand folks know."

It was like a blow in the face to him. Not many but their friends! And she was taking him in confidently because he was her friend. What sort of a friend was he? he asked himself. He could not perform the task to which he was pledged without striking home at her. If he succeeded in ferreting out the Squaw Creek raiders he must send to the penitentiary, perhaps to death, her neighbors, and possibly her relatives. She had told him her father was not implicated, but a daughter's faith in her parent was not convincing proof of his innocence. If not her father, a brother might be involved. And she was innocently making it easy for him to meet on a friendly footing these hospitable, unsuspecting savages, who had shed human blood because of the unleashed passions in them!

In that moment, while he looked away toward Lost Valley, he sickened of the task that lay before him. What would she think of him if she knew?

Arlie, too, had been looking down the gulch toward the valley. Now her gaze came slowly round to him and caught the expression of his face.

"What's the matter?" she cried.

"Nothing. Nothing at all. An old heart pain that caught me suddenly."

"I'm sorry. We'll soon be home now. We'll travel slowly."

Her voice was tender with sympathy; so, too, were her eyes when he met them.

He looked away again and groaned in his heart.

CHAPTER IV — THE WARNING OF MANTRAP GULCH

THEY FOLLOWED THE TRAIL down into the cañon. As the ponies slowly picked their footing on the steep narrow path, he asked:

"Why do they call it Mantrap Gulch?"

"It got its name before my time in the days when outlaws hid here. A hunted man came to Lost Cañon, a murderer wanted by the law for more crimes than one. He was well treated by the settlers. They gave him shelter and work. He was safe, and he knew it. But he tried to make his peace with the law outside by breaking the law of the valley. He knew that two men were lying hid in a pocket gulch, opening from the valley—men who were wanted for train robbery. He wrote to the company offering to betray these men if they would pay him the reward and see that he was not punished for his crimes.

"It seems he was suspected. His letter was opened, and the exits from the valley were both guarded. Knowing he was discovered, he tried to slip out by the river way. He failed, sneaked through the settlement at night, and slipped into the cañon here. At this end of it he found armed men on guard. He ran back and found the entrance closed. He was in a trap. He tried to climb one of the walls. Do you see that point where the rock juts out?"

"About five hundred feet up? Yes."

"He managed to climb that high. Nobody ever knows how he did it, but when morning broke there he was, like a fly on a wall. His hunters came and saw him. I suppose he could hear them laughing as their voices came echoing up to him. They shot above him, below him, on either side of him. He knew they were playing with him, and that they would finish him when they got ready. He must have been half crazy with fear. Anyhow, he lost his hold and fell. He was dead before they reached him. From that day this has been called Mantrap Gulch."

The ranger looked up at the frowning walls which shut out the sunlight. His imagination pictured the drama—the hunted man's wild flight up the gulch; his dreadful discovery that it was closed; his desperate attempt to climb by moonlight the impossible cliff, and the tragedy that overtook him.

The girl spoke again softly, almost as if she were in the presence of that far-off Nemesis. "I suppose he deserved it. It's an awful thing to be a traitor; to sell the people who have befriended you. We can't put ourselves in his place and know why he did it. All we can say is that we're glad—glad that we have never known men who do such things. Do you think people always felt a sort of shrinking when they were near him, or did he seem just like other men?"

Glancing at the man who rode beside her, she cried out at the stricken look on his face. "It's your heart again. You're worn out with anxiety and privations. I should have remembered and come slower," she reproached herself.

"I'm all right—now. It passes in a moment," he said hoarsely.

But she had already slipped from the saddle and was at his bridle rein. "No—no. You must get down. We have plenty of time. We'll rest here till you are better."

There was nothing for it but to obey. He dismounted, feeling himself a humbug and a scoundrel. He sat down on a mossy rock, his back against another, while she trailed the reins and joined him.

"You are better now, aren't you?" she asked, as she seated herself on an adjacent boulder.

Gruffly he answered: "I'm all right."

She thought she understood. Men do not like to be coddled. She began to talk cheerfully of the first thing that came into her head. He made the necessary monosyllabic responses when her speech put it up to him, but she saw that his mind was brooding over something else. Once she saw his gaze go up to the point on the cliff reached by the fugitive.

But it was not until they were again in the saddle that he spoke.

"Yes, he got what was coming to him. He had no right to complain."

"That's what my father says. I don't deny the justice of it, but whenever I think of it, I feel sorry for him."

"Why?"

Despite the quietness of the monosyllable, she divined an eager interest back of his question.

"He must have suffered so. He wasn't a brave man, they say. And he was one against many. They didn't hunt him. They just closed the trap and let him wear himself out trying to get through. Think of that awful week of hunger and exposure in the hills before the end!"

"It must have been pretty bad, especially if he wasn't a game man. But he had no legitimate kick coming. He took his chance and lost. It was up to him to pay."

"His name was David Burke. When he was a little boy I suppose his mother used to call him Davy. He wasn't bad then; just a little boy to be cuddled and petted. Perhaps he was married. Perhaps he had a sweetheart waiting for him outside, and praying for him. And they snuffed his life out as if he had been a rattlesnake."

"Because he was a miscreant and it was best he shouldn't live. Yes, they did right. I would have helped do it in their place."

"My father did," she sighed.

They did not speak again until they had passed from between the chill walls to the warm sunshine of the valley beyond. Among the rocks above the trail, she glimpsed some early anemones blossoming bravely.

She drew up with a little cry of pleasure. "They're the first I have seen. I must have them."

Fraser swung from the saddle, but he was not quick enough. She reached them before he did, and after they had gathered them she insisted upon sitting down again.

He had his suspicions, and voiced them. "I believe you got me off just to make me sit down."

She laughed with deep delight. "I didn't, but since we are here we shall." And she ended debate by sitting down tailor-fashion, and beginning to arrange her little bouquet.

A meadow lark, troubadour of spring, trilled joyously somewhere in the pines above. The man looked up, then down at the vivid creature busy with her flowers at his feet. There was kinship between the two. She, too, was athrob with the joy note of spring.

"You're to sit down," she ordered, without looking up from the sheaf of anemone blossoms she was arranging.

He sank down beside her, aware vaguely of something new and poignant in his life.

CHAPTER V — JED BRISCOE TAKES A HAND

SUDDENLY A FOOTFALL, AND a voice:

"Hello, Arlie! I been looking for you everywhere."

The Texan's gaze took in a slim dark man, goodlooking after a fashion, but with dissipation written on the rather sullen face.

"Well, you've found me," the girl answered coolly.

"Yes, I've found you," the man answered, with a steady, watchful eye on the Texan.

Miss Dillon was embarrassed at this plain hostility, but indignation too sparkled in her eye. "Anything in particular you want?"

The newcomer ignored her question. His hard gaze challenged the Southerner; did more than challenge—weighed and condemned.

But this young woman was not used to being ignored. Her voice took on an edge of sharpness.

"What can I do for you, Jed?"

"Who's your friend?" the man demanded bluntly, insolently.

Arlie's flush showed the swift, upblazing resentment she immediately controlled. "Mr. Fraser—just arrived from Texas. Mr. Fraser, let me introduce to you Mr. Briscoe."

The Texan stepped forward to offer his hand, but Briscoe deliberately put both of his behind him.

"Might I ask what Mr. Fraser, just arrived from Texas, is doing here?" the young man drawled, contriving to make an insult of every syllable.

The girl's eyes flashed dangerously. "He is here as my guest."

"Oh, as your guest!"

"Doesn't it please you, Jed?"

"Have I said it didn't please me?" he retorted smoothly.

"Your looks say it."

He let out a sudden furious oath. "Then my looks don't lie any."

Fraser was stepping forward, but with a gesture Arlie held him back. This was her battle, not his.

"What have you got to say about it?" she demanded.

"You had no right to bring him here. Who is he anyhow?"

"I think that is his business, and mine."

"I make it mine," he declared hotly. "I've heard about this fellow from your father. You met up with him on the trail. He says his name is Fraser. You don't even know whether that is true. He may be a spy. How do you know he ain't?"

"How do I know you aren't?" she countered swiftly.

"You've known me all my life. Did you ever see him before?"

"Never."

"Well, then!"

"He risked his life to save ours."

"Risked nothing! It was a trick, I tell you."

"It makes no difference to me what you tell me. Your opinion can't affect mine."

"You know the feeling of the valley just now about strangers," said Briscoe sullenly.

"It depends on who the stranger is."

"Well, I object to this one."

"So it seems; but I don't know any law that makes me do whatever you want me to." Her voice, low and clear, cut like a whiplash.

Beneath the dust of travel the young man's face burned with anger. "We're not discussing that just now. What I say is that you had no right to bring him here—not now, especially. You know why," he added, almost in a whisper.

"If you had waited and not attempted to brow-beat me, I would have shown you that that is the very reason I had to bring him."

"How do you mean?"

"Never mind what I mean. You have insulted my friend, and through him, me. That is enough for one day." She turned from him haughtily and spoke to the Texan. "If you are ready, Mr. Fraser, we'll be going now."

The ranger, whose fingers had been itching to get at the throat of this insolent young man, turned without a word and obediently brought the girl's pony, then helped her to mount. Briscoe glared, in a silent tempest of passion.

"I think I have left a glove and my anemones where we were sitting," the girl said sweetly to the Texan.

Fraser found them, tightened the saddle girth, and mounted Teddy. As they cantered away, Arlie called to him to look at the sunset behind the mountains.

From the moment of her dismissal of Briscoe the girl had apparently put him out of her thoughts. No fine lady of the courts could have done it with more disdainful ease. And the Texan, following her lead, played his part in the little comedy, ignoring the other man as completely as she did.

The young cattleman, furious, his teeth set in impotent rage, watched it all with the lust to kill in his heart. When they had gone, he flung himself into the saddle and rode away in a tumultuous fury.

Before they had covered two hundred yards Arlie turned to her companion, all contrition. "There! I've done it again. My fits of passion are always getting me into trouble. This time one of them has given you an enemy, and a bad one, too."

"No. He would have been my enemy no matter what you said. Soon as he put his eyes on me, I knew it."

"Because I brought you here, you mean?"

"I don't mean only that. Some folks are born to be enemies, just as some are born to be friends. They've only got to look in each other's eyes once to know it."

"That's strange. I never heard anybody else say that. Do you really mean it?"

"Yes."

"And did you ever have such an enemy before? Don't answer me if I oughtn't to ask that," she added quickly.

"Yes."

"Where?"

"In Texas. Why, here we are at a ranch!"

"Yes. It's ours, and yours as long as you want to stay. Did you feel that you were enemies the moment you saw this man in Texas?"

"I knew we were going to have trouble as soon as we looked at each other. I had no feeling toward him, but he had toward me."

"And did you have trouble?"

"Some, before I landed him. The way it turned out he had most of it."

She glanced quickly at him. "What do you mean by 'landed'?"

"I am an officer in the Texas Rangers."

"What are they? Something like our forest rangers?"

"No. The duty of a Texas Ranger is to enforce the law against desperadoes. We prevent crime if we can. When we can't do that, we hunt down the criminals."

Arlie looked at him in a startled silence.

"You are an officer of the law—a sort of sheriff?" she said, at last.

"Yes, in Texas. This is Wyoming." He made his distinction, knowing it was a false one. Somehow he had the feeling of a whipped cur.

"I wish I had known. If you had only told me earlier," she said, so low as to be almost a whisper.

"I'm sorry. If you like, I'll go away again," he offered.

"No, no. I'm only thinking that it gives Jed a hold, gives him something to stir up his friends with, you know. That is, it would if he knew. He mustn't find out."

"Be frank. Don't make any secret of it. That's the best way," he advised.

She shook her head. "You don't know Jed's crowd. They'd be suspicious of any officer, no matter where he came from."

"Far as I can make out, that young man is going to be loaded with suspicions of me anyhow," he laughed.

"It isn't anything to laugh at. You don't know him," she told him gravely.

"And can't say I'm suffering to," he drawled.

She looked at him a little impatiently, as if he were a child playing with gunpowder and unaware of its potentialities.

"Can't you understand? You're not in Texas with your friends all around you. This is Lost Valley—and Lost Valley isn't on the map. Men make their own law here. That is, some of them do. I wouldn't give a snap of my fingers for your life if the impression spread that you are a spy. It doesn't matter that I know you're not. Others must feel it, too."

"I see. And Mr. Briscoe will be a molder of public opinion?"

"So far as he can he will. We must forestall him."

"Beat him to it, and give me a clean bill of moral health, eh?"

She frowned. "This is serious business, my friend."

"I'm taking it that way," he said smilingly.

"I shouldn't have guessed it."

Yet for all his debonair ease the man had an air of quiet competence. His strong, bronzed face and neck, the set of his shoulders, the light poise of him in the saddle, the steady confidence of the gray eyes, all told her as much. She was aware of a curiosity about what was hidden behind that stone-wall face of his.

"You didn't finish telling me about that enemy in Texas," she suggested suddenly.

"Oh, there ain't much to tell. He broke out from the pen, where I had put him when I was a kid. He was a desperado wanted by the authorities, so I arrested him again."

"Sounds easy."

"He made some trouble, shot up two or three men first." Fraser lifted his hand absently.

"Is that scar on your hand where he shot you?" Arlie asked.

He looked up in quick surprise. "Now, how did you know that?"

"You were talking of the trouble he made and you looked at your hand," she explained. "Where is he now? In the penitentiary?"

"No. He broke away before I got him there."

She had another flash of inspiration. "And you came to Wyoming to get him again."

"Good gracious, ma'am, but you're ce'tainly a wizard! That's why I came, though it's a secret."

"What is he wanted for?"

"Robbing a train, three murders and a few other things."

As she swung from her pony in front of the old-fashioned Southern log house, Artie laughed at him over her shoulder.

"You're a fine officer! Tell all you know to the first girl you meet!"

"Well, you see, the girl happened to be—you!"

After the manner of the old-fashioned Southern house a wide "gallery" bisected it from porch to rear. Saddles hung from pegs in the gallery. Horse blankets and bridles, spurs and saddlebags, lay here and there in disarray. A disjointed rifle which some one had started to clean was on the porch. Swiftly Arlie stripped saddle, bridle, and blanket from her pony and flung them down as a contribution to the general disorder, and at her suggestion Fraser did the same. A half-grown lad came running to herd the horses into a corral close at hand.

"I want you when you've finished feeding, Bobbie," Arlie told the lad. Then briefly to her guest: "This way, please."

She led him into a large, cheerful living room, into which, through big casement windows, the light streamed. It was a pleasant room, despite its barbaric touch. There was a grizzly bear skin before the great open, stone fireplace, and Navajo rugs covered the floor and hung on the walls. The skin of a silver-tip bear was stretched beneath a writing desk, a trophy of Arlie's rifle, which hung in a rack above. Civilization had furnished its quota to the room in a piano, some books, and a few photographs.

The Texan observed that order reigned here, even though it did not interfere with the large effect of comfort.

The girl left him, to return presently with her aunt, to whom she introduced him. Miss Ruth Dillon was a little, bright-eyed old lady, whose hair was still black, and her step light. Evidently she had her instructions, for she greeted their guest with charming cordiality, and thanked him for the service he had rendered her brother and her niece.

Presently the boy Bobbie arrived for further orders. Arlie went to her desk and wrote hurriedly.

"You're to give this note to my father," she directed. "Be sure he gets it himself. You ought to find him down in Jackson's Pocket, if the drive is from Round Top to-day. But you can ask about that along the road."

When the boy had gone, Arlie turned to Fraser.

"I want to tell father you're here before Jed gets to him with his story," she explained. "I've asked him to ride down right away. He'll probably come in a few hours and spend the night here."

After they had eaten supper they returned to the living room, where a great fire, built by Jim the negro horse wrangler, was roaring up the chimney.

It was almost eleven o'clock when horses galloped up and Dillon came into the house, followed by Jed Briscoe. The latter looked triumphant, the former embarrassed as he disgorged letters and newspapers from his pocket.

"I stopped at the office to get the mail as I came down. Here's yore paper, Ruth."

Miss Dillon pounced eagerly upon the Gimlet Butte Avalanche, and disappeared with it to her bedroom. She had formerly lived in Gimlet Butte, and was still keenly interested in the gossip of the town.

Briscoe had scored one against Arlie by meeting her father, telling his side of the story, and returning with him to the house. Nevertheless Arlie, after giving him the slightest nod her duty as hostess would permit, made her frontal attack without hesitation.

"You'll be glad to know, dad, that Mr. Fraser is our guest. He has had rather a stormy time since we saw him last, and he has consented to stay with us a few days till things blow over."

Dillon, very ill at ease, shook hands with the Texan, and was understood to say that he was glad to see him.

"Then you don't look it, dad," Arlie told him, with a gleam of vexed laughter.

Her father turned reproachfully upon her. "Now, honey, yo' done wrong to say that. Yo' know Mr. Fraser is welcome to stay in my house long as he wants. I'm proud to have him stay. Do you think I forgot already what he done for us?"

"Of course not. Then it's all settled," Arlie cut in, and rushed on to another subject. "How's the round-up coming, dad?"

"We'll talk about the round-up later. What I'm saying is that Mr. Fraser has only got to say the word, and I'm there to he'p him till the cows come home."

"That's just what I told him, dad."

"Hold yore hawsses, will yo', honey? But, notwithstanding which, and not backing water on that proposition none, we come to another p'int."

"Which Jed made to you carefully on the way down," his daughter interrupted scornfully.

"It don't matter who made it. The p'int is that there are reasons why strangers ain't exactly welcome in this valley right now, Mr. Fraser. This country is full o' suspicion. Whilst it's onjust, charges are being made against us on the outside. Right now the settlers here have got to guard against furriners. Now I know yo're all right, Mr. Fraser. But my neighbors don't know it."

"It was our lives he saved, not our neighbors'," scoffed Arlie.

"K'rect. So I say, Mr. Fraser, if yo' are out o' funds, I'll finance you. Wherever you want to go I'll see you git there, but I hain't got the right to invite you to stay in Lost Valley."

"Better send him to Gimlet Butte, dad! He killed a man in helping us to escape, and he 's wanted bad! He broke jail to get here! Pay his expenses back to the Butte! Then if there's a reward, you and Jed can divide it!" his daughter jeered.

"What's that? Killed a man, yo' say?"

"Yes. To save us. Shall we send him back under a rifle guard? Or shall we have Sheriff Brandt come and get him?"

"Gracious goodness, gyurl, shet up whilst I think. Killed a man, eh? This valley has always been open to fugitives. Ain't that right, Jed?"

"To fugitives, yes," said Jed significantly. "But that fact ain't proved."

"Jed's getting right important. We'll soon be asking him whether we can stay here," said Arlie, with a scornful laugh. "And I say it is proved. We met the deputies the yon side of the big cañon."

Briscoe looked at her out of dogged, half-shuttered eyes. He said nothing, but he looked the picture of malice.

Dillon rasped his stubbly chin and looked at the Texan. Far from an alert-minded man, he came to conclusions slowly. Now he arrived at one.

"Dad burn it, we'll take the 'fugitive' for granted. Yo' kin lie up here long as yo' like, friend. I'll guarantee yo' to my neighbors. I reckon if they don't like it they kin lump it. I ain't a-going to give up the man that saved my gyurl's life."

The door opened and let in Miss Ruth Dillon. The little old lady had the newspaper in her hand, and her beady eyes were shining with excitement.

"It's all in here, Mr. Fraser—about your capture and escape. But you didn't tell us all of it. Perhaps you didn't know, though, that they had plans to storm the jail and hang you?"

"Yes, I knew that," the Texan answered coolly. "The jailer told me what was coming to me. I decided not to wait and see whether he was lying. I wrenched a bar from the window, lowered myself by my bedding, flew the coop, and borrowed a horse. That's the whole story, ma'am, except that Miss Arlie brought me here to hide me."

"Read aloud what the paper says," Dillon ordered.

His sister handed the Avalanche to her niece. Arlie found the article and began to read:

"A dastardly outrage occurred three miles from Gimlet Butte last night. While on their way home from the trial of the well-known Three Pines sheep raid case, a small party of citizens were attacked by miscreants presumed to be from the Cedar Mountain country. How many of these there were we have no means of knowing, as the culprits disappeared in the mountains after murdering William Faulkner, a well-known sheep man, and wounding Tom Long."

There followed a lurid account of the battle, written from the point of view of the other side. After which the editor paid his respects to Fraser, though not by name.

"One of the ruffians, for some unknown reason—perhaps in the hope of getting a chance to slay another victim—remained too long near the scene of the atrocity and was apprehended early this morning by that fearless deputy, James Schilling. He refused to give his name or any other information about himself. While the man is a stranger to Gimlet Butte, there can be no doubt that he is one of the Lost Valley desperadoes implicated in the Squaw Creek raid some months ago. Since the bullet that killed Faulkner was probably fired from the rifle carried by this man, it is safe to assume that the actual murderer was apprehended. The man is above medium height, well built and muscular, and carries all the earmarks of a desperate character."

Arlie glanced up from her reading to smile at Fraser. "Dad and I are miscreants, and you are a ruffian and a desperate character," she told him gayly.

"Go on, honey," her father urged.

The account told how the prisoner had been confined in the jail, and how the citizens, wrought up by the continued lawlessness of the Lost Valley district, had quietly gathered to make an example of the captured man. While condemning lynching in general, the Avalanche wanted to go on record as saying that if ever it was justifiable this was the occasion. Unfortunately, the prisoner, giving thus further evidence of his desperate nature, had cut his way out of prison with a pocketknife and escaped from town by means of a horse he found saddled and did not hesitate to steal. At the time of going to press he had not yet been recaptured, though Sheriff Brandt had several posses on his trail. The outlaw had cut the telephone wires, but it was confidently believed he would be captured before he reached his friends in the mountains.

Arlie's eyes were shining. She looked at Briscoe and handed him the paper triumphantly. This was her vindication for bringing the hunted man to Lost Valley. He had been fighting their battles and had almost lost his life in doing it. Jed might say what he liked while she had this to refute him.

"I guess that editor doesn't believe so confidently as he pretends," she said. "Anyhow, he has guessed wrong. Mr. Fraser has reached his friends, and they'll look out for him."

Her father came to her support radiantly. "You bet yore boots they will, honey. Shake hands on it, Mr. Fraser. I reckon yore satisfied too, Jed. Eh, boy?"

Briscoe viewed the scene with cynical malice. "Quite a hero, ain't he? If you want to know, I stand pat. Mr. Fraser from Texas don't draw the wool over my eyes none. Right now I serve notice to that effect. Meantime, since I don't aim to join the happy circle of his admirers, I reckon I'll duck."

He nodded impudently at Arlie, turned on his heel, and went trailing off with jingling spur. They heard him cursing at his horse as he mounted. The cruel swish of a quirt came to them, after which the swift pounding of a horse's hoofs. The cow pony had found its gallop in a stride.

The Texan laughed lightly. "Exit Mr. Briscoe, some disappointed," he murmured.

He noticed that none of the others shared his mirth.

CHAPTER VI — A SURE ENOUGH WOLF

BRISCOE DID NOT RETURN at once to the scene of the round-up. He followed the trail toward Jackson's Pocket, but diverged after he had gone a few miles and turned into one of the hundred blind gulches that ran out from the valley to the impassable mountain wall behind. It was known as Jack Rabbit Run, because its labyrinthine trails offered a retreat into which hunted men might always dive for safety. Nobody knew its recesses better than Jed Briscoe, who was acknowledged to be the leader of that faction in the valley which had brought it the bad name it held.

Long before Jed's time there had been such a faction, then the dominant one of the place, now steadily losing ground as civilization seeped in, but still strong because bound by ties of kindred and of interest to the honest law-abiding majority. Of it were the outlaws who came periodically to find shelter here, the hasty men who had struck in heat and found it necessary to get beyond the law's reach for a time, and reckless cowpunchers, who foregathered with these, because they were birds of a feather. To all such, Jack Rabbit Run was a haven of rest.

By devious paths the cattleman guided his horse until he came to a kind of pouch, guarded by a thick growth of aspens. The front of these he skirted, plunged into them at the farther edge, and followed a narrow trail which wound among them till the grove opened upon a saucer-shaped valley in which nestled a little log cabin. Lights gleamed from the windows hospitably and suggested the comfortable warmth of a log fire and good-fellowship. So many a hunted man had thought as he emerged from that grove to look down upon the valley nestling at his feet.

Jed turned his horse into a corral back of the house, let out the hoot of an owl as he fed and watered, and returning to the cabin, gave the four knocks that were the signal for admission.

Bolts were promptly withdrawn and the door thrown open by a slender, fair-haired fellow, whose features looked as if they had been roughed out and not finished. He grinned amiably at the newcomer and greeted him with: "Hello, Jed."

"Hello, Tommie," returned Briscoe, carelessly, and let his glance pass to the three men seated at the table with cards and poker chips in front of them, The man facing Briscoe was a big, heavy-set, unmistakable ruffian with long, drooping, red mustache, and villainous, fishy eyes. It was observable that the trigger finger of his right hand was missing. Also, there was a nasty scar on his right cheek running from the bridge of the nose halfway to the ear. This gave surplusage to the sinister appearance he already had. To him Briscoe spoke first, attempting a geniality he did not feel.

"How're they coming, Texas?"

"You ain't heard me kicking any, have you?" the man made sullen answer.

"Not out loud," said Briscoe significantly, his eyes narrowing after a trick they had when he was most on his guard.

"I reckon my remarks will be plumb audible when I've got any kick to register, seh."

"I hope not, Mr. Johnson. In this neck of woods a man is liable to get himself disliked if he shoots off his mouth too prevalent. Folks that don't like our ways can usually find a door open out of Lost Valley—if they don't wait too long!"

"I'm some haidstrong. I reckon I'll stay." He scowled at Jed with disfavor, meeting him eye to eye. But presently the rigor of his gaze relaxed. Me remembered that he was a fugitive from justice, and at the mercy of this man who had so far guessed his secret. Putting a temporary curb on his bilious jealousy, he sulkily added: "Leastways, if there's no objection, Mr. Briscoe. I ain't looking for trouble with anybody."

"A man who's looking for it usually finds it, Mr. Johnson. A man that ain't, lives longer and more peaceable." At this point Jed pulled himself together and bottled his arrogance, remembering that he had come to make an alliance with this man. "But that's no way for friends to talk. I got a piece of news for you. We'll talk it over in the other room and not disturb these gentlemen."

One of the "gentlemen" grinned. He was a round-bodied, bullet-headed cowpuncher, with a face like burnt leather. He was in chaps, flannel shirt, and broad-brimmed hat. From a pocket in his chaps a revolver protruded. "That's right, Jed. Wrap it up proper. You'd hate to disturb us, wouldn't you?"

"I'll not interrupt you from losing your money more than five minutes, Yorky," answered Briscoe promptly.

The third man at the table laughed suddenly. "Ay bane laik to know how yuh feel now, Yorky?" he taunted.

"It ain't you that's taking my spondulix in, you big, overgrown Swede!" returned Yorky amiably. "It's the gent from Texas. How can a fellow buck against luck that fills from a pair to a full house on the draw?"

The blond giant, Siegfried—who was not a Swede, but a Norwegian—announced that he was seventeen dollars in the game himself.

Tommie, already broke, and an onlooker, reported sadly.

"Sixty-one for me, durn it!"

Jed picked up a lamp, led the way to the other room, and closed the door behind them.

"I thought it might interest you to know that there's a new arrival in the valley, Mr. Struve," he said smoothly.

"Who says my name's Struve?" demanded the man who called himself Johnson, with fierce suspicion.

Briscoe laughed softly. "I say it—Wolf Struve. Up till last month your address for two years has been number nine thousand four hundred and thirty-two, care of Penitentiary Warden, Yuma, Arizona."

"Prove it. Prove it," blustered the accused man.

"Sure." From his inside coat pocket Jed took out a printed notice offering a reward for the capture of Nick Struve, alias "Wolf" Struve, convict, who had broken prison on the night of February seventh, and escaped, after murdering one of the guards. A description and a photograph of the man wanted was appended.

"Looks some like you. Don't it, Mr.—shall I say Johnson or Struve?"

"Say Johnson!" roared the Texan. "That ain't me. I'm no jailbird."

"Glad to know it." Briscoe laughed in suave triumph. "I thought you might be. This description sounds some familiar. I'll not read it all. But listen: 'Scar on right cheek, running from bridge of nose toward ear. Trigger finger missing; shot away when last arrested. Weight, about one hundred and ninety.' By the way, just out of curiosity, how heavy are you, Mr. Johnson? 'Height, five feet nine inches. Protuberant, fishy eyes. Long, drooping, reddish mustache.' I'd shave that mustache if I were you, Mr.—er—Johnson. Some one might mistake you for Nick

Struve."

The man who called himself Johnson recognized denial as futile. He flung up the sponge with a blasphemous oath. "What do you want? What's your game? Do you want to sell me for the reward? By thunder, you'd better not!"

Briscoe gave way to one of the swift bursts of passion to which he was subject. "Don't threaten me, you prison scum! Don't come here and try to dictate what I'm to do, and what I'm not to do. I'll sell you if I want to. I'll send you back to be hanged like a dog. Say the word, and I'll have you dragged out of here inside of forty-eight hours."

Struve reached for his gun, but the other, wary as a panther, had him covered while the convict's revolver was still in his pocket.

"Reach for the roof! Quick—or I'll drill a hole in you! That's the idea. I reckon I'll collect your hardware while I'm at it. That's a heap better."

Struve glared at him, speechless.

"You're too slow on the draw for this part of the country, my friend," jeered Briscoe. "Or perhaps, while you were at Yuma, you got out of practice. It's like stealing candy from a kid to beat you to it. Don't ever try to draw a gun again in Lost Valley while you're asleep. You might never waken."

Jed was in high good humor with himself. His victim looked silent murder at him.

"One more thing, while you're in a teachable frame of mind," continued Briscoe. "I run Lost Valley. What I say, goes here. Get that soaked into your think-tank, my friend. Ever since you came, you've been disputing that in your mind. You've been stirring up the boys against me. Think I haven't noticed it? Guess again, Mr. Struve. You'd like to be boss yourself, wouldn't you? Forget it. Down in Texas you may be a bad, bad man, a sure enough wolf, but in Wyoming you only stack up to coyote size. Let this slip your mind, and I'll be running Lost Valley after your bones are picked white by the buzzards."

"I ain't a-goin' to make you any trouble. Didn't I tell you that before?" growled Struve reluctantly.

"See you don't, then. Now I'll come again to my news. I was telling you that there's another stranger in this valley, Mr. Struve. Hails from Texas, too. Name of Fraser. Ever hear of him?"

Briscoe was hardly prepared for the change which came over the Texan at mention of that name. The prominent eyes stared, and a deep, apoplectic flush ran over the scarred face. The hand that caught at the wall trembled with excitement.

"You mean Steve Fraser—Fraser of the Rangers!" he gasped.

"That's what I'm not sure of. I got to milling it over after I left him, and it come to me I'd seen him or his picture before. You still got that magazine with the article about him?"

"Yes."

"I looked it over hurriedly. Let me see his picture again, and I'll tell you if it's the same man."

"It's in the other room."

"Get it."

Struve presently returned with the magazine, and, opening it, pointed to a photograph of a young officer in uniform, with the caption underneath:

LIEUTENANT STEPHEN FRASER OF THE TEXAS RANGERS
Who, single-handed, ran down and brought to justice the worst gang of outlaws known in recent years.

"It's the same man," Briscoe announced.

The escaped convict's mouth set in a cruel line.

"One of us, either him or me, never leaves this valley alive," he announced.

Jed laughed softly and handed back the revolver. "That's the way to talk. My friend, if you mean that, you'll need your gun. Here's hoping you beat him to it."

"It won't be an even break this time if I can help it."

"I gather that it was, last time."

"Yep. We drew together." Struve interlarded his explanation with oaths. "He's a devil with a gun. See that?" He held up his right band.

"I see you're shy your most useful finger, if that's what you mean."

"Fraser took it off clean at twenty yards. I got him in the hand, too, but right or left he's a dead shot. He might 'a' killed me if he hadn't wanted to take me alive. Before I'm through with him he'll wish he had."

"Well, you don't want to make any mistake next time. Get him right."

"I sure will." Hitherto Struve had been absorbed in his own turbid emotions, but he came back from them now with a new-born suspicion in his eyes. "Where do you come in, Mr. Briscoe? Why are you so plumb anxious I should load him up with lead? If it's a showdown, I'd some like to see your cards too."

Jed shrugged. "My reasons ain't urgent like yours. I don't favor spies poking their noses in here. That's all there's to it."

Jed had worked out a plot as he rode through the night from the Dillon ranch—one so safe and certain that it pointed to sure success. Jed was no coward, but he had a spider-like cunning that wove others as dupes into the web of his plans.

The only weakness in his position lay in himself, in that sudden boiling up of passion in him that was likely to tear through his own web and destroy it. Three months ago he had given way to one of these outbursts, and he knew that any one of four or five men could put a noose around his neck. That was another reason why such a man as this Texas ranger must not be allowed to meet and mix with them.

It was his cue to know as much as he could of every man that came into the valley. Wherefore he had run down the record of Struve from the reward placard which a detective agency furnished him of hundreds of criminals who were wanted. What could be more simple than to stir up the convict, in order to save himself, to destroy the ranger who had run him down before? There would be a demand so insistent for the punishment of the murderer that it could not be ignored. He would find some pretext to lure Struve from the valley for a day or two, and would arrange it so that he would be arrested while he was away. Thus he would be rid of both these troublesome intruders without making a move that could be seen.

It was all as simple as A B C. Already Struve had walked into the trap. As Jed sat down to take a hand in the poker game that was in progress, he chuckled quietly to himself. He was quite sure that he was already practically master of the situation.

CHAPTER VII — THE ROUND-UP

"WOULD YOU LIKE TO take in the round-up to-day?"

Arlie flung the question at Fraser with a frank directness of sloe-black eyes that had never known coquetry. She was washing handkerchiefs, and her sleeves were rolled to the elbows of the slender, but muscular, coffee-brown arms.

"I would."

"If you like you may ride out with me to Willow Spring. I have some letters to take to dad."

"Suits me down to the ground, ma'am."

It was a morning beautiful even for Wyoming. The spring called potently to the youth in them. The fine untempered air was like wine, and out of a blue sky the sun beat pleasantly down through a crystal-clear atmosphere known only to the region of the Rockies. Nature was preaching a wordless sermon on the duty of happiness to two buoyant hearts that scarce needed it.

Long before they reached the scene of the round-up they could hear the almost continual bawl of worried cattle, and could even see the cloud of dust they stirred. They passed the remuda, in charge of two lads lounging sleepily in their saddles with only an occasional glance at the bunch of grazing horses they were watching. Presently they looked down from a high ridge at the busy scene below.

Out of Lost Valley ran a hundred rough and wooded gulches to the impassable cliff wall which bounded it. Into one of these they now descended slowly, letting their ponies pick a way among the loose stones and shale which covered the steep hillside.

What their eyes fell upon was cattle-land at its busiest. Several hundred wild hill cattle were gathered in the green draw, and around them was a cordon of riders holding the gather steady. Now and again one of the cows would make a dash to escape, and instantly the nearest rider would wheel, as on a batter's plate, give chase, and herd the animal back after a more or less lengthy pursuit.

Several of the riders were cutting out from the main herd cows with unmarked calves, which last were immediately roped and thrown. Usually it took only an instant to determine with whose cow the calf had been, and a few seconds to drive home the correct brand upon the sizzling flank. Occasionally the discussion was more protracted, in order to solve a doubt as to the ownership, and once a calf was released that it might again seek its mother to prove identity.

Arlie observed that Fraser's eyes were shining.

"I used to be a puncher myse'f," he explained. "I tell you it feels good to grip a saddle between your knees, and to swallow the dust and hear the bellow of the cows. I used to live in them days. I sure did."

A boyish puncher galloped past with a whoop and waved his hat to Arlie. For two weeks he had been in the saddle for fourteen hours out of the twenty-four. He was grimy with dust, and hollow-eyed from want of sleep. A stubbly beard covered his brick-baked face. But the unquenchable gayety of the youthful West could not be extinguished. Though his flannel shirt gaped where the thorns had torn it, and the polka-dot bandanna round his throat was discolored with sweat, he was as blithely debonair as ever.

"That's Dick France. He's a great friend of mine," Arlie explained.

"Dick's in luck," Fraser commented, but whether because he was enjoying himself so thoroughly or because he was her friend the ranger did not explain.

They stayed through the day, and ate dinner at the tail of the chuck wagon with the cattlemen. The light of the camp fires, already blazing in the nipping night air, shone brightly. The ranger rode back with her to the ranch, but next morning he asked Arlie if she could lend him an old pair of chaps discarded by her father.

She found a pair for him.

"If you don't mind, I'll ride out to the round-up and stay with the boys a few days," he suggested.

"You're going to ride with them," she accused.

"I thought I would. I'm not going to saddle myse'f on you two ladies forever."

"You know we're glad to have you. But that isn't it. What about your heart? You know you can't ride the range."

He flushed, and knew again that feeling of contempt for himself, or, to be more exact, for his position.

"I'll be awful careful, Miss Arlie," was all he found to say.

She could not urge him further, lest he misunderstand her.

"Of course, you know best," she said, with a touch of coldness.

He saddled Teddy and rode back. The drive for the day was already on, but he fell in beside young France and did his part. Before two days had passed he was accepted as one of these hard-riding punchers, for he was a competent vaquero and stood the grueling work as one born to it. He was, moreover, well liked, both because he could tell a good story and because these sons of Anak recognized in him that dynamic quality of manhood they could not choose but respect. In this a fortunate accident aided him.

They were working Lost Creek, a deep and rapid stream at the point where the drive ended. The big Norwegian, Siegfried, trying to head off a wild cow racing along the bank with tail up, got too near the edge. The bank caved beneath the feet of his pony, and man and horse went head first into the turbid waters. Fraser galloped up at once, flung himself from his saddle, and took in at a glance the fact that the big blond Hercules could not swim.

The Texan dived for him as he was going down, got hold of him by the hair, and after a struggle managed somehow to reach the farther shore. As they both lay there, one exhausted, and the other fighting for the breath he had nearly lost forever, Dillon reached the bank.

"Is it all right, Steve?" he called anxiously.

"All right," grinned the ranger weakly. "He'll go on many a spree yet. Eh, Siegfried?"

The Norwegian nodded. He was still frightened and half drowned. It was not till they were riding up the creek to find a shallow place they could ford that he spoke his mind.

"Ay bane all in ven you got me, pardner."

"Oh, you were still kicking."

"Ay bane t'ink Ay had van chance not to get out. But Ay bane not forget dees. Eef you ever get in a tight place, send vor Sig Siegfried."

"That's all right, Sig."

Nobody wasted any compliments on him. After the fashion of their kind, they guyed the Norwegian about the bath he had taken. Nevertheless, Fraser knew that he had won the liking of these men, as well as their deep respect. They began to call him by his first name, which hitherto only Dillon had done, and they included him in the rough, practical jokes they played on each other.

One night they initiated him—an experience to be both dreaded and desired. To be desired because it implies the conferring of the thirty-second degree of the freemasonry of Cattleland's approval; to be dreaded because hazing is mild compared with some features of the exercises.

Fraser was dragged from sweet slumber, pegged face down on his blankets, with a large-sized man at the extremity of each arm and leg, and introduced to a chapping. Dick France wielded the chaps vigorously upon the portions of his anatomy where they would do the most execution. The Texan did not enjoy it, but he refrained from saying so. When he was freed, he sat down painfully on a saddle and remarked amiably:

"You're a beautiful bunch, ain't you? Anybody got any smoking?"

This proper acceptance of their attentions so delighted these overgrown children that they dug up three bottles of whisky that were kept in camp for rattlesnake bites, and made Rome howl. They had ridden all day, and for many weary days before that; but they were started toward making a night of it when Dillon appeared.

Dillon was boss of the round-up—he had been elected by general consent, and his word was law. He looked round upon them with a twinkling eye, and wanted to know how long it was going to last. But the way he put his question was:

"How much whisky is there left?"

Finding there was none, he ordered them all back to their blankets. After a little skylarking, they obeyed. Next day Fraser rode the hills, a sore, sore man. But nobody who did not know could have guessed it. He would have died before admitting it to any of his companions. Thus he won the accolade of his peers as a worthy horseman of the hills.

CHAPTER VIII — THE BRONCHO BUSTERS

JED BRISCOE REJOINED THE round-up the day following Fraser's initiation. He took silent note of the Texan's popularity, of how the boys all called him "Steve" because he had become one of them, and were ready either to lark with him or work with him. He noticed, too, that the ranger did his share of work without a whimper, apparently enjoying the long, hard hours in the saddle. The hill riding was of the roughest, and the cattle were wild as deers and as agile. But there was no break-neck incline too steep for Steve Fraser to follow.

Once Jed chanced upon Steve stripped for a bath beside the creek, and he understood the physical reason for his perfect poise. The wiry, sinuous muscles, packed compactly without obtrusion, played beneath the skin like those of a panther. He walked as softly and as easily as one, with something of the rippling, unconscious grace of that jungle lord. It was this certainty of himself that vivified the steel-gray eyes which looked forth unafraid, and yet amiably, upon a world primitive enough to demand proof of every man who would hold the respect of his fellows.

Meanwhile, Briscoe waited for Struve and his enemy to become entangled in the net he was spinning. He made no pretense of fellowship with Fraser; nor, on the other hand, did he actively set himself against him with the men. He was ready enough to sneer when Dick France grew enthusiastic about his new friend, but this was to be expected from one of his jaundiced temper.

"Who is this all-round crackerjack you're touting, Dick?" he asked significantly.

France was puzzled. "Who is he? Why, he's Steve Fraser."

"I ain't asking you what his name is. I'm asking who he is. What does he do for a living? Who recommended him so strong to the boys that they take up with him so sudden?"

"I don't care what he does for a living. Likely, he rides the range in Texas. When it comes to recommendations, he's got one mighty good one written on his face."

"You think so, do you?"

"That's what I think, Jed. He's the goods—best of company, a straight-up rider, and a first-rate puncher. Ask any of the boys."

"I'm using my eyes, Dick. They tell me all I need to know."

"Well, use them to-morrow. He's going to take a whirl at riding Dead Easy. Next day he's going to take on Rocking Horse. If he makes good on them, you'll admit he can ride."

"I ain't saying he can't ride. So can you. If it's plumb gentle, I can make out to stick on a pony myself."

"Course you can ride. Everybody knows that. You're the best ever. Any man that can win the championship of Wyoming——But you'll say yourself them strawberry roans are wicked devils."

"He hasn't ridden them yet, Dick."

"He's going to."

"We'll be there to see it. Mebbe he will. Mebbe he won't. I've known men before who thought they were going to."

It was in no moment of good-natured weakness that Fraser had consented to try riding the outlaw horses. Nor had his vanity anything to do with it. He knew a time might be coming when he would need all the prestige and all the friendship he could earn to tide him over the crisis. Jed Briscoe had won his leadership, partly because he could shoot quicker and straighter, ride harder, throw a rope more accurately, and play poker better than his companions.

Steve had a mind to show that he, too, could do some of these things passing well. Wherefore, he had let himself be badgered good-naturedly into trying a fall with these famous buckers. As the heavy work of the round-up was almost over, Dillon was glad to relax discipline enough to give the boys a little fun.

The remuda was driven up while the outfit was at breakfast. His friends guyed Steve with pleasant prophecy.

"He'll be hunting leather about the fourth buck!"

"If he ain't trying to make of himse'f one of them there Darius Green machines!" suggested another.

"Got any last words, Steve? Dead Easy most generally eats 'em alive," Dick derided.

"Sho! Cayn't you see he's so plumb scared he cayn't talk?"

Fraser grinned and continued to eat. When he had finished he got his lariat from the saddle, swung to Siegfried's pony, and rode unobtrusively forward to the remuda. The horses were circling round and round, so that it was several minutes before he found a chance. When he did, the rope snaked forward and dropped over the head of the strawberry roan. The horse stood trembling, making not the least resistance, even while the ranger saddled and cinched.

But before the man settled to the saddle, the outlaw was off on its furious resistance. It went forward and up into the air with a plunging leap. The rider swung his hat and gave a joyous whoop. Next instant there was a scatter of laughing men as the horse came toward them in a series of short, stiff-legged bucks which would have jarred its rider like a pile driver falling on his head had he not let himself grow limp to meet the shock.

All the tricks of its kind this unbroken five-year-old knew. Weaving, pitching, sunfishing, it fought superbly, the while Steve rode with the consummate ease of a master. His sinuous form swayed instinctively to every changing motion of his mount. Even when it flung itself back in blind fury, he dropped lightly from the saddle and into it again as the animal struggled to its feet.

The cook waved a frying pan in frantic glee. "Hurra-ay! You're the goods, all right, all right."

"You bet. Watch Steve fan him. And he ain't pulled leather yet. Not once."

An unseen spectator was taking it in from the brow of a little hill crowned with a group of firs. She had reached this point just as the Texan had swung to the saddle, and she watched the battle between horse and man intently. If any had been there to see, he might have observed a strange fire smouldering in her eyes. For the first time there was filtering through her a vague suspicion of this man who claimed to have heart trouble, and had deliberately subjected himself to the terrific strain of such a test. She had seen broncho busters get off bleeding at mouth and nose and ears after a hard fight, and she had never seen a contest more superbly fought than this one. But full of courage as the horse was, it had met its master and began to know it.

The ranger's quirt was going up and down, stinging Dead Easy to more violent exertions, if possible. But the outlaw had shot its bolt. The plunges grew less vicious, the bucks more feeble. It still pitched, because of the unbroken gameness that defied defeat, but so mechanically that the motions could be forecasted.

Then Steve began to soothe the brute. Somehow the wild creature became aware that this man who was his master was also disposed to be friendly. Presently it gave up the battle, quivering in every limb. Fraser slipped from the saddle, and putting his arm across its neck began to gentle the outlaw. The animal had always looked the incarnation of wickedness. The red eyes in its ill-shaped head were enough to give one bad dreams. A quarter of an hour before, it had bit savagely at him. Now it stood breathing deep, and trembling while its master let his hand pass gently over the nose and neck with soft words that slowly won the pony back from the terror into which it had worked itself.

"You did well, Mr. Fraser from Texas," Jed complimented him, with a smile that thinly hid his malice. "But it won't do to have you going back to Texas with the word that Wyoming is shy of riders. I ain't any great shakes, but I reckon I'll have to take a whirl at Rocking Horse." He had decided to ride for two reasons. One was that he had glimpsed the girl among the firs; the other was to dissipate the admiration his rival had created among the men.

Briscoe lounged toward the remuda, rope in hand. It was his cue to get himself up picturesquely in all the paraphernalia of the cowboy. Black-haired and white-toothed, lithe as a wolf, and endowed with a grace almost feline, it was easy to understand how this man appealed to the imagination of the reckless young fellows of this primeval valley. Everything he did was done well. Furthermore, he looked and acted the part of leader which he assumed.

Rocking Horse was in a different mood from its brother. It was hard to rope, and when Jed's raw-hide had fallen over its head it was necessary to reënforce the lariat with two others. Finally the pony had to be flung down before a saddle could be put on. When Siegfried, who had been kneeling on its head, stepped back, the outlaw staggered to its feet, already badly shaken, to find an incubus clamped to the saddle.

No matter how it pitched, the human clothespin stuck to his seat, and apparently with as little concern as if he had been in a rowboat gently moved to and fro by the waves. Jed rode like a centaur, every motion attuned to those of the animal as much as if he were a part of it. No matter how it pounded or tossed, he stuck securely to the hurricane deck of the broncho.

Once only he was in danger, and that because Rocking Horse flung furiously against the wheel of a wagon and ground the rider's leg till he grew dizzy with the pain. For an instant he caught at the saddle horn to steady himself as the roan bucked into the open again.

"He's pulling leather!" some one shouted.

"Shut up, you goat!" advised the Texan good-naturedly. "Can't you see his laig got jammed till he's groggy? Wonder is, he didn't take the dust! They don't raise better riders than he is."

"By hockey! He's all in. Look out! Jed's falling," France cried, running forward.

It looked so for a moment, then Jed swam back to clear consciousness again, and waved them back. He began to use his quirt without mercy.

"Might know he'd game it out," remarked Yorky.

He did. It was a long fight, and the horse was flecked with bloody foam before its spirit and strength failed. But the man in the saddle kept his seat till the victory was won.

Steve was on the spot to join heartily the murmur of applause, for he was too good a sportsman to grudge admiration even to his enemy.

"You're the one best bet in riders, Mr. Briscoe. It's a pleasure to watch you," he said frankly.

Jed's narrowed eyes drifted to him. "Oh, hell!" he drawled with insolent contempt, and turned on his heel.

From the clump of firs a young woman was descending, and Jed went to meet her.

"You rode splendidly," she told him with vivid eyes. "Were you hurt when you were jammed again the wagon? I mean, does it still hurt?" For she noticed that he walked with a limp.

"I reckon I can stand the grief without an amputation. Arlie, I got something to tell you."

She looked at him in her direct fashion and waited.

"It's about your new friend." He drew from a pocket some leaves torn out of a magazine. His finger indicated a picture. "Ever see that gentleman before?"

The girl looked at it coolly. "It seems to be Mr. Fraser taken in his uniform; Lieutenant Fraser, I should say."

The cattleman's face fell. "You know, then, who he is, and what he's doing here."

Without evasion, her gaze met his. "I understood him to say he was an officer in the Texas Rangers. You know why he is here."

"You're right, I do. But do you?"

"Well, what is it you mean? Out with it, Jed," she demanded impatiently.

"He is here to get a man wanted in Texas, a man hiding in this valley right now."

"I don't believe it," she returned quickly. "And if he is, that's not your business or mine. It's his duty, isn't it?"

"I ain't discussing that. You know the law of the valley, Arlie."

"I don't accept that as binding, Jed. Lots of people here don't. Because Lost Valley used to be a nest of miscreants, it needn't always be. I don't see what right we've got to set ourselves above the law."

"This valley has always stood by hunted men when they reached it. That's our custom, and I mean to stick to it."

"Very well. I hold you to that," she answered quickly. "This man Fraser is a hunted man. He's hunted because of what he did for me and dad. I claim the protection of the valley for him."

"He can have it—if he's what he says he is. But why ain't he been square with us? Why didn't he tell who he was?"

"He told me."

"That ain't enough, Arlie. If he did, you kept it quiet. We all had a right to know."

"If you had asked him, he would have told you."

"I ain't so sure he would. Anyhow, I don't like it. I believe he is here to get the man I told you of. Mebbe that ain't all."

"What more?" she scoffed.

"This fellow is the best range detective in the country. My notion is he's spying around about that Squaw Creek raid."

Under the dusky skin she flushed angrily. "My notion is you're daffy, Jed. Talk sense, and I'll listen to you. You haven't a grain of proof."

"I may get some yet," he told her sulkily.

She laughed her disbelief. "When you do, let me know."

And with that she gave her pony the signal to more forward.

Nevertheless, she met the ranger at the foot of the little hill with distinct coldness. When he came up to shake hands, she was too busy dismounting to notice.

"Your heart must be a good deal better. I suppose Lost Valley agrees with you." She had swung down on the other side of the horse, and her glance at him across the saddle seat was like a rapier thrust.

He was aware at once of being in disgrace with her, and it chafed him that he had no adequate answer to her implied charge.

"My heart's all right," he said a little gruffly.

"Yes, it seems to be, lieutenant."

She trailed the reins and turned away at once to find her father. The girl was disappointed in him. He had, in effect, lied to her. That was bad enough; but she felt that his lie had concealed something, how much she scarce dared say. Her tangled thoughts were in chaos. One moment she was ready to believe the worst; the next, it was impossible to conceive such a man so vile a spy as to reward hospitality with treachery.

Yet she remembered now that it had been while she was telling of the fate of the traitor Burke that she had driven him to his lie. Or had he not told it first when she pointed out Lost Valley at his feet? Yes, it was at that moment she had noticed his pallor. He had, at least, conscience enough to be ashamed of what he was doing. But she recognized a wide margin of difference between the possibilities of his guilt. It was one thing to come to the valley for an escaped murderer; it was quite another to use the hospitality of his host as a means to betray the friends of that host. Deep in her heart she could not find it possible to convict him of the latter alternative. He was too much a man, too vitally dynamic. No; whatever else he was, she felt sure he was not so hopelessly lost to decency. He had that electric spark of self-respect which may coexist with many faults, but not with treachery.

CHAPTER IX — A SHOT FROM BALD KNOB

A BUNCH OF YOUNG steers which had strayed from their range were to be driven to the Dillon ranch, and the boss of the rodeo appointed France and Fraser to the task.

"Yo'll have company home, honey," he told his daughter, "and yo'll be able to give the boys a hand if they need it. These hill cattle are still some wild, though we've been working them a week. Yo're a heap better cowboy than some that works more steady at the business."

Briscoe nodded. "You bet! I ain't forgot that day Arlie rode Big Timber with me two years ago. She wasn't sixteen then, but she herded them hill steers like they belonged to a milk bunch."

He spoke his compliment patly enough, but somehow the girl had an impression that he was thinking of something else. She was right, for as he helped gather the drive his mind was busy with a problem. Presently he dismounted to tighten a cinch, and made a signal to a young fellow known as Slim Leroy. The latter was a new and tender recruit to Jed's band of miscreants. He drew up beside his leader and examined one of the fore hoofs of his pony.

"Slim, I'm going to have Dillon send you for the mail to-day. When he tells you, that's the first you know about it. Understand? You'll have to take the hill cut to Jack Rabbit Run on your way in. At the cabin back of the aspens, inquire for a man that calls himself Johnson. If he's there, give him this message: 'This afternoon from Bald Knob.' Remember! Just those words, and nothing more. If he isn't there, forget the message. You'll know the man you want because he is shy his trigger finger and has a ragged scar across his right cheek. Make no mistake about this, Slim."

"Sure I won't."

Briscoe, having finished cinching, swung to his saddle and rode up to say good-by to Arlie.

"Hope you'll have no trouble with this bunch. If you push right along you'd ought to get home by night," he told her.

Arlie agreed carelessly. "I don't expect any trouble with them. So-long, Jed."

It would not have been her choice to ride home with the lieutenant of rangers, but since her father had made the appointment publicly she did not care to make objection. Yet she took care to let Fraser see that he was in her black books. The men rode toward the rear of the herd, one on each side, and Arlie fell in beside her old playmate, Dick. She laughed and talked with him about a hundred things in which Steve could have had no part, even if he had been close enough to catch more than one word out of twenty. Not once did she even look his way. Quite plainly she had taken pains to forget his existence.

"It was Briscoe's turn the other day," mused the Texan. "It's mine now. I wonder when it will be Dick's to get put out in the cold!"

Nevertheless, though he tried to act the philosopher, it cut him that the high-spirited girl had condemned him. He felt himself in a false position from which he could not easily extricate himself. The worst of it was that if it came to a showdown he could not expect the simple truth to exonerate him.

From where they rode there drifted to him occasionally the sound of the gay voices of the young people. It struck him for the first time that he was getting old. Arlie could not be over eighteen, and Dick perhaps twenty-one. Maybe young people like that thought a fellow of twenty-seven a Methusaleh.

After a time the thirsty cattle smelt water and hit a bee line so steadily for it that they needed no watching. Every minute or two one of the leaders stretched out its neck and let out a bellow without slackening its pace.

Steve lazed on his pony, shifting his position to ease his cramped limbs after the manner of the range rider. In spite of himself, his eyes would drift toward the jaunty little figure on the pinto. The masculine in him approved mightily her lissom grace and the proud lilt of her dark head, with its sun-kissed face set in profile to him. He thought her serviceable costume very becoming, from the pinched felt hat pinned to the dark mass of hair, and the red silk kerchief knotted loosely round the pretty throat, to the leggings beneath the corduroy skirt and the flannel waist with sleeves rolled up in summer-girl fashion to leave the tanned arms bare to the dimpled elbows.

The trail, winding through a narrow defile, brought them side by side again.

"Ever notice what a persistent color buckskin is, Steve?" inquired France, by way of bringing him into the conversation. "It's strong in every one of these cattle, though the old man has been trying to get rid of it for ten years."

"You mustn't talk to me, Dick," responded his friend gravely. "Little Willie told a lie, and he's being stood in a corner."

Arlie flushed angrily, opened her mouth to speak, and, changing her mind, looked at him witheringly. He didn't wither, however. Instead, he smiled broadly, got out his mouth organ, and cheerfully entertained them with his favorite, "I Met My Love In the Alamo."

The hot blood under dusky skin held its own in her cheeks. She was furious with him, and dared not trust herself to speak. As soon as they had passed through the defile she spurred forward, as if to turn the leaders. France turned to his friend and laughed ruefully.

"She's full of pepper, Steve."

The ranger nodded. "She's all right, Dick. If you want to know, she's got a right to make a doormat of me. I lied to her. I was up against it, and I kinder had to. You ride along and join her. If you want to get right solid, tell her how many kinds of a skunk I am. Worst of it is, I ain't any too sure I'm not."

"I'm sure for you then, Steve," the lad called back, as he loped forward after the girl.

He was so sure, that he began to praise his friend to Arlie, to tell her of what a competent cowman he was, how none of them could make a cut or rope a wild steer like him. She presently wanted to know whether Dick could not find something more interesting to talk about.

He could not help smiling at her downright manner. "You've surely got it in for him, Arlie. I thought you liked him."

She pulled up her horse, and looked at him. "What made you think that? Did he tell you so?"

Dick fairly shouted. "You do rub it in, girl, when you've got a down on a fellow. No, he didn't tell me. You did."

"Me?" she protested indignantly. "I never did."

"Oh, you didn't say so, but I don't need a church to fall on me before I can take a hint. You acted as though you liked him that day you and him came riding into camp."

"I didn't do any such thing, Dick France. I don't like him at all," very decidedly.

"All the boys do—all but Jed. I don't reckon he does."

"Do I have to like him because the boys do?" she demanded.

"O' course not." Dick stopped, trying to puzzle it out. "He says you ain't to blame, that he lied to you. That seems right strange, too. It ain't like Steve to lie."

"How do you know so much about him? You haven't known him a week."

"That's what Jed says. I say it ain't a question of time. Some men I've knew ten years I ain't half so sure of. He's a man from the ground up. Any one could tell that, before they had seen him five minutes."

Secretly, the girl was greatly pleased. She so wanted to believe that Dick was right. It was what she herself had thought.

"I wish you'd seen him the day he pulled Siegfried out of Lost

Creek. Tell you, I thought they were both goners," Dick continued.

"I expect it was most ankle-deep," she scoffed. "Hello, we're past Bald Knob!"

"They both came mighty nigh handing in their checks."

"I didn't know that, though I knew, of course, he was fearless," Arlie said.

"What's that?" Dick drew in his horse sharply, and looked back.

The sound of a rifle shot echoed from hillside to hillside. Like a streak of light, the girl's pinto flashed past him. He heard her give a sobbing cry of anguish. Then he saw that Steve was slipping very slowly from his saddle.

A second shot rang out. The light was beginning to fail, but he made out a man's figure crouched among the small pines on the shoulder of Bald Knob. Dick jerked out his revolver as he rode back, and fired twice. He was quite out of pistol range, but he wanted the man in ambush to see that help was at hand. He saw Arlie fling herself from her pony in time to support the Texan just as he sank to the ground.

"She'll take care of Steve. It's me for that murderer," the young man thought.

Acting upon that impulse, he slid from his horse and slipped into the sagebrush of the hillside. By good fortune he was wearing a gray shirt of a shade which melted into that of the underbrush. Night falls swiftly in the mountains, and already dusk was softly spreading itself over the hills.

Dick went up a draw, where young pines huddled together in the trough; and from the upper end of this he emerged upon a steep ridge, eyes and ears alert for the least sign of human presence. A third shot had rung out while he was in the dense mass of foliage of the evergreens, but now silence lay heavy all about him. The gathering darkness blurred detail, so that any one of a dozen boulders might be a shield for a crouching man.

Once, nerves at a wire edge from the strain on him, he thought he saw a moving figure. Throwing up his gun, he fired quickly. But he must have been mistaken, for, shortly afterward, he heard some one crashing through dead brush at a distance.

"He's on the run, whoever he is. Guess I'll get back to Steve," decided France wisely.

He found his friend stretched on the ground, with his head in Arlie's lap.

"Is it very bad?" he asked the girl.

"I don't know. There's no light. Whatever shall we do?" she moaned.

"I'm a right smart of a nuisance, ain't I?" drawled the wounded man unexpectedly.

She leaned forward quickly. "Where are you hit?"

"In the shoulder, ma'am."

"Can you ride, Steve? Do you reckon you could make out the five miles?" Dick asked.

Arlie answered for him. She had felt the inert weight of his heavy body and knew that he was beyond helping himself. "No. Is there no house near? There's Alec Howard's cabin."

"He's at the round-up, but I guess we had better take Steve there—if we could make out to get him that far."

The girl took command quietly. "Unsaddle Teddy."

She had unloosened his shirt and was tying her silk kerchief over the wound, from which blood was coming in little jets.

"We can't carry him," she decided. "It's too far. We'll have to lift him to the back of the horse, and let him lie there. Steady, Dick. That's right. You must hold him on, while I lead the horse."

Heavy as he was, they somehow hoisted him, and started. He had fainted again, and hung limply, with his face buried in the mane of the pony. It seemed an age before the cabin loomed, shadow-like, out of the darkness. They found the door unlocked, as usual, and carried him in to the bed.

"Give me your knife, Dick," Arlie ordered quietly. "And I want water. If that's a towel over there, bring it."

"Just a moment. I'll strike a light, and we'll see where we're at."

"No. We'll have to work in the dark. A light might bring them down on us." She had been cutting the band of the shirt, and now ripped it so as to expose the wounded shoulder.

Dick took a bucket to the creek, and presently returned with it. In his right hand he carried his revolver. When he reached the cabin he gave an audible sigh of relief and quickly locked the door.

"Of course you'll have to go for help, Dick. Bring old Doc Lee."

"Why, Arlie, I can't leave you here alone. What are you talking about?"

"You'll have to. It's the only thing to do. You'll have to give me your revolver. And, oh, Dick, don't lose a moment on the way."

He was plainly troubled. "I just can't leave you here alone, girl. What would your father say if anything happened? I don't reckon anything will, but we can't tell. No, I'll stay here, too. Steve must take his chance."

"You'll not stay." She flamed round upon him, with the fierce passion of a tigress fighting for her young. "You'll go this minute—this very minute!"

"But don't you see I oughtn't to leave you? Anybody would tell you that," he pleaded.

"And you call yourself his friend," she cried, in a low, bitter voice.

"I call myself yours, too," he made answer doggedly.

"Then go. Go this instant. You'll go, anyway; but if you're my friend, you'll go gladly, and bring help to save us both."

"I wisht I knew what to do," he groaned.

Her palms fastened on his shoulders. She was a creature transformed. Such bravery, such feminine ferocity, such a burning passion of the spirit, was altogether outside of his experience of her or any other woman. He could no more resist her than he could fly to the top of Bald Knob.

"I'll go, Arlie."

"And bring help soon. Get Doc Lee here soon as you can. Leave word for armed men to follow. Don't wait for them."

"No."

"Take his Teddy horse. It can cover ground faster than yours."

"Yes."

With plain misgivings, he left her, and presently she heard the sound of his galloping horse. It seemed to her for a moment as if she must call him back, but she strangled the cry in her throat. She locked the door and bolted it, then turned back to the bed, upon which the wounded man was beginning to moan in his delirium.

CHAPTER X — DOC LEE

ARLIE KNEW NOTHING OF wounds or their treatment. All she could do was to wash the shoulder in cold water and bind it with strips torn from her white underskirt. When his face and hands grew hot with the fever, she bathed them with a wet towel. How badly he was hurt— whether he might not even die before Dick's return—she had no way of telling. His inconsequent babble at first frightened her, for she had never before seen a person in delirium, nor heard of the insistence with which one harps upon some fantasy seized upon by a diseased mind.

"She thinks you're a skunk, Steve. So you are. She's dead right— dead right—dead right. You lied to her, you coyote! Stand up in the corner, you liar, while she whangs at you with a six-gun! You're a skunk—dead right."

So he would run on in a variation of monotony, the strong, supple, masterful man as helpless as a child, all the splendid virility stricken from him by the pressure of an enemy's finger. The eyes that she had known so full of expression, now like half-scabbarded steel, and now again bubbling from the inner mirth of him, were glazed and unmeaning. The girl had felt in him a capacity for silent self-containment; and here he was, picking at the coverlet with restless fingers, prattling foolishly, like an infant.

She was a child of impulse, sensitive and plastic. Because she had been hard on him before he was struck down, her spirit ran open-armed to make amends. What manner of man he was she did not know. But what availed that to keep her, a creature of fire and dew, from the clutch of emotions strange and poignant? He had called himself a liar and a coyote, yet she knew it was not true, or at worst, true in some qualified sense. He might be hard, reckless, even wicked in some ways. But, vaguely, she felt that if he were a sinner he sinned with self-respect. He was in no moral collapse, at least. It was impossible to fit him to her conception of a spy. No, no! Anything but that!

So she sat there, her fingers laced about her knee, as she leaned forward to wait upon the needs she could imagine for him, the dumb tragedy of despair in her childish face.

The situation was one that made for terror. To be alone with a wounded man, his hurt undressed, to hear his delirium and not to know whether he might not die any minute—this would have been enough to cause apprehension. Add to it the darkness, her deep interest in him, the struggle of her soul, and the dread of unseen murder stalking in the silent night.

Though her thought was of him, it was not wholly upon him. She sat where she could watch the window, Dick's revolver in another chair beside her. It was a still, starry night, and faintly she could see the hazy purple, mountain line. Somewhere beneath those uncaring stars was the man who had done this awful thing. Was he far, or was he near? Would he come to make sure he had not failed? Her fearful heart told her that he would come.

She must have fought her fears nearly an hour before she heard the faintest of sounds outside. Her hand leaped to the revolver. She sat motionless, listening, with nerves taut. It came again presently, a deadened footfall, close to the door. Then, after an eternity, the latch clicked softly. Some one, with infinite care, was trying to discover whether the door was locked.

His next move she anticipated. Her eyes fastened on the window, while she waited breathlessly. Her heart was stammering furiously. Moments passed, in which she had to set her teeth to keep from screaming aloud. The revolver was shaking so that she had to steady the barrel with her left hand. A shadow crossed one pane, the shadow of a head in profile, and pushed itself forward till shoulders, arm, and poised revolver covered the lower sash. Very, very slowly the head itself crept into sight.

Arlie fired and screamed simultaneously. The thud of a fall, the scuffle of a man gathering himself to his feet again, the rush of retreating steps, all merged themselves in one single impression of fierce, exultant triumph.

Her only regret was that she had not killed him. She was not even sure that she had hit him, for her bullet had gone through the glass within an inch of the inner woodwork. Nevertheless, she knew that he had had a shock that would carry him far. Unless he had accomplices with him—and of that there had been no evidence at the time of the attack from Bald Knob—he would not venture another attempt. Of one thing she was sure. The face that had looked in at the window was one she had never seen before, In this, too, she found relief—for she knew now that the face she had expected to see follow the shadow over the pane had been that of Jed Briscoe; and Jed had too much of the courage of Lucifer incarnate in him to give up because an unexpected revolver had been fired in his face.

Time crept slowly, but it could hardly have been a quarter of an hour later that she heard the galloping of horses.

"It is Dick!" she cried joyfully, and, running to the door, she unbolted and unlocked it just as France dragged Teddy to a halt and flung himself to the ground.

The young man gave a shout of gladness at sight of her.

"Is it all right, Arlie?"

"Yes. That is—I don't know. He is delirious. A man came to the window, and I shot at him. Oh, Dick, I'm so glad you're back."

In her great joy, she put her arms round his neck and kissed him. Old Doctor Lee, dismounting more leisurely, drawled his protest.

"Look-a-here, Arlie. I'm the doctor. Where do I come in?"

"I'll kiss you, too, when you tell me he'll get well." The half-hysterical laugh died out of her voice, and she caught him fiercely by the arm. "Doc, doc, don't let him die," she begged.

He had known her all her life, had been by the bedside when she came into the world, and he put his arm round her shoulders and gave her a little hug as they passed into the room.

"We'll do our level best, little girl."

She lit a lamp, and drew the window curtain, so that none could see from the outside. While the old doctor arranged his instruments and bandages on chairs, she waited on him. He noticed how white she was, for he said, not unkindly:

"I don't want two patients right now, Arlie. If you're going to keel over in a faint right in the middle of it, I'll have Dick help."

"No, no, I won't, doc. Truly, I won't," she promised.

"All right, little girl. We'll see how game you are. Dick, hold the light. Hold it right there. See?"

The Texan had ceased talking, and was silent, except for a low moan, repeated at regular intervals. The doctor showed Arlie how to administer the anaesthetic after he had washed the wound. While he was searching for the bullet with his probe she flinched as if he had touched a bare nerve, but she stuck to her work regardless of her feelings, until the lead was found and extracted and the wound dressed.

Afterward, Dick found her seated on a rock outside crying hysterically. He did not attempt to cope with the situation, but returned to the house and told Lee.

"Best thing for her. Her nerves are overwrought and unstrung. She'll be all right, once she has her cry out. I'll drift around, and jolly her along."

The doctor presently came up and took a seat beside her.

"Wha—what do you think, doctor?" she sobbed.

"Well, I think it's tarnation hot operating with a big kerosene lamp six inches from your haid," he said, as he mopped his forehead.

"I mean—will he—get well?"

Lee snorted. "Well, I'd be ashamed of him if he didn't. If he lets a nice, clean, flesh wound put him out of business he don't deserve to live. Don't worry any about him, young lady. Say, I wish I had zwei beer right now, Arlie."

"You mean it? You're not just saying it to please me?"

"Of course, I mean it," he protested indignantly. "I wish I had three."

"I mean, are you sure he'll get well?" she explained, a faint smile touching her wan face.

"Yes, I mean that, too, but right now I mean the beer most. Now, honest, haven't I earned a beer?"

"You've earned a hundred thousand, doc. You're the kindest and dearest man that ever lived," she cried.

"Ain't that rather a large order, my dear?" he protested mildly. "I couldn't really use a hundred thousand. And I'd hate to be better than Job and Moses and Pharaoh and them Bible characters. Wouldn't I have to give up chewing? Somehow, a halo don't seem to fit my haid. It's most too bald to carry one graceful.... You may do that again if you want to." This last, apropos of the promised reward which had just been paid in full.

Arlie found she could manage a little laugh by this time.

"Well, if you ain't going to, we might as well go in and have a look at that false-alarm patient of ours," he continued. "We'll have to sit up all night with him. I was sixty-three yesterday. I'm going to quit this doctor game. I'm too old to go racing round the country nights just because you young folks enjoy shooting each other up. Yes, ma'am, I'm going to quit. I serve notice right here. What's the use of having a good ranch and some cattle if you can't enjoy them?"

As the doctor had been serving notice of his intention to quit doctoring for over ten years, Arlie did not take him too seriously. She knew him for what he was—a whimsical old fellow, who would drop in the saddle before he would let a patient suffer; one of the old school, who loved his work but liked to grumble over it.

"Maybe you'll be able to take a rest soon. You know that young doctor from Denver, who was talking about settling here——"

This, as she knew, was a sore point with him. "So you're tired of me, are you? Want a new-fangled appendix cutter from Denver, do you? Time to shove old Doc Lee aside, eh?"

"I didn't say that, doc," she repented.

"Huh! You meant it. Wonder how many times he'd get up at midnight and plow through three-foot snow for six miles to see the most ungrateful, squalling little brat——"

"Was it me, doc?" she ungrammatically demanded.

"It was you, Miss Impudence."

They had reached the door, but she held him there a moment, while she laughed delightedly and hugged him. "I knew it was me. As if we'd let our old doc go, or have anything to do with a young ignoramus from Denver! Didn't you know I was joking? Of course you did."

He still pretended severity. "Oh, I know you. When it comes to wheedling an old fool, you've got the rest of the girls in this valley beat to a fare-you-well."

"Is that why you always loved me?" she asked, with a sparkle of mischief in her eye.

"I didn't love you. I never did. The idea!" he snorted. "I don't know what you young giddy pates are coming to. Huh! Love you!"

"I'll forgive you, even if you did," she told him sweetly.

"That's it! That's it!" he barked. "You forgive all the young idiots when they do. And they all do—every last one of them. But I'm too old for you, young lady. Sixty-three yesterday. Huh!"

"I like you better than the younger ones."

"Want us all, do you? Young and old alike. Well, count me out."

He broke away, and went into the house. But there was an unconquerably youthful smile dancing in his eyes. This young lady and he had made love to each other in some such fashion ever since she had been a year old. He was a mellow and confirmed old bachelor, but he proposed to continue their innocent coquetry until he was laid away, no matter which of the young bucks of the valley had the good fortune to win her for a wife.

CHAPTER XI — THE FAT IN THE FIRE

FOR TWO DAYS FRASER remained in the cabin of the stockman Howard, France making it his business to see that the place was never left unguarded for a moment. At the end of that time the fever had greatly abated, and he was doing so well that Doctor Lee decided it would be better to move him to the Dillon ranch for the convenience of all parties.

This was done, and the patient continued steadily to improve. His vigorous constitution, helped by the healthy, clean, outdoor life he had led, stood him in good stead. Day by day he renewed the blood he had lost. Soon he was eating prodigious dinners, and between meals was drinking milk with an egg beaten in it.

On a sunny forenoon, when he lay in the big window of the living room, reading a magazine, Arlie entered, a newspaper in her hand. Her eyes were strangely bright, even for her, and she had a manner of repressed excitement, Her face was almost colorless.

"Here's some more in the Avalanche about our adventure near Gimlet Butte," she told him, waving the paper.

"Nothing like keeping in the public eye," said Steve, grinning. "I don't reckon our little picnic at Bald Knob is likely to get in the Avalanche, though. It probably hasn't any correspondent at Lost Valley. Anyhow, I'm hoping not."

"Mr. Fraser, there is something in this paper I want you to explain. But tell me first when it was you shot this man Faulkner. I mean at just what time in the fight."

"Why, I reckon it must have been just before I ducked."

"That's funny, too." She fixed her direct, fearless gaze on him. "The evidence at the coroner's jury shows that it was in the early part of the fight he was shot, before father and I left you."

"No, that couldn't have been, Miss Arlie, because——"

"Because——" she prompted, smiling at him in a peculiar manner.

He flushed, and could only say that the newspapers were always getting things wrong.

"But this is the evidence at the coroner's inquest," she said, falling grave again on the instant. "I understand one thing now, very clearly, and that is that Faulkner was killed early in the fight, and the other man was wounded in the ankle near the finish."

He shook his head obstinately. "No, I reckon not."

"Yet it is true. What's more, you knew it all the time."

"You ce'tainly jump to conclusions, Miss Arlie."

"And you let them arrest you, without telling them the truth! And they came near lynching you! And there's a warrant out now for your arrest for the murder of Faulkner, while all the time I killed him, and you knew it!"

He gathered together his lame defense. "You run ahaid too fast for me, ma'am. Supposing he was hit while we were all there together, how was I to know who did it?"

"You knew it couldn't have been you, for he wasn't struck with a revolver. It couldn't have been dad, since he had his shotgun loaded with buckshot."

"What difference did it make?" he wanted to know impatiently. "Say I'd have explained till kingdom come that I borrowed the rifle from a friend five minutes after Faulkner was hit—would anybody have believed me? Would it have made a bit of difference?"

Her shining eyes were more eloquent than a thousand tongues. "I don't say it would, but there was always the chance. You didn't take it. You would have let them hang you, without speaking the word that brought me into it. Why?"

"I'm awful obstinate when I get my back up," he smiled.

"That wasn't it. You did it to save a girl you had never seen but once. I want to know why."

"All right. Have it your own way. But don't ask me to explain the whyfors. I'm no Harvard professor."

"I know," she said softly. She was not looking at him, but out of the window, and there were tears in her voice.

"Sho! Don't make too much of it. We'll let it go that I ain't all coyote, after all. But that don't entitle me to any reward of merit. Now, don't you cry, Miss Arlie. Don't you."

She choked back the tears, and spoke in deep self-scorn. "No! You don't deserve anything except what you've been getting from me—suspicion and distrust and hard words! You haven't done anything worth speaking of—just broke into a quarrel that wasn't yours, at the risk of your life; then took it on your shoulders to let us escape; and, afterward, when you were captured, refused to drag me in, because I happen to be a girl! But it's not worth mentioning that you did all this for strangers, and that later you did not tell even me, because you knew it would trouble me that I had killed him, though in self-defense. And to think that all the time I've been full of hateful suspicions about you! Oh, you don't know how I despise myself!"

She let her head fall upon her arm on the table, and sobbed.

Fraser, greatly disturbed, patted gently the heavy coil of blue-black hair.

"Now, don't you, Arlie; don't you. I ain't worth it. Honest, I ain't. I did what it was up to me to do. Not a thing more. Dick would have done it. Any of the boys would. Now, let's look at what you've done for me."

From under the arm a muffled voice insisted she had done nothing but suspect him.

"Hold on, girl. Play fair. First off you ride sixty miles to help me when I'm hunted right hard. You bring me to your home in this valley where strangers ain't over and above welcome just now. You learn I'm an officer and still you look out for me and fight for me, till you make friends for me. It's through you I get started right with the boys. On your say-so they give me the glad hand. You learn I've lied to you, and two or three hours later you save my life. You sit there steady, with my haid in your lap, while some one is plugging away at us. You get me to a house, take care of my wounds, and hold the fort alone in the night till help comes. Not only that, but you drive my enemy away. Later, you bring me home, and nurse me like I was a long-lost brother. What I did for you ain't in the same class with what you've done for me."

"But I was suspicious of you all the time."

"So you had a right to be. That ain't the point, which is that a girl did all that for a man she thought might be an enemy and a low-down spy. Men are expected to take chances like I did, but girls ain't. You took 'em. If I lived a thousand years, I couldn't tell you all the thanks I feel."

"Ah! It makes it worse that you're that kind of a man. But I'm going to show you whether I trust you." Her eyes were filled with the glad light of her resolve. She spoke with a sort of proud humility. "Do you know, there was a time when I thought you might have—I didn't really believe it, but I thought it just possible—that you might have come here to get evidence against the Squaw Creek raiders? You'll despise me, but it's the truth."

His face lost color. "And now?" he asked quietly.

"Now? I would as soon suspect my father—or myself! I'll show you what I think. The men in it were Jed Briscoe and Yorky and Dick France."

"Stop," he cried hoarsely.

"Is it your wound?" she said quickly.

"No. That's all right. But you musn't tell——"

"I'm telling, to show whether I trust you. Jed and Yorky and Dick and Slim——"

She stopped to listen. Her father's voice was calling her. She rose from her seat.

"Wait a moment. There's something I've got to tell you," the Texan groaned.

"I'll be back in a moment. Dad wants to see me about some letters."

And with that she was gone. Whatever the business was, it detained her longer than she expected. The minutes slipped away, and still she did not return. A step sounded in the hall, a door opened, and Jed Briscoe stood before him.

"You're here, are you?" he said.

The Texan measured looks with him. "Yes, I'm here."

"Grand-standing still, I reckon."

"If you could only learn to mind your own affairs," the Texan suggested evenly.

"You'll wish I could before I'm through with you."

"Am I to thank you for that little courtesy from Bald Knob the other evening?"

"Not directly. At three hundred yards, I could have shot a heap straighter than that. The fool must have been drunk."

"You'll have to excuse him. It was beginning to get dark. His intentions were good."

There was a quick light step behind him, and Arlie came into the room. She glanced quickly from one to the other, and there was apprehension in her look.

"I've come to see Lieutenant Fraser on business," Briscoe explained, with an air patently triumphant.

Arlie made no offer to leave the room. "He's hardly up to business yet, is he?" she asked, as carelessly as she could.

"Then we'll give it another name. I'm making a neighborly call to ask how he is, and to return some things he lost."

Jed's hand went into his pocket and drew forth leisurely a photograph. This he handed to Arlie right side up, smiling the while, with a kind of masked deviltry.

"Found it in Alec Howard's cabin. Seems your coat was hanging over the back of a chair, lieutenant, and this and a paper fell out. One of the boys must have kicked it to one side, and it was overlooked. Later, I ran across it. So I'm bringing it back to you."

In spite of herself Arlie's eyes fell to the photograph. It was a snapshot of the ranger and a very attractive young woman. They were smiling into each other's eyes with a manner of perfect and friendly understanding. To see it gave Arlie a pang. Flushing at her mistake, she turned the card over and handed it to the owner.

"Sorry. I looked without thinking," she said in a low voice.

Fraser nodded his acceptance of her apology, but his words and his eyes were for his enemy. "You mentioned something else you had found, seems to me."

Behind drooping eyelids Jed was malevolently feline. "Seems to me I did."

From his pocket came slowly a folded paper. He opened and looked it over at leisure before his mocking eyes lifted again to the wounded man. "This belongs to you, too, but I know you'll excuse me if I keep it to show to the boys before returning it."

"So you've read it," Arlie broke in scornfully.

He grinned at her, and nodded. "Yes, I've read it, my dear. I had to read it, to find out whose it was. Taken by and large, it's a right interesting document, too."

He smiled at the ranger maliciously, yet with a certain catlike pleasure in tormenting his victim. Arlie began to feel a tightening of her throat, a sinking of the heart. But Fraser looked at the man with a quiet, scornful steadfastness. He knew what was coming, and had decided upon his course.

"Seems to be a kind of map, lieutenant. Here's Gimlet Butte and the Half Way House and Sweetwater Dam and the blasted pine. Looks like it might be a map from the Butte to this part of the country. Eh, Mr. Fraser from Texas?"

"And if it is?"

"Then I should have to ask you how you come by it, seeing as the map is drawn on Sheriff Brandt's official stationery," Jed rasped swiftly.

"I got it from Sheriff Brandt, Mr. Briscoe, since you want to know. You're not entitled to the information, but I'll make you a gift of it. He gave it to me to guide me here."

Even Briscoe was taken aback. He had expected evasion, denial, anything but a bold acceptance of his challenge. His foe watched the wariness settle upon him by the narrowing of his eyes.

"So the sheriff knew you were coming?"

"Yes."

"I thought you broke jail. That was the story I had dished up to me."

"I did, with the help of the sheriff."

"Oh, with the help of the sheriff? Come to think of it, that sounds right funny—a sheriff helping his prisoner to escape."

"Yet it is true, as it happens."

"I don't doubt it, lieutenant. Fact is, I had some such notion all the time. Now, I wonder why-for he took so friendly an interest in you."

"I had a letter of introduction to him from a friend in Texas. When he knew who I was, he decided he couldn't afford to have me lynched without trying to save me."

"I see. And the map?"

"This was the only part of the country in which I would be safe from capture. He knew I had a claim on some of the Cedar Mountain people, because it was to help them I had got into trouble."

"Yes, I can see that." Arlie nodded quickly. "Of course, that is just what the sheriff would think."

"Folks can always see what they want to, Arlie," Jed commented. "Now, I can't see all that, by a lot."

"It isn't necessary you should, Mr. Briscoe," Fraser retorted.

"Or else I see a good deal more, lieutenant," Jed returned, with his smooth smile. "Mebbe the sheriff helped you on your way because you're such a good detective. He's got ambitions, Brandt has. So has Hilliard, the prosecuting attorney. Happen to see him, by the way?"

"Yes."

Jed nodded. "I figured you had. Yes, it would be Hilliard worked the scheme out, I expect."

"You're a good deal of a detective yourself, Mr. Briscoe," the Texan laughed hardily. "Perhaps I could get you a job in the rangers."

"There may be a vacancy there soon," Jed agreed.

"What's the use of talking that way, Jed? Are you threatening Mr.

Fraser? If anything happens to him, I'll remember this," Arlie told him.

"Have I mentioned any threats, Arlie? It is well known that Lieutenant Fraser has enemies here. It don't take a prophet to tell that, after what happened the other night."

"Any more than it takes a prophet to tell that you are one of them."

"I play my own hand. I don't lie down before him, or any other man. He'd better not get in my way, unless he's sure he's a better man than I am."

"But he isn't in your way," Arlie insisted. "He has told a plain story. I believe every word of it."

"I notice he didn't tell any of his plain story until we proved it on him. He comes through with his story after he's caught with the goods. Don't you know that every criminal that is caught has a smooth explanation?"

"I haven't any doubt Mr. Briscoe will have one when his turn comes," the ranger remarked.

Jed wheeled on him. His eyes glittered menace. "You've said one word too much. I'll give you forty-eight hours to get out of this valley."

"How dare you, Jed—and in my house!" Arlie cried. "I won't have it. I won't have blood shed between you."

"It's up to him," answered the cattleman, his jaw set like a vise. "Persuade him to git out, and there'll be no blood shed."

"You have no right to ask it of him. You ought not——" She stopped, aware of the futility of urging a moral consideration upon the man, and fell back upon the practical. "He couldn't travel that soon, even if he wanted to. He's not strong enough. You know that."

"All right. We'll call it a week. If he's still here a week from to-day, there will be trouble."

With that, he turned on his heel and left the room. They heard his spurs trailing across the porch and jingling down the steps, after which they caught a momentary vision of him, dark and sinister, as his horse flashed past the window.

The ranger smiled, but rather seriously. "The fat's in the fire now, sure enough, ma'am."

She turned anxiously upon him. "Why did you tell him all that? Why did you let him go away, believing you were here as a spy to trap him and his friends?"

"I let him have the truth. Anyhow, I couldn't have made good with a denial. He had the evidence. I can't keep him from believing what he wants to."

"He'll tell all his friends. He'll exaggerate the facts and stir up sentiment against you. He'll say you came here as a detective, to get evidence against the Squaw Creek raiders."

"Then he'll tell the truth!"

She took it in slowly, with a gathering horror. "The truth!" she repeated, almost under her breath. "You don't mean——You can't mean——Are you here as a spy upon my friends?"

"I didn't know they were your friends when I took the job. If you'll listen, I'll explain."

Words burst from her in gathering bitterness.

"What is there to explain, sir? The facts cry to heaven. I brought you into this valley, gave you the freedom of our home against my father's first instinct. I introduced you to my friends, and no doubt they told you much you wanted to know. They are simple, honest folks, who don't know a spy when they see one. And I—fool that I am—I vouched for you. More, I stood between you and the fate you deserved. And, lastly, in my blind conceit, I have told you the names of the men in the Squaw Creek trouble. If I had only known—and I had all the evidence, but I was so blind I would not see you were a snake in the grass."

He put out a hand to stop her, and she drew back as if his touch were pollution. From the other side of the room, she looked across at him in bitter scorn.

"I shall make arrangements to have you taken out of the valley at once, sir."

"You needn't take the trouble, Miss Arlie. I'm not going out of the valley. If you'll have me taken to Alec Howard's shack, which is where you brought me from, I'll be under obligations to you."

"Whatever you are, I'm not going to have your blood on my hands. You've got to leave the valley."

"I have to thank you for all your kindness to me. If you'd extend it a trifle further and listen to what I've got to say, I'd be grateful."

"I don't care to hear your excuses. Go quickly, sir, before you meet the end you deserve, and give up the poor men I have betrayed to you." She spoke in a choked voice, as if she could scarce breathe.

"If you'd only listen before you——"

"I've listened to you too long. I was so sure I knew more than my father, than my friends. I'll listen no more."

The Texan gave it up. "All right, ma'am. Just as you say. If you'll order some kind of a rig for me, I'll not trouble you longer. I'm sorry that it's got to be this way. Maybe some time you'll see it different."

"Never," she flashed passionately, and fled from the room.

He did not see her again before he left. Bobbie came to get him in a light road trap they had. The boy looked at him askance, as if he knew something was wrong. Presently they turned a corner and left the ranch shut from sight in a fold of the hills.

At the first division of the road Fraser came to a difference of opinion with Bobbie.

"Arlie said you was going to leave the valley. She told me I was to take you to Speed's place."

"She misunderstood. I am going to Alec Howard's."

"But that ain't what she told me."

Steve took the reins from him, and turned into the trail that led to Howard's place. "You can explain to her, Bobbie, that you couldn't make me see it that way."

An hour later, he descended upon Howard—a big, rawboned ranchman, who had succumbed quickly to a deep friendship for this "Admirable Crichton" of the plains.

"Hello, Steve! Glad to death to see you. Hope you've come to stay, you old pie eater," he cried joyously, at sight of the Texan.

Fraser got down. "Wait here a moment, Bobbie. I want to have a talk with Alec. I may go on with you."

They went into the cabin, and Fraser sat down. He was still far from strong.

"What's up, Steve?" the rancher asked.

"You asked me to stay, Alec. Before I say whether I will or not, I've got a story to tell you. After I've told it, you can ask me again if you want me to stop with you. If you don't ask me, I'll ride off with the boy."

"All right. Fire ahead, old hoss. I'll ask you fast enough."

The Texan told his story from the beginning. Only one thing he omitted—that Arlie had told him the name of the Squaw Creek raiders.

"There are the facts, Alec. You've got them from beginning to end. It's up to you. Do you want me here?"

"Before I answer that, I'll have to put a question myse'f, Steve. Why do you want to stay? Why not leave the valley while you're still able to?"

"Because Jed Briscoe put it up to me that I'd got to leave within a week. I'll go when I'm good and ready."

Alec nodded his appreciation of the point. "Sure. You don't want to sneak out, with yore tail betwixt yore laigs. That brings up another question, Steve. What about the Squaw Creek sheep raiders? Just for argument, we'll put it that some of them are my friends. You understand—just for argument. Are you still aiming to run them down?"

Fraser met his frank question frankly. "No, Alec, I've had to give up that notion long since—soon as I began to guess they were friends of Miss Arlie. I'm going back to tell Hilliard so. But I ain't going to be run out by Briscoe."

"Good enough. Put her there, son. This shack's yore home till hell freezes over, Steve."

"You haven't any doubts about me, Alec. If you have, better say so now."

"Doubts? I reckon not. Don't I know a man when I see one? I'm plumb surprised at Arlie." He strode to the door, and called to Bobbie: "Roll along home, son. Yore passenger is going to stay a spell with me."

"Of course, I understand what this means, Alec. Jed and his crowd aren't going to be any too well pleased when they learn you have taken me in. They may make you trouble," the ranger said.

The big cow man laughed. "Oh, cut it out, Steve. Jed don't have to O. K. my guest list. Not on yore life. I'm about ready for a ruction with that young man, anyway. He's too blamed bossy. I ain't wearing his brand. Fact is, I been having notions this valley has been suffering from too much Briscoe. Others are sharing that opinion with me. Ask Dick France. Ask Arlie, for that matter."

"I'm afraid I'm off that young lady's list of friends."

"Sho! She'll come round. She's some hot-haided. It always was her way to get mad first, and find out why afterward. But don't make any mistake about her, Steve. She's the salt of the earth, Arlie Dillon is. She figured it out you wasn't playing it quite on the square with her. Onct she's milled it around a spell, she'll see things different. I've knowed her since she was knee-high, and I tell you she's a game little thoroughbred."

The Texan looked at him a moment, then stared out of the window.

"We won't quarrel about that any, Alec. I'll endorse those sentiments, and then some, even if she did call me a snake in the grass."

CHAPTER XII — THE DANCE

THE DAY AFTER FRASER changed his quarters, Dick France rode up to the Howard ranch. Without alighting, he nodded casually to Alec, and then to his guest.

"Hello, Steve! How's the shoulder?"

"Fine and dandy."

"You moved, I see." The puncher grinned.

"If you see it for yourself, I'll not attempt to deny it."

"Being stood in the corner some more, looks like! Little Willie been telling some more lies?"

"Come in, Dick, and I'll put you wise."

Steve went over the story again. When he mentioned the Squaw Creek raid, he observed that his two friends looked quickly at each other and then away. He saw, however, that Dick took his pledge in regard to the raiders at face value, without the least question of doubt. He made only one comment on the situation.

"If Jed has served notice that he's going after you, Steve, he'll ce'tainly back the play. What's more, he won't be any too particular how he gets you, just so he gets you. He may come a-shooting in the open. Then, again, he may not. All according to how the notion strikes him."

"That's about it," agreed Howard.

"While it's fresh on my mind, I'll unload some more comfort. You've got an enemy in this valley you don't know about."

"The one that shot me?"

"I ain't been told that. I was to say, 'One enemy more than he knows of.'"

"Who told you to say it?"

"I was to forget to tell you that, Steve."

"Then I must have a friend more than I know of, too."

"I ain't so sure about that. You might call her a hostile friend."

"It's a lady, then. I can guess who."

"Honest, I didn't mean to tell you, Steve. It slipped out."

"I won't hold it against you."

"She sent for me last night, and this morning I dropped round. Now, what do you reckon she wanted with me?"

"Give it up."

"I'm to take a day off and ride around among the boys, so as to see them before Jed does. I'm to load 'em up with misrepresentations about how you and the sheriff happen to be working in cahoots. I gathered that the lady is through with you, but she don't want your scalp collected by the boys."

"I'm learning to be thankful for small favors," Fraser said dryly. "She figures me up a skunk, but hates to have me massacreed in her back yard. Ain't that about it, Dick?"

"Somewheres betwixt and between," France nodded. "Say, you lads going to the dance at Millikan's?"

"Didn't know there was one."

"Sure. Big doings. Monday night. Always have a dance after the spring round-up. Jed and his friends will be there—that ought to fetch you!" Dick grinned.

"I haven't noticed any pressing invitation to my address yet," said Steve.

"I'm extending it right now. Millikan told me to pass the word among the boys. Everybody and his neighbor invited." Dick lit a cigar, and gathered up his reins. "So-long, boys. I got to be going." Over his shoulder he fired another joyous shot as he cantered away. "I reckon that hostile friend will be there, too, Steve, if that's any inducement."

Whether it was an inducement is not a matter of record, but certain it is that the Texan found it easy to decide to go. Everybody in the valley would be there, and absence on his part would be construed as weakness, even as a confession of guilt. He had often observed that a man's friends are strong for him only when he is strong for himself.

Howard and his guest drove to Millikan's Draw, for the wound of the latter was still too new to stand so long a horseback ride. They arrived late, and the dance was already in full swing. As they stabled and fed the team, they could hear the high notes of the fiddles and the singsong chant of the caller.

"Alemane left. Right han' t'yer pardner, an' gran' right and left. Ev-v-rybody swing."

The ranch house was a large one, the most pretentious in the valley. A large hall opened into a living room and a dining room, by means of large double doors, which had been drawn back, so as to make one room of them.

As they pushed their way through the crowd of rough young fellows who clustered round the door, as if afraid their escape might be cut off, Fraser observed that the floor was already crowded with dancers.

The quadrille came to an end as he arrived, and, after they had seated their partners, red-faced perspiring young punchers swelled the knot around the door.

Alec stayed to chaff with them, while the Texan sauntered across the floor and took a seat on one of the benches which lined the walls. As he did so, a man and his partner, so busy in talk with each other that they had not observed who he was, sat down beside him in such position that the young woman was next him. Without having looked directly at either of them, Fraser knew that the girl was Arlie Dillon, and her escort Jed Briscoe. She had her back half turned toward him, so that, even after she was seated she did not recognize her neighbor.

Steve smiled pleasantly, and became absorbed in a rather noisy bout of repartee going on between one swain and his lass, not so absorbed, however, as not to notice that he and his unconscious neighbors were becoming a covert focus of attention. He had already noticed a shade of self-consciousness in the greeting of those whom he met, a hint of a suggestion that he was on trial. Among some this feeling was evidently more pronounced. He met more than one pair of eyes that gave back to his genial nod cold hostility.

At such an affair as this, Jed Briscoe was always at his best. He was one of the few men in the valley who knew how to waltz well, and music and rhythm always brought out in him a gay charm women liked. His lithe grace, his assurance, his ease of manner and speech, always differentiated him from the other ranchmen.

No wonder rumor had coupled his name with that of Arlie as her future husband. He knew how to make light love by implication, to skate around the subject skilfully and boldly with innuendo and suggestion.

Arlie knew him for what he was—a man passionate and revengeful, the leader of that side of the valley's life which she deplored. She did not trust him. Nevertheless, she felt his fascination. He made that appeal to her which a graceless young villain often does to a good woman who lets herself become interested in trying to understand the sinner and his sins. There was another reason why just now she showed him special favor. She wanted to blunt the edge of his anger against the Texan ranger, though her reason for this she did not admit even to herself.

She had—oh, she was quite sure of this—no longer any interest in Fraser except the impersonal desire to save his life. Having thought it all over, she was convinced that her friends had nothing to fear from him as a spy. That was what he had tried to tell her when she would not listen.

Deep in her heart she knew why she had not listened. It had to do with that picture of a pretty girl smiling up happily into his eyes—a thing she had not forgotten for one waking moment since. Like a knife the certainty had stabbed her heart that they were lovers. Her experience had been limited. Kodaks had not yet reached Lost Valley as common possessions. In the mountains no girl had her photograph taken beside a man unless they had a special interest in each other. And the manner of these two had implied the possession of a secret not known to the world.

So Arlie froze her heart toward the Texan, all the more because he had touched her girlish imagination to sweet hidden dreams of which her innocence had been unnecessarily ashamed. He had spoken no love to her, nor had he implied it exactly. There had been times she had thought something more than friendship lay under his warm smile. But now she scourged herself for her folly, believed she had been unmaidenly, and set her heart to be like flint against him. She had been ready to give him what he had not wanted. Before she would let him guess it she would rather die, a thousand times rather, she told herself passionately.

She presently became aware that attention was being directed toward her and Jed and somebody who sat on the other side of her. Without looking round, she mentioned the fact in a low voice to her partner of the dance just finished. Jed looked up, and for the first time observed the man behind her. Instantly the gayety was sponged from his face.

"Who is it?" she asked.

"That man from Texas."

Arlie felt the blood sting her cheeks. The musicians were just starting a waltz. She leaned slightly toward Jed, and said, in a low voice:

"Did you ask me to dance this with you?"

He had not, but he did now. He got to his feet, with shining eyes, and whirled her off. The girl did not look toward the Texan.

Nevertheless, as they circled the room, she was constantly aware of him. Sitting there, with a smile on his strong face, apparently unperturbed, he gave no hint of the stern fact that he was circled by enemies, any one of whom might carry his death in a hip pocket. His gaze was serene, unabashed, even amused.

The young woman was irritably suspicious that he found her anger amusing, just as he seemed to find the dangerous position in which he was placed. Yet her resentment coexisted with a sympathy for him that would not down. She believed he was marked for death by a coterie of those present, chief of whom was the man smiling down into her face from half-shut, smouldering eyes.

Her heart was a flame of protest against their decree, all the more so because she held herself partly responsible for it. In a panic of repentance, she had told Dick of her confession to the ranger of the names of the Squaw Creek raiders, and France had warned his confederates. He had done this, not because he distrusted Fraser, but because he felt it was their due to get a chance to escape if they wanted to do so.

Always a creature of impulse, Arlie had repented her repentance when too late. Now she would have fought to save the Texan, but the horror of it was that she could not guess how the blow would fall. She tried to believe he was safe, at least until the week was up.

When Dick strolled across the floor, sat down beside Steve, and began casually to chat with him, she could have thanked the boy with tears. It was equivalent to a public declaration of his intentions. At least, the ranger was not friendless. One of the raiders was going to stand by him. Besides Dick, he might count on Howard; perhaps on others.

Jed was in high good humor. All along the line he seemed to be winning. Arlie had discarded this intruder from Texas and was showing herself very friendly to the cattleman. The suspicion of Fraser which he had disseminated was bearing fruit; and so, more potently, was the word the girl had dropped incautiously. He had only to wait in order to see his rival wiped out. So that, when Arlie put in her little plea, he felt it would not cost him anything to affect a large generosity.

"Let him go, Jed. He is discredited. Folks are all on their guard before him now. He can't do any harm here. Dick says he is only waiting out his week because of your threat. Don't make trouble. Let him sneak back home, like a whipped cur," she begged.

"I don't want any trouble with him, girl. All I ask is that he leave the valley. Let Dick arrange that, and I'll give him a chance."

She thanked him, with a look that said more than words.

It was two hours later, when she was waltzing with Jed again, that Arlie caught sight of a face that disturbed her greatly. It was a countenance disfigured by a ragged scar, running from the bridge of the nose. She had last seen it gazing into the window of Alec Howard's cabin on a certain never-to-be-forgotten night.

"Who is that man—the one leaning against the door jamb, just behind Slim Leroy?" she asked.

"He's a fellow that calls himself Johnson. His real name is Struve," Jed answered carelessly.

"He's the man that shot the Texas lieutenant," she said.

"I dare say. He's got a good reason for shooting him. The man broke out of the Arizona penitentiary, and Fraser came north to rearrest him. At least, that's my guess. He wouldn't have been here tonight if he hadn't figured Fraser too sick to come. Watch him duck when he learns the ranger's here."

At the first opportunity Arlie signaled to Dick that she wanted to see him. Fraser, she observed, was no longer in the dancing rooms. Dick took her out from the hot room to the porch.

"Let's walk a little, Dick. I want to tell you something."

They sauntered toward the fine grove of pines that ran up the hillside back of the house.

"Did you notice that man with the scar, Dick?" she presently asked.

"Yes. I ain't seen him before. Must be one of the Rabbit Run guys, I take it."

"I've seen him. He's the man that shot your friend. He was the man I shot at when he looked in the window."

"Sure, Arlie?"

"Dead sure, Dick. He's an escaped convict, and he has a grudge at your friend. He is afraid of him, too. Look out for Lieutenant Fraser tonight. Don't let him wander around outside. If he does, there may be murder done."

Even as she spoke, there came a sound from the wooded hillside—the sound of a stifled cry, followed by an imprecation and the heavy shuffling of feet.

"Listen, Dick!"

For an instant he listened. Then: "There's trouble in the grove, and I'm not armed," he cried.

"Never mind! Go—go!" she shrieked, pushing him forward.

For herself, she turned, and ran like a deer for the house.

Siegfried was sitting on the porch, whittling a stick.

"They—they're killing Steve—in the grove," she panted.

Without a word he rolled off, like a buffalo cow, toward the scene of action.

Arlie pushed into the house and called for Jed.

CHAPTER XIII — THE WOLF HOWLS

AS STEVE STROLLED OUT into the moonlight, he left behind him the monotonous thumping of heavy feet and the singsong voice of the caller.

> *"Birdie fly out,*
> *Crow hop in,*
> *Join all hands*
> *And circle ag'in."*

came to him, in the high, strident voice of Lute Perkins. He took a deep breath of fresh, clean air, and looked about him. After the hot, dusty room, the grove, with its green foliage, through which the moonlight filtered, looked invitingly cool. He sauntered forward, climbed the hill up which the wooded patch straggled, and sat down, with his back to a pine.

Behind the valley rampart, he could see the dim, saw-toothed Teton peaks, looking like ghostly shapes in the moonlight. The night was peaceful. Faint and mellow came the sound of jovial romping from the house; otherwise, beneath the distant stars, a perfect stillness held.

How long he sat there, letting thoughts happen dreamily rather than producing them of gray matter, he did not know. A slight sound, the snapping of a twig, brought his mind to alertness without causing the slightest movement of his body.

His first thought was that, in accordance with dance etiquette in the ranch country, his revolver was in its holster under the seat of the trap in which they had driven over. Since his week was not up, he had expected no attack from Jed and his friends. As for the enemy, of whom Arlie had advised him, surely a public dance was the last place to tempt one who apparently preferred to attack from cover. But his instinct was certain. He did not need to look round to know he was trapped.

"I'm unarmed. You'd better come round and shoot me from in front. It will look better at the inquest," he said quietly.

"Don't move. You're surrounded," a voice answered.

A rope snaked forward and descended over the ranger's head, to be jerked tight, with a suddenness that sent a pain like a knife thrust through the wounded shoulder. The instinct for self-preservation was already at work in him. He fought his left arm free from the rope that pressed it to his side, and dived toward the figure at the end of the rope. Even as he plunged, he found time to be surprised that no revolver shot echoed through the night, and to know that the reason was because his enemies preferred to do their work in silence.

The man upon whom he leaped gave a startled oath and stumbled backward over a root.

Fraser, his hand already upon the man's throat, went down too. Upon him charged men from all directions. In the shadows, they must have hampered each other, for the ranger, despite his wound—his shoulder was screaming with pain—got to his knees, and slowly from his knees to his feet, shaking the clinging bodies from him.

Wrenching his other hand from under the rope, he fought them back as a hurt grizzly does the wolf pack gathered for the kill. None but a very powerful man could ever have reached his feet. None less agile and sinewy than a panther could have beaten them back as at first he did. They fought in grim silence, yet the grove was full of the sounds of battle. The heavy breathing, the beat of shifting feet, the soft impact of flesh striking flesh, the thud of falling bodies—of these the air was vocal. Yet, save for the gasps of sudden pain, no man broke silence save once.

"The snake'll get away yet!" a hoarse voice cried, not loudly, but with an emphasis that indicated strong conviction.

Impossible as it seemed, the ranger might have done it but for an accident. In the struggle, the rope had slipped to a point just below his knees. Fighting his way down the hill, foot by foot, the Texan felt the rope tighten. One of his attackers flung himself against his chest and he was tripped. The pack was on him again. Here there was more light, and though for a time the mass swayed back and forth, at last they hammered him down by main strength. He was bound hand and foot, and dragged back to the grove.

They faced their victim, panting deeply from their exertions. Fraser looked round upon the circle of distorted faces, and stopped at one. Seen now, with the fury and malignancy of its triumph painted upon it, the face was one to bring bad dreams.

The lieutenant, his chest still laboring heavily, racked with the torture of his torn shoulder, looked into that face out of the only calm eyes in the group.

"So it's you, Struve?"

"Yes, it's me—me and my friends."

"I've been looking for you high and low."

"Well, you've found me," came the immediate exultant answer.

"I reckon I'm indebted to you for this." Fraser moved his shoulder slightly.

"You'll owe me a heap more than that before the night's over."

"Your intentions were good then, I expect. Being shy a trigger finger spoils a man's aim."

"Not always."

"Didn't like to risk another shot from Bald Knob, eh? Must be some discouraging to hit only once out of three times at three hundred yards, and a scratch at that."

The convict swore. "I'll not miss this time, Mr. Lieutenant."

"You'd better not, or I'll take you back to the penitentiary where I put you before."

"You'll never put another man there, you meddling spy," Struve cried furiously.

"I'm not so sure of that. I know what you've got against me, but I should like to know what kick your friends have coming," the ranger retorted.

"You may have mine, right off the reel, Mr. Fraser, or whatever you call yourself. You came into this valley with a lie on your lips. We played you for a friend, and you played us for suckers. All the time you was in a deal with the sheriff for you know what. I hate a spy like I do a rattlesnake."

It was the man Yorky that spoke. Steve's eyes met his.

"So I'm a spy, am I?"

"You know best."

"Anyhow, you're going to shoot me first, and find out afterward?"

"Wrong guess. We're going to hang you." Struve, unable to keep back longer his bitter spleen, hissed this at him.

"Yes, that's about your size, Struve. You can crow loud now, when the odds are six to one, with the one unarmed and tied at that. But what I want to know is—are you playing fair with your friends? Have you told them that every man in to-night's business will hang, sure as fate? Have you told them of those cowardly murders you did in Arizona and Texas? Have you told them that your life is forfeit, anyway? Do they know you're trying to drag them into your troubles? No? You didn't tell them that. I'm surprised at you, Struve."

"My name's Johnson."

"Not in Arizona, it isn't. Wolf Struve it is there, wanted for murder and other sundries." He turned swiftly from him to his confederates. "You fools, you're putting your heads into a noose. He's in already, and wants you in, too. Test him. Throw the end of that rope over the limb, and stand back, while he pulls me up alone. He daren't—not for his life, he daren't. He knows that whoever pulls on that rope hangs himself as surely as he hangs me."

The men looked at each other, and at Struve. Were they being led into trouble to pay this man's scores off for him? Suspicion stirred uneasily in them.

"That's right, too. Let Johnson pull him up," Slim Leroy said sullenly.

"Sure. You've got more at stake than we have. It's up to you, Johnson," Yorky agreed.

"That's right," a third chipped in.

"We'll all pull together, boys," Struve insinuated. "It's only a bluff of his. Don't let him scare you off."

"He ain't scaring me off any," declared Yorky. "He's a spy, and he's getting what is coming to him. But you're a stranger too, Johnson. I don't trust you any—not any farther than I can see you, my friend. I'll stand for being an aider and abettor, but I reckon if there's any hanging to be done you'll have to be the sheriff," replied Yorky stiffly.

Struve turned his sinister face on one and another of them. His lips were drawn back, so that the wolfish teeth gleamed in the moonlight. He felt himself being driven into a trap, from which there was no escape. He dared not let Fraser go with his life, for he knew that, sooner or later, the ranger would run him to earth, and drag him back to the punishment that was awaiting him in the South. Nor did he want to shoulder the responsibility of murdering this man before five witnesses.

Came the sound of running footsteps.

"What's that?" asked Slim nervously.

"Where are you, Steve?" called a voice.

"Here," the ranger shouted back.

A moment later Dick France burst into the group. "What's doing?" he panted.

The ranger laughed hardily. "Nothing, Dick. Nothing at all. Some of the boys had notions of a necktie party, but they're a little shy of sand. Have you met Mr. Struve, Dick? I know you're acquainted with the others, Mr. Struve is from Yuma. An old friend of mine. Fact is, I induced him to locate at Yuma."

Dick caught at the rope, but Yorky flung him roughly back.

"This ain't your put in, France," he said. "It's up to Johnson." And to the latter: "Get busy, if you're going to."

"He's a spy on you-all, just the same as he is on me," blurted the convict.

"That's a lie, Struve," pronounced the lieutenant evenly. "I'm going to take you back with me, but I've got nothing against these men. I want to announce right now, no matter who tells a different story, that I haven't lost any Squaw Creek raiders and I'm not hunting any."

"You hear? He came into this valley after me."

"Wrong again, Struve. I didn't know you were here. But I know now, and I serve notice that I'm going to take you back with me, dead or alive. That's what I'm paid for, and that's what I'm going to do."

It was amazing to hear this man, with a rope round his neck, announce calmly what he was going to do to the man who had only to pull that rope to send him into eternity. The very audacity of it had its effect.

Slim spoke up. "I don't reckon we better go any farther with this thing, Yorky."

"No, I don't reckon you had," cut in Dick sharply. "I'll not stand for it."

Again the footsteps of a running man reached them. It was Siegfried. He plunged into the group like a wild bull, shook the hair out of his eyes, and planted himself beside Fraser. With one backward buffet of his great arm he sent Johnson heels over head. He caught Yorky by the shoulders, strong man though the latter was, and shook him till his teeth rattled, after which he flung him reeling a dozen yards to the ground. The Norwegian was reaching for Dick when Fraser stopped him.

"That's enough of a clean-up right now, Sig. Dick butted in like you to help me," he explained.

"The durned coyotes!" roared the big Norseman furiously, leaping at Leroy and tossing him over his head as an enraged bull does. He turned upon the other three, shaking his tangled mane, but they were already in flight.

"I'll show them. I'll show them," he kept saying as he came back to the man he had rescued.

"You've showed them plenty, Sig. Cut out the rough house before you maim some of these gents who didn't invite you to their party."

The ranger felt the earth sway beneath him as he spoke. His wound had been torn loose in the fight, and was bleeding. Limply he leaned against the tree for support.

It was at this moment he caught sight of Arlie and Briscoe as they ran up. Involuntarily he straightened almost jauntily. The girl looked at him with that deep, eager look of fear he had seen before, and met that unconquerable smile of his.

The rope was still round his neck and the coat was stripped from his back. He was white to the lips, and she could see he could scarce stand, even with the support of the pine trunk. His face was bruised and battered. His hat was gone; and hidden somewhere in his crisp short hair was a cut from which blood dripped to the forehead. The bound arm had been torn from its bandages in the unequal battle he had fought. But for all his desperate plight he still carried the invincible look that nothing less than death can rob some men of.

The fretted moonlight, shifting with the gentle motion of the foliage above, fell full upon him now and showed a wet, red stain against the white shirt. Simultaneously outraged nature collapsed, and he began to sink to the ground.

Arlie gave a little cry and ran forward. Before he reached the ground he had fainted; yet scarcely before she was on her knees beside him with his head in her arms.

"Bring water, Dick, and tell Doc Lee to come at once. He'll be in the back room smoking. Hurry!" She looked fiercely round upon the men assembled. "I think they have killed him. Who did this? Was it you, Yorky? Was it you that murdered him?"

"I bane t'ink it take von hoondred of them to do it," said Siegfried. "Dat fallar, Johnson, he bane at the bottom of it."

"Then why didn't you kill him? Aren't you Steve's friend? Didn't he save your life?" she panted, passion burning in her beautiful eyes.

Siegfried nodded. "I bane Steve's friend, yah! And Ay bane kill Johnson eef Steve dies."

Briscoe, furious at this turn of the tide which had swept Arlie's sympathies back to his enemy, followed Struve as he sneaked deeper into the shadow of the trees. The convict was nursing a sprained wrist when Jed reached him.

"What do you think you've been trying to do, you sap-headed idiot?" Jed demanded. "Haven't you sense enough to choose a better time than one when the whole settlement is gathered to help him? And can't you ever make a clean job of it, you chuckle-minded son of a gun?"

Struve turned, snarling, on him. "That'll be enough from you, Briscoe. I've stood about all I'm going to stand just now."

"You'll stand for whatever I say," retorted Jed. "You've cooked your goose in this valley by to-night's fool play. I'm the only man that can pull you through. Bite on that fact, Mr. Struve, before you unload your bile on me."

The convict's heart sank. He felt it to be the truth. The last thing he had heard was Siegfried's threat to kill him.

Whether Fraser lived or died he was in a precarious position and he knew it.

"I know you're my friend, Jed," he whined. "I'll do what you say. Stand by me and I'll sure work with you."

"Then if you take my advice you'll sneak down to the corral, get your horse, and light out for the run. Lie there till I see you."

"And Siegfried?"

"The Swede won't trouble you unless this Texan dies. I'll send you word in time if he does."

Later a skulking shadow sneaked into the corral and out again. Once out of hearing, it leaped to the back of the horse and galloped wildly into the night.

CHAPTER XIV — HOWARD EXPLAINS

TWO HORSEMEN RODE INTO Millikan's Draw and drew up in front of the big ranch house. To the girl who stepped to the porch to meet them they gave friendly greeting. One of them asked:

"How're things coming, Arlie?"

"Better and better every day, Dick. Yesterday the doctor said he was out of danger."

"It's been a tough fight for Steve," the other broke in. "Proper nursing is what pulled him through. Doc says so."

"Did he say that, Alec? I'll always think it was doc. He fought for that life mighty hard, boys."

Alec Howard nodded: "Doc Lee's the stuff. Here he comes now, talking of angels."

Doctor Lee dismounted and grinned. "Which of you lads is she making love to now?"

Arlie laughed. "He can't understand that I don't make love to anybody but him," she explained to the younger men.

"She never did to me, doc," Dick said regretfully.

"No, we were just talking about you, doc."

"Fire ahead, young woman," said the doctor, with assumed severity. "I'm here to defend myself now."

"Alec was calling you an angel, and I was laughing at him," said the girl demurely.

"An angel—huh!" he snorted.

"I never knew an angel that chewed tobacco, or one that could swear the way you do when you're mad," continued Arlie.

"I don't reckon your acquaintance with angels is much greater than mine, Miss Arlie Dillon. How's the patient?"

"He's always wanting something to eat, and he's cross as a bear."

"Good for him! Give him two weeks now and he'll be ready to whip his weight in wild cats."

The doctor disappeared within, and presently they could hear his loud, cheerful voice pretending to berate the patient.

Arlie sat down on the top step of the porch.

"Boys, I don't know what I would have done if he had died. It would have been all my fault. I had no business to tell him the names of you boys that rode in the raid, and afterward to tell you that I told him," she accused herself.

"No, you had no business to tell him, though it happens he's safe as a bank vault," Howard commented.

"I don't know how I came to do it," the girl continued. "Jed had made me suspicious of him, and then I found out something fine he had done for me. I wanted him to know I trusted him. That was the first thing I thought of, and I told it. He tried to stop me, but I'm such an impulsive little fool."

"We all make breaks, Arlie. You'll not do it again, anyhow," France comforted.

Doctor Lee presently came out and pronounced that the wounded man was doing well. "Wants to see you boys. Don't stay more than half an hour. If they get in your way, sweep 'em out, Arlie."

The cowpunchers entered the sick room with the subdued, gingerly tread of professional undertakers.

"I ain't so bad as that yet, boys," the patient laughed. "You're allowed to speak above a whisper. Doc thinks I'll last till night, mebbe, if I'm careful."

They told him all the gossip of the range—how young Ford had run off with Sallie Laundon and got married to her down at the Butte; how Siegfried had gone up and down the valley swearing he would clean out Jack Rabbit Run if Steve died; how Johnson had had another row with Jed and had chosen to take water rather than draw. Both of his visitors, however, had something on their minds they found some difficulty in expressing.

Alec Howard finally broached it.

"Arlie told you the names of some of the boys that were in the Squaw Creek sheep raid. She made a mistake in telling you anything, but we'll let that go in the discard. It ain't necessary that you should know the names of the others, but I'm going to tell you one of them, Steve."

"No, I don't want to know."

"This is my say-so. His name is Alec Howard."

"I'm sorry to hear that, Alec. I don't know why you have told me."

"Because I want you to know the facts of that raid, Steve. No killing was on the program. That came about in a way none of us could foresee."

"This is how it was, Steve," explained Dick. "Word came that Campeau was going to move his sheep into the Squaw Creek district. Sheep never had run there. It was understood the range there was for our cattle. We had set a dead line, and warned them not to cross it. Naturally, it made us sore when we heard about Campeau.

"So some of us gathered together hastily and rode over. Our intentions were declared. We meant to drive the sheep back and patrol the dead line. It was solemnly agreed that there was to be no shooting, not even of sheep."

The story halted here for a moment before Howard took it up again. "Things don't always come out the way you figure them. We didn't anticipate any trouble. We outnumbered them two to one. We had the advantage of the surprise. You couldn't guess that for anything but a cinch, could you?"

"And it turned out different?"

"One of us stumbled over a rock as we were creeping forward. Campeau heard us and drew. The first shot came from them. Now, I'm going to tell you something you're to keep under your own hat. It will surprise you a heap when I tell you that one man on our side did all the damage. He was at the haid of the line, and it happens he is a dead shot. He is liable to rages, when he acts like a crazy man. He got one now. Before we could put a stopper on him, he had killed Campeau and Jennings, and wounded the herders. The whole thing was done before you could wink an eye six times. For just about that long we stood there like roped calves. Then we downed the man in his tracks, slammed him with the butt of a revolver."

Howard stopped and looked at the ranger before he spoke again. His voice was rough and hoarse.

"Steve, I've seen men killed before, but I never saw anything so awful as that. It was just like they had been struck by lightning for suddenness. There was that devil scattering death among them and the poor fellows crumpling up like rabbits. I tell you every time I think of it the thing makes me sick."

The ranger nodded. He understood. The picture rose before him of a man in a Berserk rage, stark mad for the moment, playing Destiny on that lonely, moonlit hill. The face his instinct fitted to the irresponsible murderer was that of Jed Briscoe. Somehow he was sure of that, beyond the shadow of a doubt. His imagination conceived that long ride back across the hills, the deep agonies of silence, the fierce moments of vindictive accusation. No doubt for long the tug of conscience was with them in all their waking hours, for these men were mostly simple-minded cattlemen caught in the web of evil chance.

"That's how it was, Steve. In as long as it takes to empty a Winchester, we were every one of us guilty of a murder we'd each have given a laig to have stopped. We were all in it, all tied together, because we had broke the law to go raiding in the first place. Technically, the man that emptied that rifle wasn't any more guilty than us poor wretches that stood frozen there while he did it. Put it that we might shave the gallows, even then the penitentiary would bury us. There was only one thing to do. We agreed to stand together, and keep mum."

"Is that why you're telling me, Alec?" Fraser smiled.

"We ain't telling you, not legally," the cow-puncher answered coolly. "If you was ever to say we had, Dick and me would deny it. But we ain't worrying any about you telling it. You're a clam, and we know it. No, we're telling you, son, because we want you to know about how it was. The boys didn't ride out to do murder. They rode out simply to drive the sheep off their range."

The Texan nodded. "That's about how I figured it. I'm glad you told me, boys. I reckon I don't need to tell you I'm padlocked in regard to this."

Arlie came to the door and looked in. "It's time you boys were going. Doc said a half hour."

"All right, Arlie," responded Dick. "So-long, Steve. Be good, you old pie eater."

After they had gone, the Texan lay silent for a long time. He understood perfectly their motive in telling him the story. They had not compromised themselves legally, since a denial would have given them two to one in the matter of witnesses. But they wished him to see that, morally, every man but one who rode on that raid was guiltless of the Squaw Creek murders.

Arlie came in presently, and sat down near the window with some embroidery.

"Did the boys tire you?" she asked, noting his unusual silence.

"No. I was thinking about what they told me. They were giving me the inside facts of the Squaw Creek raid."

She looked up in surprise. "They were?" A little smile began to dimple the corners of her mouth. "That's funny, because they had just got through forgiving me for what I told you."

"What they told me was how the shooting occurred."

"I don't know anything about that. When I told you their names I was only telling what I had heard people whisper. That's all I knew."

"You've been troubled because your friends were in this, haven't you? You hated to think it of them, didn't you?" he asked.

"Yes. It has troubled me a lot."

"Don't let it trouble you any more. One man was responsible for all the bloodshed. He went mad and saw red for half a minute. Before the rest could stop him, the slaughter was done. The other boys aren't guilty of that, any more than you are or I."

"Oh, I'm glad—I'm glad," she cried softly. Then, looking up quickly to him: "Who was the man?" she asked.

"I don't know. It is better that neither of us should know that."

"I'm glad the boys told you. It shows they trust you."

"They figure me out a decent man," he answered carelessly.

"Ah! That's where I made my mistake." She looked at him bravely, though the color began to beat into her cheeks beneath the dusky tan. "Yet I knew it all the time—in my heart. At least, after I had given myself time to think it over. I knew you couldn't be that. If I had given you time to explain—but I always think too late."

His eyes, usually so clear and steely, softened at her words. "I'm satisfied if you knew—in your heart."

"I meant——" she began, with a flush.

"Now, don't spoil it, please," he begged.

Under his steady, half-smiling gaze, her eyes fell. Two weeks ago she had been a splendid young creature, as untaught of life as one of the wild forest animals and as unconsciously eager for it. But there had come a change over her, a birth of womanhood from that night when she had stood between Stephen Fraser and death. No doubt she would often regret it, but she had begun to live more deeply. She could never go back to the care-free days when she could look all men in the face with candid, girlish eyes. The time had come to her, as it must to all sensitive of life, when she must drink of it, whether she would or no.

"Because I'd rather you would know it in your heart than in your mind," he said.

Something sweet and terrifying, with the tingle and warmth of rare wine in it, began to glow in her veins. Eyes shy, eager, frightened, met his for an instant. Then she remembered the other girl. Something hard as steel ran through her. She turned on her heel and left the room.

CHAPTER XV — THE TEXAN PAYS A VISIT

FROM THAT DAY FRASER had a new nurse. Arlie disappeared, and her aunt replaced her a few hours later and took charge of the patient. Steve took her desertion as an irritable convalescent does, but he did not let his disappointment make him unpleasant to Miss Ruth Dillon.

"I'm a chump," he told himself, with deep disgust. "Hadn't any more sense than to go scaring off the little girl by handing out a line of talk she ain't used to. I reckon now she's done with me proper."

He continued to improve so rapidly that within the prescribed two weeks he was on horseback again, though still a little weak and washed out. His first ride of any length was to the Dillon ranch. Siegfried accompanied him, and across the Norwegian's saddle lay a very business-like rifle.

As they were passing the mouth of a cañon, the ranger put a casual question: "This Jack Rabbit Run, Sig?"

"Yah. More men wanted bane lost in that gulch than any place Ay knows of."

"That so? I'm going in there to-morrow to find that man Struve," his friend announced carelessly.

The big blonde giant looked at him. "Yuh bain't, Steve? Why, yuh bain't fit to tackle a den uh wild cats." An admiring grin lit the Norwegian's face. "Durn my hide, yuh've got 'em all skinned for grit, Steve. Uh course, Ay bane goin' with yuh."

"If it won't get you in bad with your friends I'll be glad to have you, Sig."

"They bain't my friends. Ay bane shook them, an' served notice to that effect."

"Glad of it."

"Yuh bane goin' in after Struve only?"

"Yes. He's the only man I want."

"Then Ay bane go in, and bring heem out to yuh."

Fraser shook his head. "No, old man, I've got to play my own hand."

"Ay t'ink it be a lot safer f'r me to happen in an' get heem," remonstrated Siegfried.

"Safer for me," corrected the lieutenant, smiling. "No, I can't work that way. I've got to take my own chances. You can go along, though, on one condition. You're not to interfere between me and Struve. If some one else butts in, you may ask him why, if you like.

"Ay bane t'ink yuh von fool, Steve. But Ay bane no boss. Vat yuh says goes."

They found Arlie watering geraniums in front of the house. Siegfried merely nodded to her and passed on to the stables with the horses. Fraser dismounted, offering her his hand and his warm smile.

He had caught her without warning, and she was a little shy of him. Not only was she embarrassed, but she saw that he knew it. He sat down on the step, while she continued to water her flowers.

"You see your bad penny turned up again, Miss Arlie," he said.

"I didn't know you were able to ride yet, Lieutenant Fraser."

"This is my first try at it. Thought I'd run over and say 'Thank you' to my nurse."

"I'll call auntie," she said quickly.

He shook his head. "Not necessary, Miss Arlie. I settled up with her. I was thinking of the nurse that ran off and left me."

She was beginning to recover herself. "You want to thank her for leaving while there was still hope," she said, with a quick little smile.

"Why did you do it? I've been mighty lonesome the past two weeks," he said quietly.

"You would be, of course. You are used to an active outdoor life, and I suppose the boys couldn't get round to see you very often."

"I wasn't thinking of the boys," he meditated aloud.

Arlie blushed; and to hide her embarrassment she called to Jimmie, who was passing: "Bring up Lieutenant Fraser's Teddy. I want him to see how well we're caring for his horse."

As a diversion, Teddy served very well. Horse and owner were both mightily pleased to see each other. While the animal rubbed its nose against his coat, the ranger teased and petted it.

"Hello, you old Teddy hawss. How air things a-comin', pardner?" he drawled, with a reversion to his Texas speech. "Plumb tickled to death to meet up with yore old master, ain't you? How come it you ain't fallen in love with this young lady and forgot Steve?"

"He thinks a lot of me, too," Arlie claimed promptly.

"Don't blame you a bit, Teddy. I'll ce'tainly shake hands with you on that. But life's jest meetin' and partin', old hawss. I got to take you away for good, day after to-morrow."

"Where are you going?" the girl asked quickly. Then, to cover the swift interest of her question: "But, of course, it is time you were going back to your business."

"No, ma'am, that is just it. Seems to me either too soon or too late to be going."

She had her face turned from him, and was busy over her plants, to hide the tremulous dismay that had shaken her at his news.

She did not ask him what he meant, nor did she ask again where he was going. For the moment, she could not trust her voice to say more.

"Too late, because I've seen in this valley some one I'll never forget, and too soon because that some one will forget me, sure as a gun," he told her.

"Not if you write to him."

"It isn't a him. It's my little nurse."

"I'll tell auntie how you feel about it, and I'm sure she won't forget you."

"You know mighty well I ain't talking about auntie."

"Then I suppose you must mean me."

"That's who I'm meaning."

"I think I'll be able to remember you if I try—by Teddy," she answered, without looking at him, and devoted herself to petting the horse.

"Is it—would it be any use to say any more, Arlie?" he asked, in a low voice, as he stood beside her, with Teddy's nose in his hands.

"I—I don't know what you mean, sir. Please don't say anything more about it." Then again memory of the other girl flamed through her. "No, it wouldn't—not a bit of use, not a bit," she broke out fiercely.

"You mean you couldn't——"

The flame in her face, the eyes that met his, as if drawn by a magnet, still held their anger, but mingled with it was a piteous plea for mercy. "I—I'm only a girl. Why don't you let me alone?" she cried bitterly, and hard upon her own words turned and ran from the room.

Steve looked after her in amazed surprise. "Now don't it beat the band the way a woman takes a thing."

Dubiously he took himself to the stable and said good-by to Dillon.

An hour later she went down to dinner still flushed and excited. Before she had been in the room two minutes her father gave her a piece of startling news.

"I been talking to Steve. Gracious, gyurl, what do you reckon that boy's a-goin' to do?"

Arlie felt the color leap into her cheeks.

"What, dad?"

"He's a'goin' back to Gimlet Butte, to give himself up to Brandt, day after to-morrow."

"But—what for?" she gasped.

"Durned if I know! He's got some fool notion about playin' fair. Seems he came into the Cedar Mountain country to catch the Squaw Creek raiders. Brandt let him escape on that pledge. Well, he's give up that notion, and now he thinks, dad gum it, that it's up to him to surrender to Brandt again."

The girl's eyes were like stars. "And he's going to go back there and give himself up, to be tried for killing Faulkner."

Dillon scratched his head. "By gum, gyurl, I didn't think of that. We cayn't let him go."

"Yes, we can."

"Why, honey, he didn't kill Faulkner, looks like. We cayn't let him go back there and take our medicine for us. Mebbe he would be lynched. It's a sure thing he'd be convicted."

"Never mind. Let him go. I've got a plan, dad." Her vivid face was alive with the emotion which spoke in it. "When did he say he was going?" she asked buoyantly.

"Day after to-morrow. Seems he's got business that keeps him hyer to-morrow. What's yore idee, honey?"

She got up, and whispered it in his ear. His jaw dropped, and he stared at her in amazement.

CHAPTER XVI — THE WOLF BITES

STEVE CAME DROWSILY TO consciousness from confused dreams of a cattle stampede and the click of rifles in the hands of enemies who had the drop on him. The rare, untempered sunshine of the Rockies poured into his window from a world outside, wonderful as the early morning of creation. The hillside opposite was bathed miraculously in a flood of light, in which grasshoppers fiddled triumphantly their joy in life. The sources of his dreams discovered themselves in the bawl of thirsty cattle and the regular clicking of a windmill.

A glance at his watch told him that it was six o'clock.

"Time to get up, Steve," he told himself, and forthwith did.

He chose a rough crash towel, slipped on a pair of Howard's moccasins, and went down to the river through an ambient that had the sparkle and exhilaration of champagne. The mountain air was still finely crisp with the frost, in spite of the sun warmth that was beginning to mellow it. Flinging aside the Indian blanket he had caught up before leaving the cabin, he stood for an instant on the bank, a human being with the physical poise, compactness, and lithe-muscled smoothness of a tiger.

Even as he plunged a rifle cracked. While he dived through the air, before the shock of the icy water tingled through him, he was planning his escape. The opposite bank rose ten feet above the stream. He kept under the water until he came close to this, then swam swiftly along it with only his head showing, so as to keep him out of sight as much as possible.

Half a stone's throw farther the bank fell again to the water's edge, the river having broadened and grown shallow, as mountain creeks do. The ranger ran, stooping, along the bank, till it afforded him no more protection, then dashed across the stony-bottomed stream to the shelter of the thick aspens beyond.

Just as he expected, a shot rang from far up the mountainside. In another instant he was safe in the foliage of the young aspens.

In the sheer exhilaration of his escape he laughed aloud.

"Last show to score gone, Mr. Struve. I figured it just right. He waited too long for his first shot. Then the bank hid me. He wasn't expecting to see me away down the stream, so he hadn't time to sight his second one."

Steve wound his way in and out among the aspens, working toward the tail of them, which ran up the hill a little way and dropped down almost to the back door of the cabin. Upon this he was presently pounding.

Howard let him in. He had a revolver in his hand, the first weapon he could snatch up.

"You durned old idiot! It's a wonder you ain't dead three ways for Sunday," he shouted joyfully at sight of him. "Ain't I told you 'steen times to do what bathin' you got to do, right here in the shack?"

The Texan laughed again. Naked as that of Father Adam, his splendid body was glowing with the bath and the exercise.

"He's ce'tainly the worst chump ever, Alec. Had me in sight all the way down to the creek, but waited till I wasn't moving. Reckon he was nervous. Anyhow, he waited just one-tenth of a second too late. Shot just as I leaned forward for my dive. He gave me a free hair-cut though."

A swath showed where the bullet had mowed a furrow of hair so close that in one place it had slightly torn the scalp.

"He shot again, didn't he?"

"Yep. I swam along the far bank, so that he couldn't get at me, and crossed into the aspens. He got another chance as I was crossing, but he had to take it on the fly, and missed."

The cattleman surveyed the hillside cautiously through the front window. "I reckon he's pulled his freight, most likely. But we'll stay cooped for a while, on the chance. You're the luckiest cuss I ever did see. More lives than a cat."

Howard laid his revolver down within reach, and proceeded to light a fire in the stove, from which rose presently the pleasant odors of aromatic coffee and fried ham and eggs.

"Come and get it, Steve," said Howard, by way of announcing breakfast. "No, you don't. I'll take the window seat, and at that we'll have the curtain drawn."

They were just finishing breakfast when Siegfried cantered up.

"You bane ready, Steve?" he called in.

Howard appeared in the doorway. "Say, Sig, go down to the corral and saddle up Teddy for Steve, will you? Some of his friends have been potshotting at him again. No damage done, except to my feelings, but there's nothing like being careful."

Siegfried's face darkened. "Ay bane like for know who it vas?"

Howard laughed. "Now, if you'll tell Steve that he'll give you as much as six bits, Sig. He's got notions, but they ain't worth any more than yours or mine. Say, where you boys going to-day? I've a notion to go along."

"Oh, just out for a little *pasear*," Steve answered casually. "Thought you were going to work on your south fence to-day."

"Well, I reckon I better. It sure needs fixing. You lads take good care of yourselves. I don't need to tell you not to pass anywhere near the run, Sig," he grinned, with the manner of one giving a superfluous warning.

Fraser looked at Siegfried, with a smile in his eyes. "No, we'll not pass the run to-day, Alec."

A quarter of an hour later they were in the saddle and away. Siegfried did not lead his friend directly up the cañon that opened into Jack Rabbit Run, but across the hills to a pass, which had to be taken on foot. They left the horses picketed on a grassy slope, and climbed the faint trail that went steeply up the boulder-strewn mountain.

The ascent was so steep that the last bit had to be done on all fours. It was a rock face, though by no means an impossible one, since projecting ledges and knobs offered a foothold all the way. From the summit, the trail edged its way down so precipitously that twice fallen pines had to be used as ladders for the descent.

As soon as they were off the rocks, the big blonde gave the signal for silence. "Ay bane t'ink we might meet up weeth some one," he whispered, and urged Steve to follow him as closely as possible.

It was half an hour later that Sig pointed out a small clearing ahead of them. "Cabin's right oop on the edge of the aspens. See it?"

The ranger nodded assent.

"Ay bane go down first an' see how t'ings look."

When the Norwegian entered the cabin, he saw two men seated at a table, playing seven up. The one facing him was Tommie, the cook; the other was an awkward heavy-set fellow, whom he knew for the man he wanted, even before the scarred, villainous face was twisted toward him.

Struve leaped instantly to his feet, overturning his chair in his haste. He had not met the big Norseman since the night he had attempted to hang Fraser.

"Ay bane not shoot yuh now," Siegfried told him.

"Right sure of that, are you?" the convict snarled, his hand on his weapon. "If you've got any doubts, now's the time to air them, and we'll settle this thing right now."

"Ay bane not shoot, Ay tell you."

Tommie, who had ducked beneath the table at the prospect of trouble, now cautiously emerged.

"I ain't lost any pills from either of your guns, gents," he explained, with a face so laughably and frankly frightened that both of the others smiled.

"Have a drink, Siegfried," suggested Struve, by way of sealing the treaty. "Tommie, get out that bottle."

"Ay bane t'ink Ay look to my horse first," the Norwegian answered, and immediately left by way of the back door not three minutes before Jed Briscoe entered by the front one.

Jed shut the door behind him and looked at the convict.

"Well?" he demanded.

Struve faced him sullenly, without answering.

"Tommie, *vamos*," hinted Briscoe gently, and as soon as the cook had disappeared, he repeated his monosyllable: "Well?"

"It didn't come off," muttered the other sulkily.

"Just what I expected. Why not?"

Struve broke into a string of furious oaths. "Because I missed him—missed him twice, when he was standing there naked before me. He was coming down to the creek to take a bath, and I waited till he was close. I had a sure bead on him, and he dived just as I fired. I got another chance, when he was running across, farther down, and, by thunder, I missed again."

Jed laughed, and the sound of it was sinister.

"Couldn't hit the side of a house, could you? You're nothing but a cheap skate, a tin-horn gambler, run down at the heels. All right. I'm through with you. Lieutenant Fraser, from Texas, can come along and collect whenever he likes. I'll not protect a false alarm like you any longer."

Struve looked at him, as a cornered wolf might have done. "What will you do?"

"I'll give you up to him. I'll tell him to come in and get you. I'll show him the way in, you white-livered cur!" bullied the cattleman, giving way to one of his rages.

"You'd better not," snarled the convict. "Not if you want to live."

As they stood facing each other in a panting fury the door opened, to let in Siegfried and the ranger.

Jed's rage against Struve died on the spot. He saw his enemy, the ranger, before him, and leaped to the conclusion that he had come to this hidden retreat to run him down for the Squaw Creek murders. Instantly, his hand swept to the hilt of his revolver.

That motion sealed his doom. For Struve knew that Siegfried had brought the ranger to capture him, and suspected in the same flash that Briscoe was in on the betrayal. Had not the man as good as told him so, not thirty seconds before? He supposed that Jed was drawing to kill or cover him, and, like a flash of lightning, unscabbarded and fired.

"You infernal Judas, I'll get you anyhow," he cried.

Jed dropped his weapon, and reeled back against the wall, where he hung for a moment, while the convict pumped a second and a third bullet into his body. Briscoe was dead before Fraser could leap forward and throw his arms round the man who had killed him.

Between them, they flung Struve to the ground, and disarmed him. The convict's head had struck as he went down, and it was not for some little time that he recovered fully from his daze. When he did his hands were tied behind him.

"I didn't go for to kill him," he whimpered, now thoroughly frightened at what he had done. "You both saw it, gentlemen. You did, lieutenant. So did you, Sig. It was self-defense. He drew on me. I didn't go to do it."

Fraser was examining the dead man's wounds. He looked up, and said to his friend: "Nothing to do for him, Sig. He's gone."

"I tell you, I didn't mean to do it," pleaded Struve. "Why, lieutenant, that man has been trying to get me to ambush you for weeks. I'll swear it." The convict was in a panic of terror, ready to curry favor with the man whom he held his deadliest enemy. "Yes, lieutenant, ever since you came here. He's been egging me on to kill you."

"And you tried it three times?"

"No, sir." He pointed vindictively at the dead man, lying face up on the floor. "It was him that ambushed you this morning. I hadn't a thing to do with it."

"Don't lie, you coward."

They carried the body to the next room and put it on a bed. Tommie was dispatched on a fast horse for help.

Late in the afternoon he brought back with him Doctor Lee, and half an hour after sunset Yorky and Slim galloped up. They were for settling the matter out of hand by stringing the convict Struve up to the nearest pine, but they found the ranger so very much on the spot that they reconsidered.

"He's my prisoner, gentlemen. I came in here and took him—that is, with the help of my friend Siegfried. I reckon if you mill it over a spell, you'll find you don't want him half as bad as we do," he said mildly.

"What's the matter with all of us going in on this thing, lieutenant?" proposed Yorky.

"I never did see such a fellow for necktie parties as you are, Yorky. Not three weeks ago, you was invitin' me to be chief mourner at one of your little affairs, and your friend Johnson was to be master of ceremonies. Now you've got the parts reversed. No, I reckon we'll have to disappoint you this trip."

"What are you going to do with him?" asked Yorky, with plain dissatisfaction.

"I'm going to take him down to Gimlet Butte. Arizona and Wyoming and Texas will have to scrap it out for him there."

"When, you get him there," Yorky said significantly.

"Yes, when I get him there," answered the Texan blandly, carefully oblivious of the other's implication.

The moon was beginning to show itself over a hill before the Texan and Siegfried took the road with their captive. Fraser had carelessly let drop a remark to the effect that they would spend the night at the Dillon ranch.

His watch showed eleven o'clock before they reached the ranch, but he pushed on without turning in and did not stop until they came to the Howard place.

They roused Alec from sleep, and he cooked them a post-midnight supper, after which he saddled his cow pony, buckled on his belt, and took down his old rifle from the rack.

"I'll jog along with you lads and see the fun," he said.

Their prisoner had not eaten. The best he could do was to gulp down some coffee, for he was in a nervous chill of apprehension. Every gust of wind seemed to carry to him the patter of pursuit. The hooting of an owl sent a tremor through him.

"Don't you reckon we had better hurry?" he had asked with dry lips more than once, while the others were eating.

He asked it again as they were setting off.

Howard looked him over with rising disgust, without answering. Presently, he remarked, apropos of nothing: "Are all your Texas wolves coyotes, Steve?"

He would have liked to know at least that it was a man whose life he was protecting, even though the fellow was also a villain. But this crumb of satisfaction was denied him.

CHAPTER XVII — ON THE ROAD TO GIMLET BUTTE

"WE'LL GO OUT BY the river way," said Howard tentatively. "Eh, what think, Sig? It's longer, but Yorky will be expecting us to take the short cut over the pass."

The Norwegian agreed. "It bane von chance, anyhow."

By unfrequented trails they traversed the valley till they reached the cañon down which poured Squaw Creek on its way to the outside world. A road ran alongside this for a mile or two, but disappeared into the stream when the gulch narrowed. The first faint streaks of gray dawn were lightening the sky enough for Fraser to see this. He was riding in advance, and commented upon it to Siegfried, who rode with him.

The Norwegian laughed. "Ay bane t'ink we do some wadin'."

They swung off to the right, and a little later splashed through the water for a few minutes and came out into a spreading valley beyond the sheer walls of the retreat they had left. Taking the road again, they traveled faster than they had been able to do before.

"Who left the valley yesterday for Gimlet Butte, Sig?" Howard asked, after it was light enough to see. "I notice tracks of two horses."

"Ay bane vondering. Ay t'ink mebbe West over——"

"I reckon not. This ain't the track of his big bay. Must 'a' been yesterday, too, because it rained the night before."

For some hours they could see occasionally the tracks of the two horses, but eventually lost them where two trails forked.

"Taking the Sweetwater cutout to the Butte, I reckon," Howard surmised.

They traveled all day, except for a stop about ten o'clock for breakfast, and another late in the afternoon, to rest the horses. At night, they put up at a ranch house, and were in the saddle again early in the morning. Before noon, they struck a telephone line, and Fraser called up Brandt at a ranch.

"Hello! This Sheriff Brandt? Lieutenant Fraser, of the Texas Rangers, is talking. I'm on my way to town with a prisoner. We're at Christy's, now. There will, perhaps, be an attempt to take him from us. I'll explain the circumstances later.... Yes.... Yes.... We can hold him, I think, but there may be trouble.... Yes, that's it. We have no legal right to detain him, I suppose.... That's what I was going to suggest. Better send about four men to meet us. We'll come in on the Blasted Pine road. About nine to-night, I should think."

As they rode easily along the dusty road, the Texan explained his plan to his friends.

"We don't want any trouble with Yorky's crowd. We ain't any of us deputies, and my commission doesn't run in Wyoming, of course. My notion is to lie low in the hills two or three hours this afternoon, and give Brandt a chance to send his men out to meet us. The responsibility will be on them, and we can be sworn in as deputies, too."

They rested in a grassy draw, about fifteen miles from town, and took the trail again shortly after dark. It was an hour later that Fraser, who had an extraordinary quick ear, heard the sound of men riding toward them. He drew his party quickly into the shadows of the hills, a little distance from the road.

They could hear voices of the advancing party, and presently could make out words.

"I tell you, they've got to come in on this road, Slim," one of the men was saying dogmatically. "We're bound to meet up with them. That's all there is to it."

"Yorky," whispered Howard, in the ranger's ear.

They rode past in pairs, six of them in all. As chance would have it, Siegfried's pony, perhaps recognizing a friend among those passing, nickered shrilly its greeting. Instantly, the riders drew up.

"Where did that come from?" Yorky asked, in a low voice.

"From over to the right. I see men there now See! Up against that hill." Slim pointed toward the group in the shadow.

Yorky hailed them. "That you, Sig?"

"Yuh bane von good guesser," answered the Norwegian.

"How many of you are there?"

"Four, Yorky," Fraser replied.

"There are six of us. We've got you outnumbered, boys."

Very faintly there came to the lieutenant the beat of horses' feet. He sparred for time.

"What do you want, Yorky?"

"You know what we want. That murderer you've got there—that's what we want."

"We're taking him in to be tried, Yorky. Justice will be done to him."

"Not at Gimlet Butte it won't. No jury will convict him for killing Jed Briscoe, from Lost Valley. We're going to hang him, right now."

"You'll have to fight for him, my friend, and before you do that I want you to understand the facts."

"We understand all the facts we need to, right now."

The lieutenant rode forward alone. He knew that soon they too would hear the rhythmic beat of the advancing posse.

"We've got all night to settle this, boys. Let's do what is fair and square. That's all I ask."

"Now you're shouting, lieutenant. That's all we ask."

"It depends on what you mean by fair and square," another one spoke up.

The ranger nodded amiably at him. "That you, Harris? Well, let's look at the facts right. Here's Lost Valley, that's had a bad name ever since it was inhabited. Far as I can make out its settlers are honest men, regarded outside as miscreants. Just as folks were beginning to forget it, comes the Squaw Creek raid. Now, I'm not going into that, and I'm not going to say a word against the man that lies dead up in the hills. But I'll say this: His death solves a problem for a good many of the boys up there. I'm going to make it my business to see that the facts are known right down in Gimlet Butte. I'm going to lift the blame from the boys that were present, and couldn't help what happened."

Yorky was impressed, but suspicion was not yet banished from his mind. "You seem to know a lot about it, lieutenant."

"No use discussing that, Yorky. I know what I know. Here's the great big point: If you lynch the man that shot Jed, the word will go out that the valley is still a nest of lawless outlaws. The story will be that the Squaw Creek raiders and their friends did it. Just as the situation is clearing up nicely, you'll make it a hundred times worse by seeming to endorse what Jed did on Squaw Creek."

"By thunder, that's right," Harris blurted.

Fraser spoke again. "Listen, boys. Do you hear horses galloping? That is Sheriff Brandt's deputies, coming to our assistance. You've lost the game, but you can save your faces yet. Join us, and kelp escort the prisoner to town. Nobody need know why you came out. We'll put it that it was to guard against a lynching."

The men looked at each other sheepishly. They had been outwitted, and in their hearts were glad of it. Harris turned to the ranger with a laugh. "You're a good one, Fraser. Kept us here talking, while your reënforcements came up. Well, boys, I reckon we better join the Sunday-school class."

So it happened that when Sheriff Brandt and his men came up they found the mountain folk united. He was surprised at the size of the force with the Texan.

"You're certainly of a cautious disposition, lieutenant. With eight men to help you, I shouldn't have figured you needed my posse," he remarked.

"It gives you the credit of bringing in the prisoner, sheriff," Steve told him unblushingly, voicing the first explanation that came to his mind.

CHAPTER XVIII — A WITNESS IN REBUTTAL

TWO HOURS LATER, LIEUTENANT Fraser was closeted with Brandt and Hilliard. He told them his story—or as much of it as he deemed necessary. The prosecuting attorney heard him to an end before he gave a short, skeptical laugh.

"It doesn't seem to me you've quite lived up to your reputation, lieutenant," he commented.

"I wasn't trying to," retorted Steve.

"What do you mean by that?"

"I have told you how I got into the valley. I couldn't go in there and betray my friends."

Hilliard wagged his fat forefinger. "How about betraying our trust? How about throwing us down? We let you escape, after you had given us your word to do this job, didn't we?"

"Yes. I had to throw you down. There wasn't any other way."

"You tell a pretty fishy story, lieutenant. It doesn't stand to reason that one man did all the mischief on that Squaw Creek raid."

"It is true. Not a shadow of a doubt of it. I'll bring you three witnesses, if you'll agree to hold them guiltless."

"And I suppose I'm to agree to hold you guiltless of Faulkner's death, too?" the lawyer demanded.

"I didn't say that. I'm here, Mr. Hilliard, to deliver my person, because I can't stand by the terms of our agreement. I think I've been fair with you."

Hilliard looked at Brandt, with twinkling eyes. It struck Fraser that they had between them some joke in which he was not a sharer.

"You're willing to assume full responsibility for the death of Faulkner, are you? Ready to plead guilty, eh?"

Fraser laughed. "Just a moment. I didn't say that. What I said was that I'm here to stand my trial. It's up to you to prove me guilty."

"But, in point of fact, you practically admit it."

"In point of fact, I would prefer not to say so. Prove it, if you can."

"I have witnesses here, ready to swear to the truth, lieutenant."

"Aren't your witnesses prejudiced a little?"

"Maybe." The smile on Hilliard's fat face broadened. "Two of them are right here. Suppose we find out."

He stepped to the door of the inner office, and opened it. From the room emerged Dillon and his daughter. The Texan looked at Arlie in blank amazement.

"This young lady says she was present, lieutenant, and knows who fired the shot that killed Faulkner."

The ranger saw only Arlie. His gaze was full of deep reproach. "You came down here to save me," he said, in the manner of one stating a fact.

"Why shouldn't I? Ought I to have let you suffer for me? Did you think I was so base?"

"You oughtn't to have done it. You have brought trouble on yourself."

Her eyes glowed with deep fires. "I don't care. I have done what was right. Did you think dad and I would sit still and let you pay forfeit for us?"

The lieutenant's spirits rejoiced at the thing she had done, but his mind could not forget what she must go through.

"I'm glad and I'm sorry," he said simply.

Hilliard came, smiling, to relieve the situation. "I've got a piece of good news for both of you. Two of the boys that were in that shooting scrap three miles from town came to my office the other day and admitted that they attacked you. It got noised around that there was a girl in it, and they were anxious to have the thing dropped. I don't think either of you need worry about it any more."

Dillon gave a shout. "Glory, hallelujah!" He had been much

troubled, and his relief shone on his face. "I say, gentlemen, that's the best news I've heard in twenty years. Let's go celebrate it with just one."

Brandt and Hilliard joined him, but the Texan lingered.

"I reckon I'll join you later, gentlemen," he said.

While their footsteps died away he looked steadily at Arlie. Her eyes met his and held fast. Beneath the olive of her cheeks, a color began to glow.

He held out both his hands. The light in his eyes softened, transfigured his hard face. "You can't help it, honey. It may not be what you would have chosen, but it has got to be. You're mine."

Almost beneath her breath she spoke. "You forgot—the other girl."

"What other girl? There is none—never was one."

"The girl in the picture."

His eyes opened wide. "Good gracious! She's been married three months to a friend of mine. Larry Neill his name is."

"And she isn't your sweetheart at all? Never was?"

"I don't reckon she ever was. Neill took that picture himself. We were laughing, because I had just been guying them about how quick they got engaged. She was saying I'd be engaged myself before six months. And I am. Ain't I?"

She came to him slowly—first, the little outstretched hands, and then the soft, supple, resilient body. Slowly, too, her sweet reluctant lips came round to meet his.

"Yes, Steve, I'm yours. I think I always have been, even before I knew you."

"Even when you hated me?" he asked presently.

"Most of all, when I hated you," She laughed happily. "That was just another way of love."

"We'll have fifty years to find out all the different ways," the man promised.

"Fifty years. Oh, Steve!"

She gave a happy little sigh, and nestled closer.

Printed in Great Britain
by Amazon.co.uk, Ltd.,
Marston Gate.